BARRY LEMMING & THE DEMON'S BLUFF

jeff rahim bronner

ISBN: 0692976957
ISBN 13: 9780692976951

To my best friend.
Maryam, I love you.

PROLOGUE

Wikipedia Journal Entry on 'Lemmings':

- A **lemming** is a small rodent, usually found in or near the Arctic.
- The misconception of lemming "mass suicide" is long-standing and has been popularized by a number of factors.
- The 1958 Disney film *White Wilderness*, which won an Academy Award for Documentary Feature, staged footage with lemmings jumping into certain death after faked scenes of mass migration. A Canadian Broadcasting Corporation documentary, *Cruel Camera*, found the lemmings used for *White Wilderness* were flown from Hudson Bay to Calgary, Alberta, Canada, where they did not jump off the cliff, but were in fact forced off the cliff by the camera crew.
- Because of their association with this odd behavior, lemming "suicide" is a frequently used metaphor in reference to people who go along unquestioningly

with popular opinion, with potentially dangerous or fatal consequences.

- Re-printed directly from Wikipedia by permission of CC-BY-SA; https://en.wikipedia.org/wiki/Lemming to see more.

1

I t was like being in a dream. Barry stood at the railing, the Commons Building and cafeteria behind him, Marty goofing off besides him as usual. The Tuesday afternoon's blue sky had Barry just starting to think about skipping his next Lit class when he saw her: Patricia, his snow-white queen, his future everything, striding across the Quad.

He felt a light come into his forehead.

Barry shifted his weight, squinted his eyes and looked up into the brilliant Riverside sun. *Who was she? And why hadn't he seen her before?* He gripped the steel railing a little tighter. She was medium height, thin, narrow hips, perfectly-snow-white skin, beautiful, subtle body, and maple brown hair. Her nose turned just slightly to the left and reminded him of a hawk, even though he knew in the moment that that was not a rational connection. She was perfect. Still maybe forty feet away, she wore jeans, a pink sweater, and a brown belt that matched her loafers. He was in love.

"Marty, you see that girl over there?" he said, pointing.

Marty finished his farting noise, pushed their stud-jock-buddy Louis off of him and accidentally took a step back into Barry. "Which one? The one with the hot red Mohawk?"

"No, the one next to her, idiot. Right there. The one who's walking by herself, in the pink sweater."

"That's Patricia Meyer," Marty said, getting a shove from Louis and pretending to hit his chin on the metal railing. "English major, loner. You'll never get within twenty feet of her."

"I'm going to marry that girl," Barry said. "I don't know how, but you watch, two years from now, you'll be getting drunk at our wedding." Barry smiled as he said this, his eyes focused and intense. Patricia was now thirty feet away and Barry could picture the whole thing: her stepping out of the shower, towel on her head, nothing covering her gorgeous, white, freckled body. Barry kicking it in the corner of their shared, second-story bedroom, just hanging out while she goes about getting dressed, Barry doing nothing but watching her.

There is something fantastic about women, Barry thought, smiling. He felt a tingle in his chest, closed his eyes to enjoy it.

Louis snapped him out of his reverie. Louis, the basketball Riverside God with shaggy brown bangs in his eyes and the uncanny ability to bed any girl in the school. Both Barry and Marty hated him for it. "Good luck, Romeo. She's hot, she reads all day long, and no one ever talks to her and she never talks to anyone. She's the human equivalent of the Willy Wonka Chocolate Factory: closed until further notice."

Barry didn't care. He was too busy shielding his eyes from the afternoon sun, trying to get another look at her. She was now twenty feet away, still walking towards them. *She was so gorgeous!* But that wasn't it. It was something in her walk, her presence. Like she knew who she was. Five hundred people in his view at the UC Riverside Quad, and Patricia, this mysterious loner, this woman that no one could talk to, was the only person he could see.

⟋

"Bunch of people have tried dating her," Marty said, confessing. "Shit, I tried to talk to her once. No luck."

"What'd she say?" Barry looked up from his meatloaf, mashed potatoes and peas, finally interested in something one of them had to say. It was early evening and the Three Amigos were enjoying another nutritious meal from the Tower – their dorm and residence for their junior year at UCR.

"She was over at Dodd in the stacks. I walked in, saw her, and asked if I could sit at her table."

"And she said no?" he asked.

"She didn't say anything. She just kept reading her book, didn't even look at me. Rude. Incredibly rude," Marty answered, shaking his head, still smarting from the rejection.

"Maybe she's deaf," Louis offered, his massive hand grabbing what looked like a tiny fork and shoveling in slabs of meatloaf while he spoke. "Or maybe she was just being polite."

"How is her not even acknowledging my presence being polite?" Marty protested.

"Because maybe saying nothing was nicer than what she wanted to say," Louis quipped, whacking Marty on the back of the head.

"Maybe she's shy," Barry said quietly, widening his view across the dorm cafeteria and spilling a few peas onto the mound of potatoes. "Hot girls who are shy are always thought to be cruel. But I don't think she is cruel. I think she's just highly intelligent, and maybe a little socially challenged. I'm going to talk to her."

"No way," Marty said, elbowing him in the ribs. "You've never done anything like that in your life."

"How old am I?" Barry asked sincerely.

"Twenty," Marty responded. "And I've known you since you were five, and you've never talked to a girl you didn't know. You always had me do it."

"Not this time," Barry said, polishing off his plate in four gigantic bites and letting out a humongous belch. "The next time I see her, you bet, I'm giving it a shot."

♈

They say at the moment of your death, your spirit detaches from your body and you begin to see crucial moments from your life.

Well, he wasn't seeing crucial moments, but Barry was definitely detached from his body. He could feel his legs moving forward, could in fact look down at his legs and say, definitively, *Yes, those are my legs moving forward.* But could he feel them? Could he realize that Patricia was now ten feet in front of him and he didn't have a clue what he was about to say? He'd been waiting three months since his declaration in the cafeteria to see her again: three months of hunkering down by the Quad, staring at drunken, half-lit faces at parties, three months of ribbing from the guys. And just when he was ready to give up, ready to either commit to life-long celibacy, become gay, or take the simple route and look for another girl, there she was, alone, about to walk right past him.

"Hi," he said, reaching out his hand towards her. "I'm Barry. Barry Lemming. My friends dared me to come over and say hi to you."

Patricia stopped, startled by his voice. She stared at his outstretched hand, not sure what to do, sort of like it might have dog shit on it.

"You can shake my hand," Barry said. "I don't bite."

"I'm sure you don't," she said, tossing her perfect hair back over her perfect shoulder. "But I don't know you, and I don't shake hands with strangers. Sorry." She kept on walking, hugging her book bag a bit tighter.

"You could get to know me," he said, taking a step in tow with her. *Where was he getting his courage?* For the first time in his young life, Barry felt completely absent of fear: no fear of the future, no fear of impending doom, no fear of anything actually. He was walking besides enigmatic, beautiful, challenging Patricia, and she was now talking to him.

"I don't think so," she said in a lower tone, turning away from him and heading towards the cafeteria.

"You getting some lunch?" he said. "Maybe I could join you."

She stopped on that. Turning, Barry had a full five seconds to drink her in. She was, in fact, incredibly beautiful: light, snow-white colored skin; a high, arching nose; piercing blue eyes that radiated out with a laser-like quality. She was a princess. She was a queen. She was getting ready to tell him 'no' in the most polite of ways.

"Look, Barry, I appreciate you coming over and saying hi. But that's about as far as I want it to go, okay?"

"Okay," he said. "No hard feelings. You change your mind, you let me know. Barry Lemming. English major. Junior.

Going to be a novelist some day. But that doesn't really concern you…sorry to bother you." He started to walk away, his face painfully red. He could see Marty and Louis gawking at him from the railing; they had taken up the hobby of watching Barry waiting for Patricia and they were now loving every second of his demise. *This was why he didn't try things.* He just wanted to get away, to get this day, and especially this moment, over with.

"What kind of novelist?" she said, opening the conversation back up, calling out to him as he was now ten, twelve, fifteen feet away.

"I don't know," he said, turning back around. "A good one. Someone who captures people and pulls them in. Character based, but where shit still happens. A Toni Morrison, maybe, except I'm white, and I'm a guy."

Patricia smiled. A genuine, open-mouthed smile. Her eyes softened and for a moment Barry thought maybe they could be friends. "Toni Morrison's good. You like <u>Sula</u> or <u>The Bluest Eye</u>?"

"I like <u>Song of Solomon</u> best. It was the story, especially the ending, with Milkman and Guitar. That was awesome."

"Yep, me, too. We read that last quarter. Okay, Barry Lemming, I'll see ya around." She gave a small wave and started up the stairs towards the Commons.

He watched her go, saw her smile back over her shoulder once at him, like he had penetrated some kind of invisible force field. *How many people spoke to her in a day? How lonely was she?* He felt this incredible shiver move through him like God himself had come down and touched him.

2

A week later, after Barry had spent major amounts of time day-dreaming, wondering what it would be like to meet her, to know her, even one day to hold her, he and Marty leaned against the same center-quad railing, staring off across the square and killing time before their next class.

"You see the sports section?" Marty asked.

"Nope," Barry said, squeezing a pimple on his left arm, hoping to make the little white pus come squirting out.

"Stop it, dude. That's nasty. Leave that alone. No wonder you don't have a girlfriend. If some girl saw you doing that..." Marty shook his head in disgust. Marty didn't have a girlfriend either. "Anyway, Gibson had three more hits. I'm killing in that fantasy league. I'll win the beer-money hands down this week."

"Good for you, Marty. I could care less."

"You really should try it," Marty continued. "It would help you bond with the fellas."

Barry turned and looked at his friend. Marty played lead in most of the college plays, had an exuberance and magnetism that Barry could only dream about. But up close, Marty was short and not that interesting to look at. His nose was round, his skin was pock-marked. Barry wondered if Marty liked himself. "Honestly, Marty. You've known me since I was five years old. I'll watch hoops and maybe hockey during the playoffs; that's about the most you'll get out of me."

"It would help you with chicks," Marty said.

Now he had Barry's attention. Barry even stood up a little straighter. "How would caring about sports and joining a fantasy-league with eight other sports nerds who drink beer and fart while picking their favorite sports gods help me with women?"

Marty flashed his winning, center-stage smile. "I don't know. It just seems to have some effect. Like, 'Hey, baby. I'm Marty and I'm winning in the fantasy league. What's your name?'"

Barry laughed. His best friend always had an angle.

He turned away from Marty and looked back over the Quad...and there she was, walking directly towards them.

"Oh my God," Barry said.

"What?" Marty asked.

"Here she comes."

"Who?" Marty craned his neck to see.

Barry gripped the rail tighter, then tried to relax. He tried to breathe down into his toes. Nothing worked. Small jolts of nervous-excitement pulsed through his body and there was nothing Barry could do to stop it, so he gave in and just stared. Patricia was wearing a gray halter top with blue jeans, her chalk-white midriff showing the hundreds of crunches Barry imagined her doing every morning while listening to *The Indigo Girls* on her Walkman.

"I need to go talk to her," Barry said, his tongue suddenly thick and made of cotton.

"The tall one in the leotard?" Marty asked, shielding his eyes in the sun.

"No, you fantasy-league idiot. That one. Patricia. The short one with the gray top and tummy showing. Remember? Last week?" Barry continued to stare. "Wow, she's coming right towards us."

"Stop staring!" Marty said. "Here, kiss me or something."

"You idiot," Barry said. "Here she comes. I've got to do something."

Barry thought about pulling some slick move he'd seen on television, but instead ended up geeking it up like a total imbecile: he stood slack-jawed as twenty-year old Patricia Meyer, the brilliant loner who never said hi to anyone, made her way up the Commons steps, gave him a quick smile as a way of saying hello again, then proceeded to walk right past them.

He tried not to stare. He tried to do something heroic or brilliant; nothing came. Instead, he just turned in rhythm with her steps, keeping a perfect lock on her as she walked past, her backside disappearing into the Commons with a throng of other students.

"Wow," Barry said, waiting a full ten seconds before continuing. "Three years in college and I just had my first epiphany: I really am going to marry that girl!"

"All right," Marty responded, open-mouthed and shaking his head at the smile his friend had just received. "She wouldn't even talk to me in the library. Maybe you don't need those fantasy leagues after all."

For the next semester, Barry's life became about two things: turning in his essays and short stories on time, and finding out everything he could about her. Patricia Meyer. The great looking girl with the ripped tummy. The brilliant loner who no one seemed to know all that well. He employed best friends Marty and Louis as lead investigators. They turned one whole wall of their adjoining dorm rooms into a gathering center, posting new findings on a dry erase or bulletin board, until one day when Barry realized he would die of embarrassment if Patricia ever came back to his room and saw the board.

He made them take it down the next week.

"But what about all this cool information?" Marty whined.

"We'll keep it here," Barry said, flipping open two large three-ring binders with sticky pages and laminate sleeves. "For once in our life, let's be cool."

"We've never been cool with anything!" Marty snapped.

"Right!" Barry said, taking down the first page of notes.

The first month went pretty quickly.

"She's an English major," Marty would yell throughout the house, excitedly writing his new fact in the binder on the left.

"Then why have I never seen her in class?" Barry responded from his top spot in the dorm bunk bed, a beer in one hand, Toni Morrison novel in the other.

"She's a loner, definitely a loner," Louis said slowly over spaghetti one night. "I've been watching her. She does not do the crowd thing. I don't know how you're going to meet

her." Louis, the jock-stud who had his pick of girls at frat parties each and every week, seemed to be getting some vicarious
thrill from helping out this way.

"I'm working on that," Barry pointed out as he sucked in a
long strand of fettucine. "Don't forget about Divine interven-
tion. God loves to bring people together."

"But you don't believe in God," Marty protested.

"Now's not a bad time to start," Barry said, cracking a
smile.

One month turned into two. Barry hung out in the quad,
read his assigned James Joyce novels in the stairwell of the
English department, did anything he could think of to spend
extra time on campus.

Nothing. Not even so much as seeing her from a distance,
which was bizarre given the dynamics of the UC Riverside student body. Back in the early 90's, there were still only five or
six thousand students, so you'd see the same people every couple of days. You couldn't count on where or when, but you'd
see their face, notice their posture as they went into the work-
out room, maybe got into their car after an exam. Compared
to UCLA, which was a city unto itself, where you might rea-
sonably go six months without seeing somebody. But not at
Riverside.

So what was the deal? Was it not meant to be?

Late one night, Barry lay in bed, thinking about her face. He
had had a date with a cousin's friend and it had gone just aw-
fully, so bad in fact that Barry had feigned a sore throat and
dropped off the homely, 6'2" girl right after the Bond movie

had ended. Barry had then raced home to lie in bed and think about Patricia. Could you fall in love with someone's face? She had a softness, a kindness. He couldn't picture her getting mad or upset. He realized, of course, that this wasn't the real Patricia; it was the idealized version of herself, the only one he'd gotten to know so far.

He flicked on the light and whipped out his notebook.

*Dear God...*he began, feeling silly because of all the years his mother had insisted that God did actually exist, all the time Barry arguing, telling her to shut up, to stop, he didn't want to hear one more word about some beneficent Supreme Being.

"If God is watching over all things..." Barry would yell at her, "then how come you and Dad still got divorced? How come Dad got sick? Why am I still so unhappy even though I'm doing what I think I'm supposed to be doing?"

He took a deep breath, let the memory go. Now was not the time to air his list of complaints. He knew that list all too well. Now was the time to try something new. Something positive. Oprah would be proud.

Dear God...

Barry let his pen linger on the page. Did he really want to go through this door? Was he about to become a 'believer'? Afraid to take a breath or go to the bathroom without attributing it to God? And what if God was busy, or worse yet, didn't exist at all?

I need your help.

It was the strangest thing. He had never thought to ask God for help before. But there it was, a question. No, a plea, inside his head. His voice, asking, begging, pleading... something out there...for help.

He waited. And he waited some more. And then his hand began to move across the page, all on its own.

Dear God, I know I haven't written to you before, and the truth is I don't even know if you exist. But if you do, I'd really like to meet this girl. It's hard to explain, but she seems like someone very special and I don't know if I'm right for her or not, but can you give me a chance to find out? I know you're busy, what with the wars and politics and President Clinton trying to get re-elected (which I hope he does and if you can help with that, both my mom and I would appreciate it greatly), but I'd like to make this one small prayer: if I can meet Patricia Meyer to see if we'd like each other, well, that'd be just great.

Sorry I've been so mad at you. I just really miss my dad.

Thank you very much, Barry Lemming

He turned out the light. Moonlight streamed in through his open window and he couldn't help but shiver and smile, feeling like something magical might happen, lying there with a foolish grin on his face all by himself in the dark.

3

Barry strutted from the parking lot towards the quad. Today was going to be the day. He could feel it. Would she like him? Shoot him down? He didn't care. At last, three months of planning and fretting would be over. Today was the day he would meet Patricia Meyer and they'd see what the Universe had in store for them.

She had a beauty that fascinated him. Short, commanding, he'd seen her only those two times but still he couldn't forget the presence she carried. *Hadrat* was the word for presence in Arabic. Barry had learned it in his Persian Lit class. *Hadrat.* Patricia definitely had that. Presence. She was different: her beauty was inside, a light that came through her eyes. *Like she knows who she is.* Barry was amazed that more people didn't know about her. But maybe that's what it is like when you're starting to fall in love. You wonder, secretly, why no one else realizes how amazing this person is? Was he crazy? Obsessed? He'd wondered about it several times during the past month. But he was twenty-one, he had a little more than a year left in his college career.

Now was the time to go nuts over a girl.

Barry had pieced together several observations from the tidbits of information that Louis and Marty turned up, things like: she, too, was an English major -- although Barry had never seen her in one of his classes or in the English department building, making him wonder if she wasn't actually a mole for the CIA, KGB, or some other government agency with three random letters -- she spent most of her time alone but did have two best friends; she did not have a boyfriend, or if she did, they spent very little time together; she liked to read and often ate lunch outdoors under the shade of the large oak trees that dotted the perimeter of the campus; she was not gay, as far as he could tell (although he'd made that mistake before, long story, not worth going into right now), and most importantly, she was a junior like him. It really was weird that they'd never had a class together.

Barry tugged at his jacket sleeve and caught a reflection of himself in the Commons windows. He looked nervous. Rugged. Even a bit frayed in his old, perfectly worn-in blue jeans, gray t-shirt, brown hiking boots, and forest green Timberland jacket that he'd just picked up this past weekend at the mall. All of it masking his body that was more soft than toned, his sporadic work-out sessions giving way more often to Coronas and Tex-Mex instead reps on the elliptical. He'd once had the fantasy of being an athlete, using and toning his body like a piece of equipment, but that had quickly given way to partying, socializing, and trying to get laid.

Barry Lemming.

The best man most women would never know about.

His shaggy brown hair parted in the middle and kind of fell away from his forehead, revealing a face that was handsome to look at but wasn't going to win him any magazine covers anytime soon. He didn't care. He didn't have to be the best-looking man in the crowd, just the one to win this girl's heart.

♑

Barry was right. Patricia did carry something very special. And she knew it. Her parents, bless their hearts, had instilled in her a deep confidence in who she was. Either that or it was just natural to her being.

Her question was: would the right person ever come along? She felt like she was wading along in a very shallow river, watching people go by on the faster part of the current, paddling furiously, shooting rapids, apparently having the time of their lives, while she just stayed to the side, did her slow paddling, and waited.

This translated into: not getting drunk every weekend and trying to hook up with the first boy that looked her way, not going to the home basketball games and gazing longingly at the players at the end of the bench, and not batting her long, sensuous eyelashes at the lonely creative writing professor who kept making little hearts at the end of her short stories.

She wanted something more.

It almost became like a game. The Waiting Game. Waiting for Mr. Right to come and sweep her off her feet. Richard Gere with a red rose in the white limo to grab Julia Roberts before the credits rolled.

Except Patricia didn't care about the fairy tale. She'd seen enough families to know that when the movie stars rode off into the sunset at the end of the picture, most of those romances would end in a fictional divorce less than a year later. Was she cynical? Jaded? She preferred realistic. When you come from a divorced home, a home where your parents barely speak to each other anymore, where holidays and birthdays and especially Christmas become the worst days of the year, you understand that every fight could end in the Big D.

There is no happy fairy-tale ending, at least not from your inner child's point of view.

She was content to play it safe, take her time, stay in the shallow part of the water and focus on her studies. She fell in love with books, with words, with stepping inside a world that someone else had created.

She did wonder, though, if true love was possible. Could two people really make it work? What was the glue that made a marriage stick? Her parents couldn't do it. They'd lasted twenty-two years, until her mom had said, 'Enough!' and gone back to grad school where she'd wanted to study speech pathology, but instead had fallen in love with her twenty three year-old TA named Phil who had a goatee and apparently was giving her the best sex of her life (yuck!).

She and Phil now had two small twin babies together. Yes, Patricia now had a half-sister and half-brother who were both less than three years old. What was her mother thinking??

That's life right there, Patricia thought absent-mindedly one day while walking to class through the tall oaks and falling leaves surrounding the outer campus parking lot. *You think you're doing one thing, but there's a whole other thing going on.*

Patricia had only two real friends at Riverside: Jenny, her roommate, and Lynn, a stick-thin jock who for some reason had befriended her on the first day of dorm assignments. Both girls were funny and sweet and had boyfriends who took up most of their time. So Patricia stuck to herself, did her work, went to class, spent time in the library, and tried hard to ignore the lonely, empty feeling that lack of attention creates inside your heart.

She wondered sometimes if she was doing the right thing. Other girls went to parties, basketball games, got dolled up before class. They would suck down some beers at the Barn on Friday nights and go home with the best available option, usually some geek business major who looked pretty good at two in the morning. Too bad he wasn't so nice the next morning in the sun's harsh light. Patricia hadn't learned much from her mother, but she did learn two things:

First: don't spread your legs for just anybody. Her mother had said this drunk one night when she was leaving Patricia's dad and Patricia, a young seventeen, had just kind of nodded and tucked the advice away somewhere in the back of her mind.

Second: be yourself. If someone likes you, then they like you, not some picturized-perfected-version of you. In other words, don't get looking 'special' for anybody.

Unless you want to, of course. Then it was different. Then you were doing it for you, because you wanted to. Not because you felt some deep need to belong or to fit in. According to her mother, the last thing you needed to do was put on lipstick to look nice for some boy.

She could almost hear her mother's voice, crackling into the phone two weeks after she'd left her father: *You don't need a man or a boyfriend to make you whole, dear. You are fine just as you are. Look at me. I'm alone now, and don't I seem fine?*

But this morning, as Patricia passed the Commons windows and caught a passing glance of herself in her white sundress and yellow pullover, with no make-up, no sparkle, no hint whatsoever that she desperately wanted a relationship the way she did, she wondered if her mother was right.

Was her mom right to leave her father? And if none of us really needed someone to make us whole, then what was her mother doing falling in love with a twenty-three year-old and having two babies at the ripe old age of forty-seven?

Patricia smiled and ducked into the Commons bathroom to put on some lipstick. Maybe it was okay to go out of your way to look nice for someone, especially if that was what it took to bring a certain someone into the shallow part of your river.

Barry could somehow feel her loneliness. Months and months of research had led him to two giant conclusions: 1) She was beautiful -- and amazing, and special, and any other incredible adjective you want to throw in here; and, 2) She was desperately lonely. But that loneliness was buried deep behind perfectly-constructed walls so no one, and I mean no one, would notice. So here's what he did: he began to notice. He waited outside of her classroom buildings, just to watch her stride across the quad towards African lit class. He hung around the side of the Creative Writing building, hoping to catch a glimpse of her dashing through the south end of campus to avoid the rain and make it into Women's Nineteenth Century Poetry. He began to learn her class schedule by heart. He even orchestrated casual meetings with Jenny and Lynn, her best friends, saying hello to them at parties or in line at the Commons. In his mind, he'd put together a pretty accurate composite of Patricia Meyer: lonely, brilliant, a little bit cool and distant. Yet, underneath that veneer, here was someone with incredible capacity, deep sensitivity, unbearable loneliness, and, quite possibly, a heart of gold. She just needed someone to pay attention to her.

She could be the one, he would say to himself at odd times during the day.

They'd only met and talked twice. But he'd made up a whole story in the interim, and ironically, his story wasn't that far off.

"I have a plan," Barry had announced over Grape Nuts and the sports page that morning. Yes, the sports page! Marty had in fact brought him into the weird, reality-tv world of professional sports, and the truth was, Barry liked it. He liked the egos and the incredibly-toned athletes making $4 million per year doing what very few people on the planet could do. There were times that Barry would picture himself out there on the court with Magic or James Worthy, leading a fast-break towards the orange rim. But then he'd come back to reality and grab another slice of pizza, or a second beer, or in this case, another bowl of cereal. He went over the details; it only took about thirty seconds to explain it to the guys. "And that's my plan."

"Dude, three months of researching and planning, and bumping into her in the cafeteria is the best thing you can come up with?" Marty fired back.

"You got a better idea, Casanova?" Barry retorted, mouthful of Grape Nuts mumbling his words.

"Why don't you just talk to her? Meet her at a party or something." Louis said, his hair dipping slightly over his eyes.

"She doesn't go to parties, at least I've never seen her."

"Write her a note," Louis offered. "Tack it up on the board in the engineering building."

Barry laughed. "First of all, she's not an engineering major. And second, like say what? Hey babe, you look fabulous. I'm the mystery guy for you. Meet me at the gym at midnight. Love, Barry."

"No, something sweet," Louis said, scratching the side of his mouth. Louis was a tall, lanky basketball player who had never shared his secrets of bedding women. "Something like: Hi Patricia, I've noticed you several times across campus and have wanted to say hello, but have been too shy. I'm an English major, a junior, my name is Barry, I have no known sexually transmitted diseases, and I'd love to get together for coffee sometime if you'd be open to that."

"That's not bad!" Barry admitted. "I think we have to lose the 'sexually transmitted diseases' part, but I like that. Thanks, Louis."

Barry finished his cereal, decided to skip Middle English Lit and the God-awfulness of *Beowulf*, then spent two hours trying to write the perfect mystery note. After filling half his trash can, he tried desperately to remember what Louis had said and the spirit he'd said it in, then given up. He decided to go with his original plan of bumping into her in line.

And he would make it look as natural and casual as he could.

Barry rolled towards the Commons, gathering steam. He felt stronger with each step. *Did God respond to his letter?* He'd never felt anything like this in his life, and whether it was nerves, the after-glow of skipping class to write a love-note to a girl, or a very deep illusion because he was about to get shot down in the worst of ways, at the moment all he knew was he was feeling good.

He was on a mission.

Until a little voice crept into his mind and said: *What if she's not there?*

Barry pictured himself collapsing and crumpling into a little ball in the Commons cafeteria. Right outside the Taco Bell line. He could imagine the students gathering around, worried looks on their faces, knowing he was dying from a broken heart, Barry's last breaths coming out slowly, and then the paramedics and the ambulance and wondering who, if anyone, would come visit him in the hospital.

Feeling a little dramatic there, Romeo?

Barry smiled. Life was good. He was trying something he'd never tried before, and that was the key here. This was about him stepping up, taking a chance, shedding that box he'd been living in for so long.

Not about what she said.

Yeah, right. A big part of him thought he was about to make the biggest fool of himself in front of half the student body. The other part, a smaller part, thought he had maybe a 5% chance of her saying she'd go out with him.

God, he hoped she said yes.

Patricia stood in the cafeteria line at the Commons, a sloppy joe and fruit plate on her tray, pink sweater slung over one arm. She'd put on matching lipstick and was feeling good. The campus of Riverside was about an hour away from Los Angeles, nestled up against the foothills before Palm Springs and home to some of the prettiest greenery in California. Patricia had come here from San Diego and really appreciated the home-town feel that the campus created. Riverside was also, unfortunately, home to most of the smog that got blown inwards from LA and San Diego, making the air brown and heavy and creating a wheeze in your chest if you weren't careful.

There she was, standing in line, thinking more about her shallow side of the river than her upcoming essay on Shakespearian sonnets when the strangest thing happened.

A young man wearing jeans and a hunter-green Timberland jacket took two steps backwards towards her and then tripped, smashing right into her tray, causing her sloppy joe and fruit plate to go cascading down the back of his jeans, making it look like, well, you can imagine. Patricia screamed in pure delight, the entire cafeteria of three hundred students turning to look, and there stood Barry, the one she had talked to about Toni Morrison, a shit-eating grin on his face, laughing at the sloppy joe, the mess it had made over his butt, and the fact that he'd finally bumped into the woman he'd been secretly plotting to meet for months.

"It's all over your jeans," Patricia said, still giggling and smiling in spite of herself. Everyone had looked. Patricia couldn't believe it.

"How bad?" Barry said, trying to swat at it.

"Stop, stop. You'll only make it worse. Here, take these," she said, handing him a couple of napkins. "I'll go get some water."

People were still turning and looking in the direction of Patricia's scream.

"It's all right," Barry said loudly. "It's only sloppy joe on my butt."

Patricia laughed, wondering who was this crazy man she'd dumped her lunch on that everybody was now staring at. He was smiling and waving like a mayor at a parade. *Weird. They'd only seen each other twice, yet it felt like they knew each other. Does that happen?* You bump into someone who should be a stranger, yet instead of feeling nervous or scared, you feel relieved, like, *Oh, there you are. Where have you been?*

"You're sitting down," she said when she returned to the scene of the crime. "I'm sure you're getting sloppy joe all over the chair."

"I got embarrassed standing," Barry admitted. "People were staring. Besides, I put down a few towels."

"It seemed like you kind of liked the attention," Patricia said, perching on the edge of her seat. She was still smiling inwardly and outwardly. No one had ever done something like this, even if it was an accident. "Don't tell me you're actually shy underneath there."

"Incredibly shy," Barry said, grinning. "But you'd never know it from my face."

"Oh, I don't know. I could see you as an actor. Kind of a crazy, gunman type."

"Gee, thanks," he said, feigning hurt.

Patricia raised her eyebrows. "So, how do you want to get that…sloppy joe…off your jeans?"

"What do you mean?" Barry said, trying to keep up with her. She was quick, really quick. After all, he'd hatched the plan to meet her, executed it perfectly, but never pondered the possibility that it might actually go well and he would now need to have a conversation with her.

In his weird way of irrational thinking, once they met, the Universe would explode and all life on this planet would cease to exist, not that he was narcissistic or anything.

"I mean stand up and let me wipe your butt," she said.

Barry laughed. "I don't even know you. I'm not letting you anywhere near my butt."

"Yeah, right. Up you go."

Barry stood, smiling. Patricia stepped over to him and wiped his jeans without a smirk, pulling the strands of dirt-red sloppy joe off his pants and making a small pile of soiled napkins.

Barry closed his eyes. *This was a dream, right?* After all, he'd spent the last three months dreaming of something like this; yet, here they were, in the cafeteria at the Commons, talking and laughing and now she was wiping his butt. Wiping his butt? Was he crazy? People were forgetting the incident, turning back to their lunches and conversations, leaving them virtually alone in the middle of the large cafeteria. Barry could see out across the students' heads, out through the large criss-cross windows to the Quad where he'd first seen her. He almost mentioned it.

"Okay, thanks. That's great," he said.

"Wait. I'm almost finished. You really got a lot of *schmutz* on there."

"Schmutz?" he asked.

"It's Yiddish. It means dirt, yuck."

"I know what it means. I'm just surprised you do," he said, feeling happy in his heart.

"Why? I don't look Jewish?" she smirked, smiling and tossing her hair back out of her face.

"Can I at least buy you a replacement lunch?" he asked. "It was your sandwich, after all."

"Oh, I don't care. Yeah, you can do that. I'd rather you buy me a pizza."

Barry turned to her. "What'd you just say?"

"I said," Patricia explained, smiling, "that I'd rather you buy me a pizza."

"That's what I thought you said." Barry knew, and knew that Patricia knew, that the Commons did not sell pizzas.

Patricia wiped a little more, the silence turning into a tiny, gray baby elephant between them.

"How do you feel about that?" she asked.

"Good. Great. I like pizza," he answered nervously. "When were you thinking of this pizza?"

She looked at her watch. "In about fifteen minutes, unless you have more classes today."

Are you kidding me? Barry thought. Like I've spent the last three months to blow it on Nineteenth Century Women's Lit.

_

They walked out to Barry's car, enjoying the sun. He thought about taking her hand, then realized that he was supposed to have just bumped into her. *This is like a dream. I'm in a dream right now.* He watched himself open her car door, come around to his side, get into the car and drive away through the parking lot.

His right hand shook on top of the throttle, and he thought for a moment that he was going to pass out.

Just drive the car, he told himself. *Just drive the car.*

He kept wanting to do something to bring himself back into his body. Pinch himself. Hit himself. Scream at the top of his lungs.

What was that psychological term: creative disassociation?

Patricia sat in the passenger seat and looked straight ahead. "You bumped into me on purpose, didn't you?" she finally asked as they drove out of the parking lot, turning down State and heading towards the center of town.

"What? What are you talking about? I didn't even know you were there," Barry smirked as he said this, biting his lip trying not to smile.

"Okay, look, you're a really bad liar, Barry. I've seen you watching me for the last few months. I've actually been waiting for you to say something. You're a terrible voyeur, and if you ever want to leave me and our kids to become a CIA agent, I'm sorry, I think the answer's going to have to be 'no.'"

Barry looked at her. She was better than his dreams.

"You saw me, huh?"

"Only about a hundred times. No one has paid this much attention to me since David Andrews in the fourth grade and he thought I was his mother."

Barry didn't say anything. He tried to think of something. Nothing came. Just endless, black silence.

"Say something," she quipped.

Barry slid the car into third, eased around a slower moving vehicle. "I've learned a lot these last few months," he began.

"Like what?"

"It's like people don't even know you exist."

"You do," she said, smiling and putting on more lipstick in the mirror. "You're somebody."

Barry drove for a minute. "What was that you said about our kids?"

They had a great time eating pizza at Beroni's: a small, family-owned Italian joint on the corner of State and Crocker. Patricia picked out a table with a large, green overhead umbrella while Barry ordered a veggie pizza and a couple of sodas.

Now that the burden of truth was out of the way, both of them relaxed, opened up, and talked like they'd been friends for years.

"I don't know," she explained. "I think people don't know UC Riverside exists. It definitely sits in the shadows of the bigger schools: UCLA, Berkeley. But I like it here. I like being able to go to class and not get hassled. I get all the classes I want, living is affordable. I get to wear jeans and a sweatshirt if I want. Just look at the sun and the weather. What could be better than this?"

Barry stared at her, totally unaware that he was supposed to say something.

"Don't just stare at me, say something," she said finally, spreading more red pepper flakes on her slice.

"Something." He smiled, pizza filling both cheeks. Here was finally someone he could be himself with. It's like he was *in* with her.

How cool was that?

They talked about Toni Morrison and Richard Wright and all of the great black authors they both loved. Milkman and Guitar and what was that ending supposed to mean?

When Barry drove her home, the sun was just starting to set, and it felt totally natural and wonderful when they stood on the steps in front of her apartment. They'd been together for three hours. Again, Barry knew he was supposed to say something, something funny and smart that would round off their time together perfectly.

"You're supposed to say something," Patricia said.

"I know," Barry lamented. "It's awful. I can't stand the pressure."

"Well, here," Patricia inserted. "I'll give you something to talk to Marty and Louis about. They worked hard these last few months as well."

And with that, she closed her eyes, leaned in towards him, and kissed him in such a way that he thought he had died and gone to heaven.

4

Two weeks later, when they'd seen each other every day, walked over to surprise each other in front of class and then met up for pizza and beers over at The Barn, that they realized something serious was going on here.

Barry was constantly making jokes, seeing how she took it, then going in deeper and deeper. He was starting to be himself, and the more he was, the more she liked it. Patricia, for her part, was an amazing listener, and she was consciously now lowering walls and veils so he could see more of who she was. She had never done this before, not till now. Her beauty, her light, was starting to come through. And the more it did, the more he opened, and the more he opened, the more relaxed she became.

"What are you doing later?" she asked, twirling the phone cord around her fingers and looking up at her poster of Pele scoring on an awesome header.

"I was going to work on that paper for Smith. Why? What'd you have in mind?"

"I was wondering if you could come over for a few minutes. My roommate Jenny is gone to San Diego and there's something I want to show you."

"I'll be right over," he said, buttoning up his shirt and throwing on the cleanest sweatshirt he had.

"That was fast," she said, opening the door and smiling. Her fingers were curled around the edge of the door and Barry still felt like he was in a dream. Here was Patricia Meyer, the object of his affection for all these months, way out of his league, out of anyone's league for that matter, staring and smiling and beckoning him to come inside.

Barry loved her apartment. He'd only been inside a few times, but Patricia had a wonderful sense of femininity: soft pinks, yellows, greens, house plants and cushy pillows that made the two-bedroom apartment feel safe and cozy. It was completely different than the governmental dorm room that he and Marty shared: piles of laundry and empty beer bottles stashed under the bunk-bed, wrappers and trash strewn about. Even though Louis had brilliantly cut an illegal door joining his room to theirs, it was still a fact that his place was downright disgusting. He turned his nose up at the thought of it.

"What was it you wanted to show me?" he said, smiling as he drank in her surroundings.

"Come here," she said, taking him by the hand.

She led him back into her bedroom, gently shutting the door. Barry started to get butterflies in his stomach. They had kissed most days, but it was always in public, or out on her steps. They had never done anything behind closed doors.

"Lay down on the bed," she said.

He did so with only the slightest hesitation.

"Barry Lemming," she said, smiling nervously and kneeling on the edge of the bed. "Could you ever fall in love with a silly English major who doesn't know what she wants out of life and has a mother from hell?"

"I could," he said, the butterflies growing larger inside.

"Good," she said. "That's good. I'd have to think about it otherwise."

"Think about what?"

"This," she said, lifting her sweater up over her head, revealing her sweet, bare breasts. Barry stopped in mid-thought, his jaw dropping down. Her body was so white, so pure. He didn't know what to do.

"What do you think?" she asked quietly.

"I think you're beautiful," he said. "Are you sure I can't be a CIA agent?"

"Shut up. Just shut up," she laughed, closing her eyes and moving towards him.

They made love slowly, tenderly, as if it was both their first and last time. Barry had never been with a woman like this, someone he wanted to know everything about. He had only had two lovers before, and both were more drunk, late-night, two-week romps than actual girlfriends. This was the first time he had had sober sex in over two years.

For Patricia, it had been more than three years since her last sexual encounter. She had lost her virginity to a lifeguard named Dave back in her hometown of San Diego, but he had bragged about it and even posted something on Facebook letting everybody know what they'd done. Yuck. She'd had one other lover, a girlfriend's dad who was going through a divorce, and even that had only lasted two months before he decided to reconcile with his petty wife. That was it.

Neither Patricia or Barry had stacks and stacks of lovers piled up in their closets. Barry unbuttoned his shirt, then slid out of his jeans. He looked over and Patricia was undoing her jeans buckle and lowering her pants over pink silk panties. Barry couldn't fucking believe it. He was about to have sex with Patricia Meyer.

They turned towards each other, slowly, awkwardly, now stripped down to their underwear and beginning to kiss.

"The first time might be kind of fast," Barry mentioned in between kisses. "It's been a little while."

"Then we'll get it better the second time," she responded, smiling.

"I think I love you," Barry gushed, breaking every rule there was for a two-week dating timeline.

"I know," she said. "That's why we're lying here."

He felt nervous but also a growing confidence as he began to move his hands over every square inch of her body. She responded, her nipples stiffening and her breaths coming in quicker bursts as they discarded their undergarments and he moved inside of her. All thoughts stopped for him then, something he would reflect on later as the single greatest moment of his young life. There were no thoughts, no words, nothing bouncing around inside of his bouncy head; he saw only her face as she closed her eyes and arched her back and they both exploded in simultaneous orgasms before crashing down on the bed together, frothy and sweaty and both smiling from ear-to-ear.

She rolled into his shoulder and began to cry then, small tears that sort of leaked and choked themselves out of her.

"What's wrong?" he asked. "Did I do something wrong?"

"No," she explained in between crying jags. "Just the opposite. You did so much right."

"Then why are you crying?"

"I don't know," she said, wiping her eyes with the back of a hand. "I think I was so lonely, and it's been so long, and you're the first nice person to come along in a really long time." She paused then, letting it sink in. "I didn't know if anyone was going to come along. I have pretty high standards, y'know." They both laughed.

He lifted the covers and looked down at their naked bodies, still hot and sweaty, her normally chalk-white skin actually flushed and pink.

"What're you doing" she asked quietly.

"Just looking at us. Look at us! Even if this never happens again, you have made me a very, very happy man."

"Why wouldn't it happen again?" she asked.

"I don't know. Things happen, things change..." he stammered.

"Oh really?" she said, feigning anger. "Two minutes ago, you love me, but now things are changing?"

"No, y'know, you might wake up later and decide it was all a big mistake."

"Really? I might? You know what I think, Barry Lemming?"

"What? I have no idea what you're thinking, actually," he said.

"I think," she put a finger on his lips and rolled over on top of him, "that it's going to happen again right now."

☙

"No fucking way," Marty blurted out, chomping on popcorn and spitting half a mouthful all over Barry.

"Way," Barry said, leaning back calmly.

Louis chimed in with a big guffaw. "You're saying that you had sex with Patricia Meyer, goddess to men and mere mortals, in her apartment yesterday afternoon?"

"That's exactly what I'm saying," Barry responded.

"Shhh!" someone said from two rows in front of them. They were in a darkened movie theater, the Riverside multiplex, and Tom Cruise was running across the screen with a blow-torch in his hand.

"I don't believe it," Marty whispered.

"Me either," Louis quipped. "I need proof."

"Believe what you want," Barry said. "I could care less. We had sex, twice, in her apartment, yesterday afternoon."

"Where was her roommate?" Marty asked.

"Shhh!" the same person hissed before moving over three rows.

"Her roommate went home to San Diego," Barry whispered back. "Now can we just watch the movie?"

Barry leaned back in his seat, crossed his hands behind his head, and smiled. A deep, resonant smile that he hadn't felt since his father had died. Patricia Meyer, naked in bed with him. He could almost call her his girlfriend, although neither of them had used that term yet.

But hey, thought Barry, when you're talking about falling in love, saying I love you, and making jokes about kids and a possible future that only two-and-a-half weeks ago seemed completely and utterly impossible, then shit, something was definitely happening.

Barry looked over at Marty, who caught his eye and mouthed *Asshole!* at him; he then looked at Louis, who had a different girl every week but never the same girl twice, and he thought about how deeply happy he was, about how quickly the last three months had gone, and the fact that Patricia was even better in real life than she was in his dreams. Tom Cruise was now planting explosives and diving out of the way as a giant red fireball filled the screen.

Patricia Meyer, lying naked in bed beside him. They had plans later, after Barry "spent some time" with the guys. This is what happiness feels like, Barry thought, his eyes crinkling above a small smile. It made him think of his dad, his dying days in the hospital, his father grasping Barry's hand and tugging on it before the morphine took him back under. Pneumonia and lung failure were the official causes of death, but everyone knew it was the cancer that had killed him. Barry had been eighteen.

Life comes in pairs of good and bad, Barry realized. Here he was so happy about Patricia, but also missing his dad. And not the big things, like birthdays and Christmas, but the little things, like the way his dad opened the front door when he got home from school, the terribly burned steaks his dad made on the charcoal bar-b-que, the loud love ballads from Bob Dylan and Cat Stevens that poured out of the living room speakers, filling their house after his dad had moved out. Barry never really saw his dad happy after that, even with the steady parade of beautiful women that would rival Louis' anytime. He would see his dad content, yet also restless, and then after a three-year bout with cancer, he didn't see him at all.

But on this day, thinking about Patricia and their naked bodies and the fact that they had plans later, Barry was happy, and he smiled and appreciated that.

5

Two months later, he and Patricia were still going steady. They were spending three or four nights a week together, people began to know them as a couple, and Barry still wanted to pinch himself to see if he'd wake up. Patricia Meyer, loner, beautiful English major who spoke to almost no one. And that was part of the charm. With Barry's love and support, she began to grow as well, smiling at people in the halls, attending (reluctantly) weekend parties where they'd have a few cups of nasty keg beer before driving up into the desert hills or racing home to dive under the covers, make love, and then pop in a movie. They were becoming predictably boring and sweet.

When graduation came a year later, Barry's mom got to meet Patricia's mom, young husband and twin toddlers in tow, and then a few minutes later, Patricia's dad and new, 8-month pregnant wife. Everybody hugged and smiled and posed for all the right photos before eating ribs, chicken and big mounds of salad from RJ's, the best bar-b-que in Riverside.

When Barry got a sales job offer in west Los Angeles, and Patricia didn't care where they went as long as it was together, they packed up a U-Haul and drove the seventy miles from Riverside to LA. They were twenty-two years old, they were in love, and they had their whole lives ahead of them.

6

He'd been waiting all his life. Waiting for what or for whom, he wasn't sure. Maybe his death, maybe the death of his father, but definitely something.

He imagined sometimes what it'd be like, the freedom of doing and saying what he really felt, what he really wanted. The human form of a Harley Davidson doing ninety on the freeway and giving the finger to whomever he wanted.

That would be living.

"Barry, you're up," Stan blared into the microphone, his terse words echoing throughout the shiny floors of the dealership, spilling out onto Lincoln Blvd. like groceries falling out of a paper bag.

Barry stubbed out his cigarette and flicked open his pocket mirror. His skin was gaunt, pale, like he hadn't been outside in months. He had been, though, and that was the weird part. It just seemed like he hadn't. The sun wouldn't stick. Barry opened his mouth and checked out his gums.

Red. Puffy red. He needed more rest.

"Hi, I'm Barry," he heard himself say to the couple, his arm extended, his voice distended like it was coming from a Jack-in-the-box drive-thru. There was no good way to approach potential car buyers, everybody was so cynical these days. They'd already been on the Internet, already been to *kbb.com* and found out what the car was really worth, made up some crazy number inside their head of the most they'd be willing to pay. Two or three thousand under sticker. *What kind of crazy shit was that?* But more and more, the dealerships were saying yes. It was kind of sad, really, what the Internet was doing to the car business. Barry had seen his personal income decline by 30% over the past six months.

But people were still people. Barry tried to smile.

"Barry, I don't want any bullshit," the man began. "We're here and we're serious; don't play games with us."

Barry took a step back and looked at the man. Mid-forties, paunch around his waistline, thinning hair and little crows' feet around his eyes. *Definitely fooling around.*

"Sir, I wouldn't dream of playing games with you. Here at Westside Toyota, well, to be honest..." Barry leaned in and lowered his voice, catching a glimpse down the woman's blouse, the stretched skin of her right breast giving Barry a little tingle. "To be honest, they do like to fuck with people here, but I'll give it to you straight, honest, I will."

The three of them climbed into a maroon Camry and pulled out onto Lincoln, swinging past the giant whale mural, its tail arching up besides its gigantic whale-smile. It made Barry sick, this mural, although he couldn't quite say why. Maybe it was the contrast between the larger-than-life white whale teeth and the real-life pungency of the city: stale, smoggy air, the congestion, the frenetic push that pulsed through Los Angeles. Maybe it was the Whole Foods across the street, the small scraggly weeds sprouting up in the vacant lot right beside the incredibly opulent market where people would drive up in their sixty-thousand-dollar Lexus and run in for a bottle of Smart Water, stampeding past the homeless man in the cardboard box who could barely feed himself. Barry couldn't take the contrast. His heart wasn't big enough to hold it all. Why this one whale mural bothered him so much, he couldn't make out, except that maybe it should have been a shark bringing in the car customers instead of a whale. That would be closer to the truth, and some part of Barry was ready for a deeper dose of truth. He leaned forward in the passenger seat, directing the man onto the 90, heading east towards downtown.

In Los Angeles, they don't call them freeways. It's just the 405, the 90. Like some monument standing in the sky. Everyone knows what you're talking about.

"What's your business?" Barry began. He looked over his shoulder, noticed the woman running her finger over the upholstery. She was stick-thin with auburn hair and large red lips. She was at least twenty years younger than the man. "Toyota prides itself on having the nicest upholstery in the industry."

"Uh-huh," the woman said, picking her nose and wiping it onto the seat cushion, the pale-green booger sitting there like a small monument.

"What the--" Barry began.

"Yes?" the woman said, raising her eyebrows in defiance, staring straight at him.

Barry turned back around to the front, pretending he hadn't seen anything. *Assholes. I'm surrounded by assholes. A total river of cascading assholes.* He smiled at the thought.

"I'm in sales," the man said, his lips juicing a bit. "Superconductors. But it's really just like selling large lawn mowers. Shit, it might even be like selling cars."

"It's all about people," Barry said, a small wave of nausea passing through him. Barry cracked his window a touch, letting the cool air blow past his face.

The man drove for a few minutes, accelerating, decelerating, braking hard on the off-ramp and nearly spinning out towards the wall, then making a U-turn on the underpass before taking them back to the dealership. Clouds slipped by as they drove.

Back on the lot, Barry went over the features of the car, then stood back about fifteen feet and let the two of them talk. He imagined himself to be a million miles away, up on Jupiter or Pluto, looking down on a small measly planet called Earth. Focusing in even closer, he took a snapshot of the United States, then California, then Marina del Rey, and finally down into the head of one lonely car salesman named Barry who needed five more sales before Friday just to pay the rent.

The man and woman smiled at each other and nodded at Barry that they wanted to go inside. Blinded momentarily, they went from the bright sunshine of the lot to the muted shadows of the dealership office. U2's *With or Without You* bounced around the dealership walls through unseen speakers. A crumpled pink piñata sagged in the corner, a leftover from the Cinco de Mayo party two weeks earlier. Barry got them each a cup of Starbuck's Pumpkin Spice and led them over to his cubicle. A small photo of Patricia and Barry smiling at a wedding was tucked in behind his desk light. Up on the gray cubicle walls sat an old newspaper clipping of Magic Johnson's famous no-look pass, and beside it a faded ticket to Disneyland, Barry's first time there.

The couple sat down, Barry taking a seat on the opposite side of the desk. Now they were on his turf. Finally. He couldn't do a damn thing when the bitch-lady wiped her nose on the gorgeous leather seat, but now, now would be his payback. He imagined shoving that booger right up her ass until it popped out of her face, but instead he would do it with numbers, he would do it with grace, and most of all, he would do it with a smile.

"What if I could get you that brand new, gorgeous Camry for $469 a month?" Barry said, getting very quiet inside. *Once you put out a number,* his mentor had said, *then you don't say another word. Whoever speaks next, loses.* Barry would often imagine that negotiating the price of a car as a life-or-death hostage situation: both sides needed to come to an agreement before somebody got hurt.

"With how much down?" the man asked.

"Couple thou…maybe twenty-seven hundred total, tax and license included."

The man and woman looked at each other. She leaned towards the man and whispered something, Barry resisting the urge to look down her shirt one more time. Negotiating was serious business, now was not the time to fuck around.

"We want it in white, with a tan interior," the man said, the skin on his face suddenly tight, making him look about thirty years older. "And no games about warranties or any of that shit."

Barry and the man shook hands on their way out, the couple smiling as they climbed into their palatial new white Camry with the tan interior and five-disc cd changer. Barry had thrown in a sub-woofer in the trunk so they could blast their Enya or Bee Gees. They ended up purchasing the warranty after all, of course. Everybody does. Once Barry explained the Toyota standard of excellence and peace of mind, the couple turned again to each other then said, *'Well, we do want peace of mind.'* The warranty was 90% straight commission for Barry, bringing his take on the deal to just over $500. Not bad for a morning's work.

He stood in the doorway, his head cocked to the side, fingering a toothpick. His seventh sale in two weeks, putting him second on the team behind Orzo, a short, stocky man from the Middle East who chain-smoked Camel cigarettes and seemed to know everybody with olive skin in Los Angeles. Barry would never catch him. He had, in fact, given up trying. Orzo had too many friends.

Chad, a newbie with crew-cut brown hair and an outrageous sky-blue suit with purple pin-stripes, nudged Barry in the doorway. "You worked them over, huh?"

"What do you mean?" Barry asked, twirling his toothpick.

"The lease you did for them. They got screwed. $469 a month for five years? Shit. I wouldn't give that to Brian Tower."

"Who's Brian Tower?" Barry asked.

"Kid that used to beat me up in the fourth grade."

"Chad, let me tell you something." Barry said, focusing his gaze and narrowing his eyes. "There's only one thing to being a good salesman, just one."

"What's that?" Chad whispered, leaning forward a little bit like he was about to catch a glimpse of something truly special. New salesman could sense it, when an old-timer was about to give them some dope. Not dope the way most people think about it – something to snort or smoke that would numb out your senses -- but the *real dope*, knowledge that could imprint their minds and translate into hundreds of sales, thousands upon thousands of dollars, and, most importantly, more women than they knew what to do with.

Barry lowered his voice. "Help people get what they want. That's it. You become their friend and help them go where they already want to go. Everybody wants a new car. Everybody wants to look cool. Shit. Everybody wants to drive through their neighborhood and pull up into their own driveway with some new piece of sleek metal so their neighbors lean out their front doors and go, 'Ooh.'" Barry paused. Chad wasn't even breathing. "So you do it right, you stay cool and low-key and don't pressure anybody...that's what they're expecting, see? That's the picture they have coming in. That some car jockey's going to be an asshole and try to pressure them into buying. But if you're nice and honest and help them see the benefits of a new car without pushing, people will like you and want to buy cars from you. And they'll tell their friends about you." Barry lowered his voice even more to a barely audible whisper. It was sacrosanct to be giving away free information like this. But it was also a rite of passage, veterans handing on time-honored secrets to the new kids dreaming of riches and success. Plus, there was something vulnerable about Chad, something innocent and pure that Barry wanted to protect. "Be a nice guy. That's the secret. That's what the assholes who run this place don't understand. It's not about sales, it's about people. Trust me. I can be an asshole to everybody, even my girlfriend if she doesn't give it up a couple times a week. But

I'm *nice* to the customers." Barry flipped the toothpick over end-to-end with his tongue, the sharp point barely grazing the pink roof of his mouth. "But what do I know? I'm only the second-highest grossing salesman here for the last seven years. You'll see, be a nice guy and help customers get what they want, you can make a hundred grand your first year. Not a bad way to live, huh? It beats working, that's for sure."

Chad smiled, whipped out a small notepad and started writing something down.

"What are you doing?" Barry asked.

"Just making a note of what you said. Helps me if I write it down."

"Morning, Barry," April said as she passed. Barry and Chad turned and stared. Drooled is more like it. April, the twenty-two year-old receptionist, was eye-candy for every man in the store: legs up from the floor to her perfectly-angled chin, sparkly blonde hair, breasts and hips like small mountains that just wouldn't stop.

"Morning, April," Barry said. "Got another sale to ring up."

"You are the man," she said, smiling.

I would like to be, Barry thought, watching her go.

Barry let another ring go by, heard his own voice on the outgoing message. *Where was Patricia?* They usually talked at least once a day, maybe more, at least until a few weeks ago. *What had happened?* Barry tried to think: he remembered some kind of argument, remembered sleeping on the couch a few nights. Beyond that...he couldn't piece it together.

Sometimes relationships felt like a cross-country flight: you take off full of energy and promise, you watch as your energy sags during the day, then you arrive at a lay-over city and you're tired and confused and not sure whether to stay or get back on the plane.

"You going to Tex-Mex? Happy hour lasts another forty-five minutes." Paulino asked, his brown leathery face talking down at Barry at an odd angle. Paulino was a veteran salesman with skin ruined by long hours in the sun. He lived alone on a twenty-foot boat in the Marina, spent most of his time with nineteen year-old co-eds from USC: beautiful, robust beauties that he'd take for long weekends to Tahoe, Palm Springs, maybe down south to Tijuana for *migas* and Coronas. Two good weekends, maybe three, and that was it, time to move on. *I think our age difference is just too big, sweetie. You have your whole life ahead of you. You don't want to spend your whole life with an over-the-hill fucker like me.*

Paulino had been married three times and swore up, down and sideways that it wouldn't happen again.

Barry thought about the Tex-Mex offer, shook his head, mouthed the words *Rain check*, then looked back at the phone.

I shouldn't. I really shouldn't.

Before he knew it, his fingers were pushing down buttons: 7-5-4-8...

Stop. Are you crazy? They used to kill people for stuff like this, string 'em up by their balls and shit.

Shut up, you pussy. Everybody does it. Remember what Nana said?

He looked at the phone. Just an ordinary white work phone, except it now looked distorted, almost blurred. Barry glanced around the dealership; no one knew or cared what he was doing. If he kept ringing up sales like this, he could swing naked from the rafters and the team would cheer him on.

"Hellooo..." Her voice was warm and sultry, like caramel dripping on a hot apple.

"Brenda," Barry said, lowering his voice.

"Is that you, Barry? I thought it was you, you bad boy. When are you going to come see me? Or is Mr. Salesman all talk and no play?"

Barry paused. *What was he supposed to do?* Patricia came into his mind then: her slim physique, the way she smiled at him when he walked in the door. His Patricia. The woman who never looked at another man, let alone fantasized about them. What would that be like, coming home and seeing some large faceless black man riding Patricia in the middle of their brass bed? And why did this faceless man always have to be black?

"Barry, are you there, sweetie? I got something for you."

Barry smiled, felt himself stiffen. "Oh yeah, what you got for me, Brenda?" Barry looking out over the top of his cubicle, the gray-blue sky, a pair of customers holding hands and pointing out possibilities as they strolled across the lot, Barry trying to pretend that his life wasn't his just for a few seconds. That instead of a long-time girlfriend, Patricia, with no babies, he actually had a wife at home with two babies, tired but happy, and Barry was on his way to the store for Huggies and low-fat yogurt instead of sitting here talking to Brenda on the phone.

He knew it was a lie, that his relationship to Patricia was a half-lie, that the fact that people blamed Patricia instead of him for the loss of their babies was a complete lie. Barry knew people would never understand the truth: that Barry wasn't there for her. In some certain way, some crucial inner way that she needed, Barry knew he was letting her down. The problem was that he didn't know how to fix it, even if he wanted to. He heard his father's voice then: *Watch out for women, son. There is no end to their needs.* But on the outside, hey, Barry was a working man, supporting his girlfriend and their house, bringing home the dollars to keep their life going. And Patricia? Patricia just hung out at home, sitting on the couch and sulking. It was hard to explain to people, easier just to dump it all on her.

And then Brenda's sultry voice started up again.

"You still there, Big B? You know what I got? Like taking milk from its momma, Barry. You gonna drink all my milk, that's what you gonna do, as soon as you come see me."

Barry clutched the phone tighter and took another look around the showroom: April and Stan stood talking near the front, Chad was on the internet looking for concert tickets, Orzo on the phone setting up his next deal and Paulino now heading out the front doors to claim his free happy-hour tacos and the co-eds that came with them.

Bottom line: no one knew who Barry was talking to or cared what he was doing. He swallowed hard. "Oh yeah, tell me again, Brenda."

"I'm getting hot just sitting here," she began. Barry touched himself then, dropped his hand into his right pants pocket and rubbing himself through his slacks. "You know what you can do with a lollipop, Barry? Roll it in your mouth, over your tongue, suck it till it's all gone. You want that, Barry? You want to come over here and let me do that for you?"

Barry hung up the phone and half-sprinted through the gray-carpeted halls back to the green walls of the bathroom, where he stepped into one of the stalls and jacked-off into the toilet. It felt good, wrapping his hand around himself and picturing Brenda's big mouth all over him. "She would suck it, just like that," he said out loud as he shot cum into the toilet, stood while the tingles ran down his arms and legs.

Patricia could never do this for him, would never do it for him. Sometimes a man just needed sex: stone-cold sex. Not love, not intimacy, not sharing or connection or any of that woo-woo, emotional, I want-to-feel-connected-to-you crap. *Just friction,* Patricia liked to call it, her mouth turning down as she said it.

Barry ripped off some toilet paper, wiped himself, did a once-around the toilet rim, then pulled up his pants and stepped out of the stall.

"You did good today, Barry, been on a hot streak lately," Stan his boss said, sucking in his trim stomach and running his fingers through the gray above his temples. Stan had been manager at the dealership since '99; he and Barry had been on-again/off-again since that time. "What's your secret?"

Barry played it cool. Turned on the hot water, tried to forget what had just happened seconds earlier in the toilet stall. "No secret. Just being at the right place at the right time, Stan. That and making sure I go to church on Sundays."

"Ah, it's more than that and you know it. How's Patricia?"

Barry looked in the mirror and met Stan's eyes, looked deep into them before looking away. Something was wrong with Stan's eyes, something askew that Barry couldn't quite put his finger on. "She's good. Staying busy. You all right, Stan? You look a little, I don't know, off-kilter or something."

Stan intensified his stare into the mirror, before breaking their gaze and looking away. "What the fuck are you talking about? Why wouldn't I be all right?"

"I'm not trying to make trouble." Barry ran some more hot water over his hands. *Why had he opened his big mouth?* "I don't know. You just seem a little, I don't know, different."

"The whole world is different, Barry. I'm just trying to be the same. The Internet has taken away forty percent of our business. I'm having to lay guys off like a fucking Mexican paper plant after the last tree is gone. That and Marge is talking about leaving me. You believe that? Says she's ready for something new, something different. Probably someone younger." Stan patted his hands on a paper towel, his cheeks now flushed red. "That April's a hot number, though, huh? You see those pants she's wearing today?" Stan let out a low whistle. "What I wouldn't give to jump into that ride for a while..." Barry stared at him. Stan and Marge had been married for nineteen years; they'd put three kids through college and had hosted Barry and Patricia at more than one Christmas party at their place. "The whole world is upside down, I tell you what." Stan sucked in his cheeks, looked at himself in the mirror, tried to smile. "She wants something new. What's out there that's new?" Stan dunked his towel in the swinging trash can and strode out.

Barry stood there a moment, thinking about Stan and the dealership and the crazy world he was living in. He pictured Stan and Marge at their Christmas parties: they'd been happy. Laughing and drinking punch and sitting next to each other on the couch, her arm draped casually across his leg. *You never know,* Barry thought. *You never know what goes on behind closed doors.*

Then he thought about heading over to Brenda's and taking her up on that offer. He thought about the look on Patricia's face if he did that, if he took their ten years together and flushed it down the tube with one blow job. One great, fucking blow job.

The whole thing would take about fifteen minutes. And no one would even know. Not Patricia, not his mom, not his co-workers at the dealership. Not his buddies from college who he hadn't talked to in years. No one. Except one person would know, one person would feel the stain for years to come: him. He would know. And he wasn't sure how he would deal with that knowledge.

Barry thought about his mom then, about the look on her face after she found out his dad had been cheating on her. She hadn't yelled, hadn't even cried, not that Barry could see. She'd just sort of gone away. Later, after his dad had died and Barry had a moment alone with her, he'd asked her about it, why she hadn't had some big emotional outburst, yelling and screaming and throwing dishes that broke on the kitchen walls, trying to corral his dad back into line.

His mom had looked at him plain and simple, her thin face worn and haggard, the outlines of her eyes and cheeks touched up with a bit of rouge. "Barry," she cleared her throat as she spoke, every sentence sounding a little bit like a planned speech. "If every marriage broke up on account of infidelity, there'd be no marriages left." She'd smiled a thin little smile, her tight lips turning up just a bit at the ends.

Barry hadn't known how to respond. He was nineteen when his dad had died, twenty-five at the time he and his mom had talked. He'd dropped his eyes and toed the carpet, and for some strange reason, he'd almost begun to cry.

7

Patricia couldn't remember what she used to feel like. She'd look in the mirror, see the dark gray circles under her eyes, and think, *There must be something wrong. These aren't my eyes. This isn't my face.* She'd think these things from a far away place, almost as if she was worrying about a friend she used to know.

She padded into the living room and lay down on the couch. *What time would Barry be home? What would he want for dinner? Did we have enough of his sparkling water?* It was too much to think about. That seemed to be her favorite phrase lately: *It's just too much to think about.* As if thinking was costing her something physically and emotionally.

Maybe it was.

She ran her fingers over her lips and skin. Maybe she was thirsty; her skin didn't usually feel this, what was the word? Parched. Not quite. Tight. Her skin felt tight. *I feel tight,* she thought, *my whole world feels tight.* She thought about that book she saw at Barnes & Noble: <u>You're Not Sick, You're Thirsty</u>! Maybe she wasn't sick, maybe it was all in her head. Bullshit!

Normal people didn't feel like this, even normal people who had lost two babies got back to life at some point, didn't they?

Heading into the kitchen, she grabbed a bottle of Arrowhead and scraped her way back to the couch. She was just so tired. Tired of headaches, tired of worrying, tired of thinking about all the things she should be doing.

Patricia, get a hold of yourself. You're a college graduate for chrissakes. You can do things.

Like what? Name five things you've done in the past three years.

Oh, like that will prove something.

Come on, I dare you.

Okay. I've grown those two rose bushes.

What else?

I'm still dating Barry. That counts for something.

What else?

I've lost two children.

Yes, you have, haven't you?

She wiped away a tear and drank from the water bottle. *I am not going to cry. I am not, dammit. There has got to be an end to the tears. You can't just keep going on forever like it just happened. It happened several years ago.*

Yes, but still, it happened.

Things happen. Tourists die. Planes drop out of the sky. And babies stop growing inside your tummy.

Things happen, sometimes for no rational, sane reasons. Not for a lack of love, or a lack of desire; not because she wasn't going to be a good mom or she and Barry didn't love each other enough, or any one single reason that anybody could point to.

But not to me, Patricia thought. *It wasn't supposed to turn out like this. I was supposed to be out walking them in strollers, cute little yellow or blue jumpers on their adorable little bodies, dropping in on their daddy at work and snuggling with him before heading back out into the sunshine. I've always been good. I haven't messed around, not like some people, like Jennifer-the-slut Fracas who lifted her legs every time a jock walked around the corner. So why? Why does she have three big booming boys and a husband like Jack? It's not fair. Life is not fair.*

I never promised you a fair life, a voice said inside her right ear.

Oh, shut up, will you. I don't even know who you are or who let you in here.

In here? Don't you mean inside your head? Aren't I you?

Patricia buried her face underneath a pillow, then blinked open her eyes, staring into the dark fabric. Was she hallucinating? Who or what were these strange voices that never gave her a break? Didn't people get locked up for voices like these?

She realized she was slowly beginning to not know the difference between the voices and herself, between what she thought was reality and what felt like a stifling hall-of-mirrors that she had tripped or slipped into. Was she depressed? Was she losing her mind?

The phone rang, its sharp trill echoing out across the living room. Patricia jumped three feet off the couch and grabbed it on the second ring.

"Yes...hello?"

"Patricia, dear, you sound startled."

"You scared me, Mother. What are you calling for?" Patricia hated herself for being so irritable, but there it was.

"Nothing, dear. Nothing. I just wanted to check in on my little Patricia-poo, see how you were feeling today."

Patricia looked at herself in the hall mirror, at her tired face and dark circles and tight skin and wanted to throw up at the sight. Her stomach was thin and flat, when it should be big and preggers. She needed to let this all go! Jennifer Fracas would never let herself get to such a state.

"I'm fine, Mother. Really. You need to stop worrying about me so much."

"You don't sound fine, dear. Now why don't you tell me what's the matter."

Patricia held the phone, debating. *Do I open this can of worms?* Every time she'd done it with her dear old mom, it had been an absolute disaster.

"How much do you want to know?" she asked.

"I have two hours til the twins go to track practice. I'm yours if you want me," her mother replied.

Patricia debated, shifting her weight from one foot to the other as she continued to stare at herself in the mirror.

Barry took a deep breath and pulled out into traffic. Lincoln was backed up as usual, cars lining up seven and eight deep on their commute home. Everybody hated the freeways at rush hour. To the side of Lincoln – a mini-highway if you were from a small town with three lanes heading each direction -- there was Justin's diner, next to it a model train shop that would be out of business in three months, a Wendy's drive-thru, and Bon Appetit, a travel agency which had just recently gone out of business due to the rise on the Internet. People used to be life-long friends with their travel agents, calling them up and chatting their ear off before buying two round-trip tickets to

Turkey. Now those same people just went to Orbitz or Expedia and six minutes later had paperless tickets sitting in their in-boxes. *Just like the car business,* Barry thought, wondering when the next round of lay-offs would begin. *Like a Mexican paper-plant after the last tree was gone.*

He strained to see how far back he was, cocking his head out his window and trying to see over the roofs of the cars. He couldn't quite make it out. Barry had been selling cars at Westside Toyota for the past seven years, and for the past seven years, he'd been getting in this traffic jam, wondering if there was another way home.

I'm going to do something about it this time, he thought with a crazy manic smile.

He pulled into the center lane and whipped a U-turn, heading south on Lincoln. *Where was he going?* He didn't know. He didn't care. He gunned the engine and flew down Lincoln, the stores and windows whipping by. He lowered his window, smelled the fresh smoggy air, turned up the radio almost to full blast, and sang along to a really bad Rod Stewart song. He literally had no idea where he was heading. In fact, he knew only one thing at that moment, and it wasn't about Patricia or car sales or about the stick-lady wiping her snot on a new seat cushion. It wasn't about Stan or Marge talking about leaving him or about April and those hot-candy pants. What he knew, plain and simple, was that he just couldn't sit in that traffic jam one more minute. Not on this day.

He breathed in the semi-fresh air, turned the radio up even louder, and gunned his car down Lincoln like this was the last drive he'd ever take.

Patricia started slowly, recounting the last several days, how she's seen more of Barry's back than his front. How he'd come in after she was asleep and leave before she was awake. How his daily check-in calls were becoming every other day, then sometimes she was the only one calling him. They were drifting apart, there was no denying it. It was just so sad that she had to be boo-hooing to her mom to realize it.

"Well, I think the answer is simple, dear."

"You do?" Patricia said, sounding hopeful.

"Yes, dear. You leave him."

Patricia paused. *What did her mom just say?*

"What did you just say?"

"I said, the answer is simple: you leave him. That's what I did with your father."

"I know, Mom. That's what I thought you said. And was that the right decision? Should I do what you did? Go back to grad school and fall in love with my TA who's twenty years younger and start having babies all over again?" Spittle flew out of Patricia's mouth as she barked out the words. She hadn't talked to anyone in almost twenty-four hours.

"That's different, dear," her mom said.

"Why? Why is it different? Because it was you and not me?"

Her mom was silent for a moment. "Patricia, let me ask you something. Are you happy with Barry? Does he still make you laugh?"

"We've lost two babies, Mom. We're not married. It's not that black and white."

"I realize that," her mom replied. "I just…I haven't seen you happy in a while."

Patricia wrapped the phone cord around her index finger, squeezing the white rubber until her finger started to turn blue. "And in this made-up scenario where I leave Barry, what do I do, Mom? Move back in with you and Phil and the wonder-twins?"

"You do anything you want. You're a smart girl, Patricia. First in your class in high school; way above-average student while getting your BA in college. Why do I have to remind you of these things? You could have any job you want; you know that…which, by the way, are you still looking for a job?"

"Yes," Patricia responded, lying through her teeth. She hadn't opened the Want Ads or Craigslist in months. She'd been with that Temp Agency, and before that worked with that Headhunter from Long Beach, but the truth is Barry was making great money and Patricia was content to just sit on the couch and think about things. But she wasn't writing, she wasn't painting, she wasn't *doing* anything. That was the truth. Not for the past eighteen months when the second miscarriage had happened. They were both still recovering from it, each in their own way.

"You haven't lived on your own since college. You're not married. I just think…" Her mom paused, trying to choose her words carefully. "I just think if you and Barry took a break, if you had some time on your own, maybe you'd remember how special and wonderful you are."

"It's not that simple, Mom," Patricia sighed, feeling a thousand pounds heavier than before starting the conversation.

"Yes, it is, dear. You just write a note. That's what I did with your father."

"And go where?" Patricia asked.

"You'll figure it out. You're a smart girl," her mother said, hanging up the phone.

Patricia heard the click, and couldn't believe where their conversation had gone.

Barry continued to race down Lincoln, heading out towards the dunes where he could just make out the blue of the ocean in the distance. He picked up his cell phone on the second ring, hoping it was Patricia.

"Barry, I need to talk to you." Stan's voice sounded funny, different, like a piano that wasn't hitting the right notes.

"I've left for the day, Stan." Barry was irritated, not trying to hide it.

"You just left five minutes ago. How far are you?"

Should he lie? Whoever heard of a boss that called you back to work after you left? "Out past the jetty, almost to the Warehouse. Shit, I can see the joggers, I mean the real joggers, out here with their headphones and nothing but God and miles of sky."

Stan shifted his weight. Barry could feel it through the phone. "But you live in the Palisades. You don't go past the jetty."

"Are you my boss or my mother?" Barry asked.

"That depends. How soon are you coming back here?"

Patricia stared at the sheet of paper. She'd given it a lot of thought, what her mother had said. Maybe she should leave Barry. She'd thought about it, of course; anyone would have given what they were going through. *What they were going*

through. It sounded so awful, like concentration camp victims or starvation survivors. Except she wasn't sure they were going through anything. She was clearly going through something. A mid-life crisis, Barry had called it. But he didn't seem to be going through anything. He was still the same old Barry: selling cars, drinking with friends, spending time on the weekends out in his workshop sawing and planning and building non-sensical items made of different kinds of wood. Barry. Her boyfriend. The round one who could strike up a conversation with anybody.

Except.

Except what?

Something had changed. She could see it in his eyes. Her mother was right about part of it. She put down the pen, then picked it up again.

8

Dear Barry,

   We've been growing apart for quite a while. I thought I would do you a favor and disappear. I just need some time to myself. Please don't look me up. I'll get in touch when I'm ready to talk.
Love, Patricia

9

Barry pulled into the lot and turned his ignition off. *Fuck, I can't get away from this place.* He looked at his watch: a few minutes before seven. The sun was setting low over the water and Barry caught the auburn reflection next to the supermarket across the street. There were several long boats rocking with the tide and for some reason Barry thought back to high school, to the way the girls wore their short skirts and how their skin looked in the sunset as they would wrap a sweater around their shoulders and head over to the football games. It was something about the sun on the skin that got him. Only in California or Florida would girls show that much skin: the tan coloring, the freckles, the invitation to something much more private. Barry as a fifteen year-old would stand by the side of the football stadium tunnel, watching the high school girls walk up to their seats and imagine diving inside and never coming out.

Stan met him out on the lot; that never happened. If there was ever the proverbial boss hiding in the proverbial ivory castle, Stan was it.

"Barry, we've got to talk."

Barry looked up. Stan didn't smile, didn't move actually, except for this small twitch on the right side of his mouth that made his whole face appear even more tight than before.

"What's up?" Barry asked, getting out of the car, trying to appear cool. Three guys had been let go in the last two weeks. Times were tough all over. Down the street, Buerge Ford had just let go of six of their guys, most of them new or still on their way up.

That's not going to be me, Barry thought. *You'll see. I'll take one in the backside before I go down like that.*

"Not here. Come for a walk with me," Stan clipped.

Now Barry was truly scared. He was second on the team; shouldn't that guarantee his place? Maybe he shouldn't have been such a dick with Stan in the bathroom earlier. Oh fuck.

Barry looked towards the showroom. April was just turning down the lights and locking the front door. They closed early every Wednesday, giving the guys a chance to have dinner with their girlfriends or wives. Right, more like giving Tex-Mex a chance to wrangle in guys like Paulino and add to their happy hour.

Barry smiled. He knew he could find another job. Ralph's Supermarket was hiring across the street. Maybe he'd be able to join their management program, go through all the different positions, start out as a bagger, work his way around to the register, scanning avocados for little old ladies not much taller than their carts.

Will you shut up? this voice from inside of him said, watching Stan make his way between the Corollas and Camrys.

Barry followed Stan as he reached the end of the lot, slipped underneath the rusted chain and whale sign marking the end of Westside Toyota, then headed out alongside the railroad tracks. Small sprouts of grass grew in between the faded wooden slats; Barry bent down and picked up a few blades.

"What are you doing that for?" Stan asked.

"I'm a nature lover. Actually, I'm trying to figure out what I'm going to do if you're about to fire me."

Barry looked at him straight. He wasn't usually this direct with Stan. Stan the Big Man. Stan the Boss. Stan the prick who could change some poor schmo's life with a swipe of his pen.

"I'm not here to fire you, Barry. Jesus Christ. Has everybody gone insane this week?"

Barry glanced over at him. Something told him not to talk.

"It's the new kid, Chad. He's just not working out. I want you to let him go."

"Me? Since when is that my job? You're the boss, Stan."

Stan winced. It was subtle, but Barry caught it. "I know I'm the boss, Barry. That's why I'm asking you to let him go."

Barry looked out across Lincoln Blvd., at the steady hum of traffic as it whizzed by. Across the street, the Spanish tiling on the supermarket roof glinted in the sunlight. Underneath, their managerial program beckoned him. He would never have to fire another checker; he knew it in his gut. Chad was a kid, he'd only been here six weeks; but more than that, he was the first person to listen to or take an interest in Barry in a long time. Barry squinted across the street, could see the ocean, its flat blue stretching out before him like a giant blanket.

"He's just a kid, Stan."

"I know he is. Let him go."

"Why?"

Stan tightened his shoulders. "Do you really want to know the in's and out's of this? How little money he's made? The fact that he couldn't hit water if he fell out of a boat?"

"No," Barry said, looking down at his shoes and toeing a rock. "Just tell me what I need to know."

"Like what?" Stan asked.

"Like when. When do you want me to fire the kid?" Barry asked, suddenly unafraid, looking Stan full in the face. His boss' crazy look was back and Barry wondered how long it would be till Stan cracked. Barry thought about Marge, wondered if she knew this side of him and if that was the real reason she was talking about leaving him.

"That's up to you. But soon, before the weekend," Stan answered, now talking over his shoulder, heading back towards the dealership, leaving Barry alone on the thin grass between the slats of the rusted railroad tracks.

10

There. That was easy. Surprisingly easy. My god, if she really loved him, could it or should it have been that easy?

She re-read the note. It sounded good. It sounded plausible.

Where would I go?

Montana is nice this time of year.

And what would I do to support myself? They don't have a 'Le Michele Boutique' up in Billings.

I would find something. I'm a college graduate! Anybody can work in a store and ring up a register.

Oh my God, these voices have got to stop!

She picked up the note, made a mental note to never talk to her mother again, then ripped the letter into small white pieces and dropped them into the blue plastic trash. They looked like parade confetti as they fluttered down.

❧

Patricia stayed in the house as long as she could, then hopped into her blue Toyota Prius, unsure where to go.

She headed away from the cliffs and the Pacific Ocean, turning left onto Sunset then right down Chautauqua, the road's long curvy neck bobbing back and forth between palm trees. She joined traffic heading east on Pacific Coast Highway (PCH), watching the joggers and roller-bladers mix in with people riding bikes on the boardwalk. They were in all shapes and sizes: a tall, skinny man in a yellow warm-up suit, a child in a white one-piece pushing a tricycle next to her mom in green pant slacks and a tan blouse.

Patricia longed to be one of them. Could be, in fact.

Had been is more like it.

Growing up does a funny thing to you, Patricia thought, maneuvering off PCH onto the Ocean Avenue off-ramp, knowing where she would end up. *You think it's going to make you happy; it doesn't.*

Then what does it make you?

Sad.

Angry.

Confused.

She got in the left-hand turn lane, flicked on her blinker.

She knew in that moment that it wasn't all Barry's fault. *I could have been with anybody,* she thought, *and this same result might have happened. I could have lost two babies and would be sitting here childless and purposeless no matter who my partner was.*

She fought back tears, looked at the red light and wondered if that was true.

Was it actually something between her and Barry, or could this have happened with anyone? A tear slid down her right cheek.

She knew she needed to get to a different place mentally, knew the thoughts she was having were not good. *But I have no idea how to get there,* she thought, seeing the light turn green and reluctantly sliding the Prius forwards.

The outdoor Farmer's Market took place every Tuesday in the west part of Santa Monica. They cordoned off four or five blocks just behind Ocean; the vendors showing up at eight; everybody else shopping from ten to four picking out fresh arugula, organic spinach, baby corn that you could sprinkle on a salad and then pick with your fingers.

Patricia hitched her basket up a bit higher on her hip and waded through the throng of people. With her hair pulled back, she looked and felt a bit like an Arthurian maiden: her golden-blonde hair and fair skin made her feel like she belonged in another time.

Fresh air. This was what she needed.

"How much for the tomatoes?" she yelled at the heavy-set lady with a roundish face and piercing, dark eyes. The vendor had three people vying for her attention and couldn't decide who to answer first.

"Three for a dollar, or I'll give you the whole bag for five," the lady spit out, swiveling towards Patricia and staring her full in the face.

Patricia handed over a five-dollar bill and hoisted the bag into her basket. The tomatoes were gorgeous. Television red, Patricia commented to herself.

She bought a few more veggies, corn and asparagus and two beautiful bunches of kale for dinner that night, then went over to the coffee cart and got herself a large chai. Chai was one of the great inventions of the twenty-first century, with its bittersweet tang and rich, full-body aroma. She again imagined being in another century as she breathed in the cinnamon spices, her nostrils now fully alive.

She took a sip of her drink and sat on a corner stoop, watching all the people move around her. *Had she really written that note this morning?* She needed to be careful of talking to her mother. Her mother. The woman who'd left her father when Patricia had still been a small child, saying that some things were beyond repair like televisions and broken phones and marriages where two people didn't love each other. Had Patricia's parents not loved each other? Then why did they get married in the first place? Why did they have her? Patricia's father, Stuart, had argued against this, of course. He'd said they loved each other very much, but that Patricia's mom spiraled into certain moods and didn't have the tools or motivation to get herself out. They'd tried drugs, doctors, weekends by the beach in San Diego. And then her mom had written a note, and that had been the end of their relationship. Period.

Stuart was now re-married with three young kids and a much younger wife. Beverly. Patricia couldn't stand her, although she couldn't figure out why. Was it because she was ten years younger than her dad? Because she was only ten years older than Patricia? Or was it because Patricia caught Beverly in her perfect, size-two pants sneaking candy bars when no one was looking? Patricia could have joined her, in that backroom at Thanksgiving a few years ago. It would have been easy: just sauntered over, shared a smile that said 'this will be our little secret' and dug into that Milky Way like there was no tomorrow. But she hadn't. Patricia had frozen, eyes bugging out of her head like she was catching her dad's new wife with the neighbor instead of caramel nougat. Beverly had frozen, too, her hand on the bar as it was half-way to her mouth. They should have just laughed it off, but instead they'd locked eyes: Beverly looking guilty as hell and Patricia judging her new step-mom for all she was worth before rejoining the others in the main part of the house. They'd never talked about it again.

But her dad was happy, and that was what counted.

Patricia took another sip of her chai, looked down at her basket full of gorgeous veggies, and felt a deeper question come into her heart: Did she and Barry still love each other?

They did.

For many, many years, they did.

But was that love growing?

Patricia shook her head slowly.

Had their love become stale and stagnant like water that sits too long?

"I think I'm depressed," Patricia said out loud without realizing it. An elderly bald man in a gray cardigan smiled sadly, regarding her as yet another lunatic on the streets of Los Angeles.

Patricia lowered her eyes, wildly embarrassed. In that moment, she didn't know if she and Barry really did love each other. She didn't know if their relationship would make it, if they would ever have babies, if he was really coming home for dinner that night. She didn't know. But she needed to find out.

Lifting herself off the stoop, Patricia grabbed the basket and began to awkwardly make her way through the crowd filled with senior citizens, moms with strollers, Mexican farm workers grabbing lunch from carts and vendors in the middle of a busy workday.

This scene looked so familiar.

Oh my God. Was this *that* Farmer's Market?

She looked again at the street signs. Arizona. Fourth street. She remembered the images from the television and the newspaper. The eye-witnesses saying how they saw bodies flying, the dark sedan accelerating instead of slowing down, people diving sideways, screaming, hoping to get out of the way. The driver had been eighty-five years old, confused between the brake and the gas. Six people had died, ten more injured, and it had happened right here. Five or six years ago. Patricia looked to her left, imagined an oncoming car barreling towards her. She stood stock still and didn't move a muscle.

And then in a flash it was gone, the entire scene. Patricia scooped up her basket, forgot the dead and the dying and all the crazy thoughts she'd been having, and rushed home to find out where her boyfriend was.

11

Make every day count, Barry's father had told him a few days before he died, the oxygen in his father's nose making his breath stale and raspy. David Lemming. A large man with a barrel chest, a sagging belly and a thin, bird-like nose which always gave off the impression of a hawk. Either that or looking down his nose at someone. David was a sagittarius, meaning if he thought it, he said it, which made some people love him, and some people scurry out of the room as soon as he came in.

Barry had been around his father most of his life, had seen him through two by-pass surgeries and one gnarly bout with cancer, the one that had taken his hair, his stamina, most of his weight. But his dad had never given up, never stopped fighting. Even thirty-six hours before the end, his breath coming shallow and short, David Lemming had looked Barry in the eye and said, "I'm going to beat this. You'll see."

Make every day count.

Barry lifted out his cell phone, thought about dialing Brenda's numbers, and instead called Patricia's cell.

"Hello," Patricia answered.

"Hey, you're there," Barry said, cruising to a stop at a red light. "I didn't think I'd catch you."

"Where are you?" Patricia asked. "I tried you over at the dealership."

"I just left. Made another sale this morning. That's seven for this pay period."

"Way to go, Barry. I'm proud of you." Patricia walked in the front door, dropped her groceries on the kitchen counter, headed towards the bathroom.

"You okay? You sound distracted." Barry asked, his mouth turning down.

"I'm fine. You know these cell phones hurt my head. Are you going by the market? Can you pick up some balsamic vinaigrette? I'm making us a nice salad."

"Sure," Barry said. "I'm almost there now. Stan kept me after."

"About what?" Patricia asked.

"I'll tell you when I get home. See you in twenty," Barry said, clicking off his phone, hating his lie, but knowing at the same time he had every right to go blow off steam. So why didn't he say that? Why didn't he tell his girlfriend the truth? Oh yeah, like what truth, like *Patricia, I'm going to go have a couple drinks to blow off the day and get ready to face you.* Or *Patricia, you really need to leave me. You know it and I know it. We both just don't want to say it. You're not happy. You sit at home and brood and talk with your crazy mother and we've now been together ten years and I still can't put a ring on your finger. It's like every day reminds me how much I've failed you.*

Barry looked at himself in the rear-view mirror. *You are a mental case,* Barry thought, slipping his Mustang into gear and gliding out into traffic.

Turning up the radio, Barry watched Lincoln disappear in his rear-view mirror and sped across the empty asphalt, glad to be free and able to move. *Balsamic vinaigrette for Patricia, balsamic vinaigrette for Patricia.* He made a mental note of it, hoping he wouldn't forget.

He felt the day unravel inside him. Did people do different things with their lives? Did everyone sit in some cubicle with red puffy gums, waiting for the next pair of assholes to come strutting through the double-doors and say, "Don't fuck with us"?

Barry sighed.

He'd started noticing it a year or two ago, the change in the customers. Everybody knew about car salesmen. They'd sell their mother's soul to make a sale. Even Barry. *But what about the customers?* Just recently, Barry had three different people lie to his face in a single day. That might sound trivial, but Barry had never deliberately lied to a customer. He played the game, sure, but they weren't his rules. It wasn't even his game. It was something he did from eight-to-five six days a week so he and Patricia could live in the alphabet streets of the Palisades, spend time together, do things like barbecues and cook-outs and long walks on the beach. Not that they did anymore, but, you know, they used to. They still could. He showed up for work not because he felt good about it, not because he cared about the cars or the dealership or least of all the customers. He fingered the steering wheel, stepped down harder on the accelerator, watched the needle climb to seventy as he sped down the hill towards Playa del Rey. No, he showed up for work because if he didn't, if he decided to freak out and leave his job without a trace and disappear to somewhere like Montana, he'd have to come in contact with a very scary realization: there was a chance that deep down, underneath his work and Patricia and all of his weird mental gymnastics, he didn't know who he was.

He made it past Jefferson, turned right at the Home Depot and started heading towards the beach. Brenda. *What kind of weird hold did she have on him?* He slid a hand down towards his crotch and began massaging himself there. Okay, let's look at this rationally. I'm thirty-two years old, I have a girlfriend named Patricia who I love most of the time but haven't had good sex with in years. I whack off to some broad named Brenda whom I've never even met. We tease each other on the phone, and once in a while, I dream and scheme and get real close to meeting her.

Never even met.

I'm pathetic. Totally pathetic. My life is pathetic. My sex is pathetic. My very existence is pathetic.

Barry tried to imagine his friend Taylor, the religious one. The one who says that everything is from God and we need to look to God to figure out our problems. God. Now there was a problem. *Don't get me started*, Barry thought, downshifting into second and cruising into the Tiki Hut's parking lot.

Barry sat for a minute, wondering whether he really wanted to go inside. The Tiki Hut had a large brown roof with fake bamboo pillars outside the door. He'd been coming here regularly for about six months, then stopped when some girl's biker husband had taken offense to the way Barry was looking at her.

The nerve of some people.

"What'll it be for the Big Car Salesman?" Vicki the bartender asked, pretending to shield her eyes from the radiance that Barry brought in with him. The Tiki Hut sported large bay windows that looked out onto the beach and right now the setting sun was so gorgeous Barry wanted to take a snapshot and stick it into his back pocket. He turned from the post-card sunset and looked at the bartender. She was short and cute with blonde bangs and sexy dimples, like something you might place on top of a cake.

"Hey Vick, how are you? Rum and coke please," Barry said, trying to smile. The place was a disaster: rotting tables, sawdust everywhere, pictures and mirrors hanging crookedly on dirty walls. Someone's bad dream. But the dark wood gave him the feeling of a secret hideout. He took his drink and went over to the corner.

Ten minutes, Barry thought. *Then I scream home, show up a few minutes late, and everything's good.*

Barry liked to sit in the corners. He used to think it was for safety, literally feeling protected by two sturdy walls behind him. Now he started to think it might be for something different entirely.

"Mind if I join you?"

He looked up, shielding his eyes a sec. Cigarette smoke drifted towards him in a large, hazy cloud. Barry had no idea who it was.

"I only have a few minutes," Barry offered.

"That's okay," the woman said, "I won't bite."

Barry motioned for her to sit down. He flipped out a Marlboro Light for himself and then offered her one, watching her draw out the stick and place it between her lips. Barry reached over and thumbed his lighter for her, smiling in a what-are-you-doing-at-my-table sort of way. The woman was short and stocky, with a scar along her right cheek that made her look like a pirate. Her smile was crooked but sweet; her skin a sickly kind of yellow. Barry wondered what her story was.

"How'd you get that?" Barry asked, taking a sip of his rum and coke, swirling an ice cube around in his mouth. His day was feeling farther away already.

"Husband," she said, blowing a ring of smoke up into the air. She tilted her nose and pursed her lips, like a ballerina finishing a perfect pose.

Barry smiled. "What'd you do?"

"He caught me fooling around with his brother, decided to teach me a little lesson."

"Did you learn the lesson?" Barry asked.

"Apparently not," the woman replied, smiling.

"I'm Barry. I sell cars over at Westside Toyota."

"Tina," the woman said, extending her hand and leaving it just a little too long in his. "I give blow jobs for a living."

"Get out of town," Barry said.

"Well, I might as well."

"What do you really do?" he asked.

"I work for the mayor. PR, stuff like that," she said, smiling, her eyes dancing just a bit. Barry could tell she was enjoying the conversation.

"And no one objects to that scar on your face?" The words just came out. Ordinarily, he would never say something like that. Maybe it was the rum; maybe it was talking to strangers in a strange place where you could be whomever you wanted, knowing you were never going to see them again. Sort of like a giant costume party where everyone was wearing a mask.

She scooted a little bit closer. "No one's taken such an interest in it in quite a while."

"I have a girlfriend," Barry said, backing up a bit.

"So?" Tina said, feigning hurt. "Doesn't everybody?" They sat in silence for a second. "What does that mean exactly, to you, Mr. Barry from Westside Toyota?"

Barry tried hard to focus, took another sip of his drink. "That means just like it sounds. I'm living with somebody."

He looked over at her; they both started to laugh.

He cleared his throat. "It's funny, isn't it? The time we spend away from our partners, trying to figure out what we're doing with them in the first place. I don't know anybody who has good sex with their partner." He looked down at his hands, sorry that he had said that. *Why could he be more honest with a total stranger than the woman he loved?*

"That's sad," she said, nodding up at Vicki for another margarita. "I know one couple, my friends Greg and Melanie, they're a pretty good fit. But that's it. They have great sex and great fun…other than that…serious relationships…the institution of marriage…losing battles if you ask me." Tina parceled out the words like she was making a pronouncement for all time. She took a long drag on her cigarette, stubbed it out, lit another one.

"Why'd you do that?" Barry asked.

"Do what?"

"Stub out a perfectly good one and light a new one."

The woman smiled. "You're quick, Barry. Can't get much past you. Nerves, I guess. Wondering what I'd do if my husband walked through those doors right now."

The cocktail waitress came over and set down their drinks.

"I didn't order this," Barry said.

"Vicki sent it over," the waitress said. "Might be your lucky night."

"No, thanks," Barry replied. "I have to drive home in a minute."

"Let him keep it, Ginger," Tina said, handing the waitress a ten. "Tip's on me."

Barry fingered his glass. He was already past the time he'd told Patricia and he still had twenty minutes to drive home.

He took a quick sip of his drink and started to go.

"Don't go," Tina said, reaching out to his arm. "We're just getting to know each other."

Barry smiled. "Look, Tina, you seem real nice. And I'm sure that that husband who did that to you is real nice, too. But I'm living with someone, and my girlfriend is sitting at home right now wondering where the hell I am. I gotta go."

Barry stood up and stretched his legs. He took a look around. Most of the booths were filled with an odd variety of people: locals in their khaki shorts and flip-flops, bikers, drunks, a funny-looking pair of tourists from Sweden or Denmark, their blonde hair spilling over their shoulders in waves.

"Barry," the woman said, leaning forward in the booth. "Come here a sec."

"What?" Barry asked.

"Come here. I'm not gonna bite you."

Barry stepped back to the table.

"I want to give you my card," Tina said as she fumbled through her purse. "Just, you know, for whatever."

She handed him the card, then stood up beside him, her small, rock-hard breasts pressing against his arm on the way up. "Do you think I'm cute?" she asked.

"Tina, come on. We're both with other people. Let's leave it at that."

"You didn't answer my question," she said.

"Yes, I think you're very attractive. Your husband with the knife is probably real cute, too." Barry was starting to get annoyed, could feel the dirty walls of the Tiki Hut closing in a bit. *Didn't he come here to get away from crap like this?*

"I lied about that. It was my dad, when I was a girl."

"Really?" Barry asked, suddenly interested.

"Yes. I'd like to tell you about it."

"I'm sorry, Tina. I really am, but I have to go."

Barry took a step away from her, while at the same time imagining what it would be like to move towards her and kiss her and press the rest of his body up against those breasts of hers. She just stood there, waiting. *Was she really married to a knife-wielding psychopath? Did she actually work for the mayor or was her first answer closer to the truth?* Barry sighed and nodded as he moved to the door. He was suddenly tired: tired of strange women, tired of watered-down rum, tired of avoiding what was really important.

He made it out to his car, to the now absent sun and the orange glow of the street lights throughout Playa del Rey. He was going to be forty minutes late for dinner; he just hoped that Patricia was still there when he got home.

12

Oprah cackled into the television camera. "Now tell me, people. Tell me. Why do women stay in these stupid relationships? And it's not just women. It's all people. We stay because we're afraid to leave. I'm afraid to leave. You're afraid to leave. We're afraid. But if you're not happy, if you're watching this television, talking to yourself about some other life you could be living and you just don't know where to start, then you start by talking to yourself about the possibility of walking towards that other life. You don't have to know the path. You just have to take the first step."

Patricia rinsed the lettuce under the faucet and snapped the stalk in two. *It's all around me,* she thought, people talking about leaving their spouses, people talking about how unhappy they are. Like it's all their spouses' fault. Don't people feel the way they do because of who they are inside, independent of anyone else? Or are we so entangled that our feelings are always dependent on another person? She could hear her mother inside her. *You are not a small person. Your life is not small or insignificant. You were not small in high school. You were even less small in college. You were on your way to great things, to actually being somebody.*

Define somebody, Patricia thought, now dunking the kale under the water and dropping two pats of grass-fed butter into the pan to sizzle.

I don't know. Somebody who is special. Somebody who people remember at parties, someone people look up to, someone that inspires other people. Someone that could be by themselves all day long with nothing except four white walls and still feel good about themselves. That kind of somebody.

Oh, the old crazy test.

I am not crazy. I'm not. I'm depressed. I'm sad. I've lost two babies. I'm in a difficult relationship. I don't know if my boyfriend loves me.

I don't know if I matter anymore.

That was the toughest part. Not knowing.

I wonder if my life really is small. I wonder if Barry feels my life is small.

It's easy, dear. You just write him a note.

Patricia dropped the kale into a buttered pan and tore the lettuce into small, tiny fragments, letting them fall into the bowl. She glanced outside, saw the sun disappear across the horizon. Barry should be home any minute.

Barry sat in the car, the overhead lights from their driveway creating a harsh glare that cut across the car's interior. *He's just not working out. I want you to let him go.* Stan's words sat like a bad meal inside Barry's chest. He should quit. Asking him to fire co-workers, especially young, energetic, just-off-the-turnip-truck co-workers. If Barry had any guts, any decency, he wouldn't take crap like that. *But what would he do? What could he do?* He was thirty-two years old. He'd been selling cars at Westside Toyota for the past seven years. Before that, he'd worked in four restaurants and ran one part-time marketing business his senior year that went belly up before the end of its first year.

He needed the job.

He looked towards their beige front door, thought about Patricia, and sucking it up, took one last swig of rum before popping in an altoids and heading for the door.

He opened the door and came inside. Their entryway had small, white ceramic tiles that led down two steps to the gray carpeting of the living room. Cardboard boxes lined the walls of the sunken living room, sitting around and between the white sofa sectional. A sparse plant hung in the corner. On the wall, a poster of Kobe driving to the hoop. Barry tried not to look at the boxes; instead, he hung up his suit jacket in the hall closet, dropped his briefcase next to his shoes, and went looking for Patricia.

"Patricia, I'm home," he called.

"I'm here," she answered. "In the kitchen."

Barry maneuvered his way through the entrance, past the stack of boxes that blocked the way into the dining room. He hated the boxes. They had been there for a month, then two. Now two years later, Barry realized the boxes were some kind of fortress; he just wasn't sure if they were keeping Patricia in or him out.

But for right now, the boxes weren't on his mind; right now, he wanted to find Patricia.

There she was, pulling the salad out of the frig.

"Hi," he said.

"Hi," she responded coolly, turning around briefly before heading back into the frig.

Barry waited a moment, hoping she would come give him a kiss. "What's for dinner?"

"Oh, not much. Some fresh greens and tomatoes from the Farmer's Market, baked potatoes, and some salmon from that fish market you like."

"The one over on Fourth?" he asked.

"That's the one," she said, not making eye contact.

They moved around each other cautiously, Patricia grabbing the last few things she needed for the table, Barry not sure how to be and finally bumping into her near the toaster.

"Hi," he said again. "I was hoping for a kiss."

"I just have a few more things to get, then we'll…"

Barry grabbed her face, kissing her hard on the lips. Too hard.

Patricia pulled away. "Why'd you do that?"

"Do what?" he asked, feeling the rum.

"Kiss me like that. You didn't even ask."

"Jesus Christ, Patricia, you're my girlfriend. We live together. Do I have to ask every time I want to kiss you? I said it three or four times."

Patricia looked down at her feet. "You said it once. And yes, I'd like you to ask before you kiss me."

"Why the cold shoulder?" Barry asked.

"Can we just eat?" she responded, turning towards the table.

They sat at the dining room table, passing the food back and forth. Neither one spoke, their crunching filling the air.

"Maybe we should get a dog," Barry said.

"You're allergic to dogs," she answered.

"Well, maybe I'm not anymore."

"What? You're expecting a miracle," she retorted.

"All I'm saying is, people change, Patricia. If you give them a chance."

"People don't change that much, Barry. You're in sales, you should know that."

When did she get so hostile?

"Can you pass the potatoes, please?" he asked.

When did he become so infantile? He is like a huge, overgrown baby. And I know he's going to want sex later. No way! Not until he apologizes.

"There's no way I'm giving you sex later," she said, handing him the potatoes.

"What did you say?" he laughed.

"I meant…that's not what I meant. I meant to say something else."

"It sounded like that's what you meant," he said. "What did you mean to say?"

"I don't remember now. But there. I've said it. There is no way I'm giving you sex later."

Barry looked at her, remembered Stan's words before walking away on the railroad tracks.

"Why is it yours to give?" he asked.

"C'mon, Barry, let it go. Can we just have one peaceful night?"

"Let what go?"

She sighed. "Do we have to talk about this again? We both know men will do it anytime, anyplace, with just about anyone or anything, so given that, then it's ours to give or not give."

"That is so not true, and you know it. You're just mad I came home late."

"Oh yeah," she said, smiling, "How would you like to grab a bottle of Captain Myers rum, go out in your Mustang and go do it down by the pier?"

"I'd love that," Barry said.

"I rest my case," she said, picking up her plate and heading into the kitchen.

Barry just sat there. It was like his entire day, his entire life, had spun completely out of control. He thought of smashing her head against the wall, and wondered, is this how you ended up on the seven o'clock news, doing unspeakable things to the people you loved? He balled his hands into little fists as he sat there at the table, steaming, listening to the running water as Patricia washed her plate with her back to him. Did fights like this happen to Stan or his siblings or his parents before they divorced? Did this happen to Taylor, who believed you needed to bring everything back before God? Oh Jesus, he'd like to kick Taylor in the teeth right about now.

"You ever have that feeling that things are spinning completely out of control, but you don't know why?" Barry entered the kitchen cautiously, aware that he was not on his turf.

Patricia stood by the sink, her dishes already under the water, her back to him. She didn't budge.

"Patricia, I'm talking to you, or trying to talk to you. Do you ever have that feeling, almost like you're on the deck of the Titanic, except you have no idea how you got there?"

"Yes," she said quietly. "I have that feeling quite a lot."

"And what do you do when you have it?" he asked.

You don't want to know, she thought. *Listen to my mother. Call my friends. Write you horrible little notes and then rip them up into pieces.*

"Different things," she said, turning around and facing him. She tucked her arms up around her chest, and Barry couldn't help noticing how cute she looked, standing there.

"Like?" he asked.

"Like I talk to myself."

"Out loud or inside your head?" he asked.

"Are you making fun of me?"

"No," he answered. "I'm completely serious, because for some reason, I've felt things get completely out of control the last two days, but I have no proof or reason that that is what's happening."

"What do you mean?" she said.

"Well, first, Stan wants me to fire someone, which is totally uncharacteristic of him. Then you and I have barely talked, and that's not like us. And lastly, I don't know, all I know is something weird is going on."

He took a step towards her. Both of them noticed it.

"I don't like you coming home late and leaving early. It's not okay with me."

"Okay," he said. "I won't do that anymore."

"Wait, not so fast. Back up a step."

"I'm still three steps away, honey."

"Barry, we both know what's happening here. You need to give me some time."

Barry looked at her. *Shit. Had he crossed a line? Did she somehow know about the drinks at the Tiki Hut? Was it a lie if he didn't tell her?*

"What's happening here, Patricia?"

She wrapped her arms more tightly around herself, a couple freckles on her pale skin showing up on her forearms. "Don't patronize me. We both know you've been running around, probably screwing around, and now you're trying to come home and make nice so you're sure I'm not going to pack up and head to Montana or something."

There, I've said it, she thought, proud of herself. If she was going to ignore her mother and stay in this relationship, then she was going to start speaking her mind. And if he didn't like it, well, then he could just hit the road.

"You don't even like the mountains," Barry said, smiling, trying to see how serious she was.

The corners of her mouth turned up. She tried to bite down in the middle. *Stop it, stop smiling. You are giving in to him. Again.*

"I mean it. I'll leave. If that's what I need to do, then I'll pack up and ship out."

"If that's what you need to do," he said, his smile full-born now, taking two steps towards her. "We all need something."

"You are such a schmuck. I'm not giving in to you, you charmer. I can't believe I even moved here with you. My mother was right. You're a selfish bastard and I never should have done it. Why buy the cow if you're getting the milk for free? Ten years later and you still haven't asked me to marry you."

"I love it when you talk dirty to me," he said, taking the last final step towards her.

Barry looked at the clock, barely able to make out the blue numbers in the dark of their bedroom. Ten-fifteen. Patricia rested with her back to him. Their lovemaking had been quick, satisfying, both of them reaching climax within minutes, the pent-up anger and rage moving through them and then somehow breaking with a tide of emotion and tears. It saved them, their ability to do this. He thought of all the times they didn't connect, all the aborted conversations, missed times they could have shared, and then thought of this time together and wondered why he didn't give to her more.

He slid away from her, slipping underneath the covers and towards the closet.

"Where are you going?" she muttered.

"Be right back," he said.

Out in the hallway, everything seemed different. Underwater. He knew they'd been fighting, but now he also knew that he was back. On the inside, like a closet hook that he could hang his hat on. Feeling her heart and her space almost like it was his own. Almost. He thought back to before he and Patricia were together: the three-month chase, the intense loneliness that permeated his spirit at the end of the day. *I don't ever want to feel that again. Not if I can help it. I'll do anything not to feel that.*

He padded into the kitchen, grabbed the half-eaten Cherry Garcia from the freezer, and flicked on the sports highlights. LeBron dribbling down the left side of the court, slicing into the middle and dunking on some fool's head. Barry let out a mini-yell, raising his fists in victory. Ice cream and sports. Two of the greatest American pastimes right in his very own living room.

I did it again. Goddammit. I give in to him every time. But it felt so good. Even if I didn't climax, just to have him near me, paying attention to me, that was something, wasn't it?

It's not everything, though. He thinks you came. He thinks he satisfies you.

He does satisfy me, sort of.

Sort of? How satisfying is that?

Like almost getting something that your heart really needs. Almost.

Patricia rolled away from the wall, put her hand out to the space where Barry had been and felt around for a minute, thinking maybe he'd magically appear.

C'mon, Lakers. Share the ball. Too many stars on one team: the Mailman, the Glove, Shaq, Kobe. Barry thought back to Kobe's trial, wondered if he really raped that blonde hotel maid the way she said: putting his hands on her throat, forcing her to have sex through falling tears. She was twenty-two years old. To this day, Kobe still claims it was consensual, but no one knew for sure. They just knew it was settled out of court, with Kobe writing a very big check as settlement. Buying her silence. *How could Barry still cheer for him? How could the thousands of people in the crowd still cheer for him, not knowing for sure?*

Patricia could hear the muffled sound of sports through the wall. She rolled over onto her back, thought about different things she might do the next day. *What made me say Montana?*

I've never even been to Montana. I've been to Colorado, though. Colorado is lovely. That place right outside Boulder where the air gets crisp and the sky blue and all you think about is how much freedom you have from everything in your life that you can't stand.

I wonder if Montana has that same thing.

Hmmm.

❧

Barry opened the door and peered inside. Patricia was still in bed. He took off his pajama bottoms and slid in close. *So good to be back in good.* Barry thought of his day, the weird conversation with Stan, the scar-faced lady from the Tiki Hut. *Why do I keep doing things like that? I've never messed around on Patricia, I probably never will.*

It's the chase, the tease, seeing how close he could get without getting caught.

I'm sick, Barry thought, *really sick.*

"You awake?" he asked.

"Sort of," she said.

"What'cha doing?" he lowered his voice, putting a cold hand on her back.

"Ooh, that's cold. Have you been eating ice cream?"

"Cherry Garcia. The only way to fly."

"And you didn't bring me any?" she asked, a note of hurt in her voice.

"Do you want some? There's still a few bites left."

"No," she said. "I shouldn't. I'll regret it in the morning."

They paused. Barry had his hand up under the back of her top, rubbed the skin between her shoulder blades. Patricia made a small noise and closed her eyes.

"You want to do something Thursday? It's my day off."

"Like what?" she asked.

"I don't know. We could go down to the boat, make a picnic. Whatever you want."

She rolled over and faced him. Even in the dark, Barry could see the memorized picture of her face: the tightly-drawn cheeks, perfect button nose, the small flared nostrils that gave away every time she was lying. Barry still thought she was beautiful. *I love this woman. I really do love this woman.* He could feel the struggle in his heart, though, the deep pain of still not knowing exactly what he wanted.

"Can I ask you something?" she said quietly.

"Of course," he said.

"Do you respect me?"

"What do you mean? Respect you how? Like respect the fact that we're living together, respect the fact that you're a woman?"

"Not like that," she began. "Just plain respect. Like would you respect me if I decided to leave you?"

13

Barry huddled in the shower, the walls closing in. She'd said it so straight, so honestly. How could you argue with that? He knew this day was coming. All the times they'd been happy, all the times they'd shared making love, going for hikes, dancing and laughing and making believe that life could be good.

He knew it was coming.

But don't I deserve it? Me, the one who goes out to the Tiki Hut and seduces women just to the point where they want me...the one who's constantly looking at women's asses, tits, wondering what they'd be like under the hood. Me, the bastard of a car salesman who'd turn over his mother for a higher commission.

Hey, that's over the line. I have bills to pay.

Still, you have to admit. Patricia has a point. I'd leave me, too.

He leaned back against the white-tiled shower wall, letting the warm water wash over him. It soaked into his scalp, his ears, ran in little rivulets down his face and onto his chest.

She hasn't left yet, a little voice inside him said.

Yeah, but she's talking about leaving.

But talking and leaving are two different things.
What are you saying?
What I'm saying, idiot, is maybe there's something we can do.
Like what? Like change?
At age thirty-two, am I even capable of change?

Barry sat in his gray cubicle, trying to pretend she hadn't said what she said. *Maybe she was kidding. Maybe she was.* He thought about her eyes, the shape of her mouth as she'd said it. She wasn't kidding.

"Barry, you're up," Stan blared into the microphone.

Barry flicked open his green pocket mirror, checked out his gums and hobbled out the double doors. His feet felt ice cold, like he was walking on pins and needles.

"Hi, I'm Barry, welcome to Westside Toyota," Barry said, extending his hand.

"Hi, Barry. I'm Colleen. Nice to see you," the tallish-blonde woman said as she smiled and took his hand.

"What kind of car are you looking for?" he asked. She was still holding his hand.

"I'm not really sure, maybe one that I could test drive for a while." Barry tried to pull his hand back; she tightened her grip.

"What's the idea?" he said, frowning.

"You don't remember me, do you?"

He stole a quick look over his shoulder: no one was paying them any attention. Barry looked at her face. She had narrow eyes, pretty, but something was off: her nose, her eyes. Something. Like someone had done something to her face they couldn't undo. Plastic surgery, maybe? Something Barry couldn't quite put his finger on.

"Do we know each other?" Barry said, taking his hand back with a snap.

"You bought me drinks at The Gaslight. Pineapple and vodkas all night long. You don't remember? Told me all the sweet, vicious things you were going to do to my body."

Barry took her by the elbow, steered her away from the showroom. "Say what now? How long ago was this?"

"About three months. You said to look you up if I ever needed a car deal."

"And do you?"

The woman smiled. "I need something."

"Do you want money?" Barry asked, reaching for his wallet.

"Honey, if I wanted money, do you think I'd be coming to you? You're a used car salesman. I want a date." She smiled as she said this, a thick, honey-dripping smile.

"You do?"

"Yep, you bet. Pineapple and vodkas, all night long," she said, an even larger smirk across her lips. She flicked a bright red tongue out, ran it over her mile-high teeth. "And this time, I want you to do those things to me you promised."

Barry shifted his weight, looked out over her head to the skyscrapers surrounding the dealership. This just wasn't his week.

Back inside, the blast of cold manufactured air hit him across the face and cheeks.

"Patricia's on four, Barry," April said, giving him a wink as he passed by.

Barry took a deep breath and stared at the phone on his desk. *What did he do? What didn't he do? Oh, fucking shit.*

"Hello," he creaked, his mouth super dry all of a sudden.

"Hey, Stranger. Just thought I'd call, see how you were holding up," she said.

"Oh, you know, about as well as any boyfriend when his girlfriend mentions she might be moving to Montana." Barry lowered his voice and ducked inside his cubicle. He stared up at the wall clock, watched the second hand spin past the numbers.

"What time did you leave this morning?" Patricia asked.

"About seven. I went for a quick run on the beach before heading over here."

"Did you get a shower?" she asked.

"Yeah, down at the marina. Why the motherly concern all of a sudden, Patricia? You afraid I won't be able to clean myself once you're gone?"

Silence. Barry bit his lip. *Was that last phrase a little harsh?* He hadn't meant for it to come out that sharp, but there it was.

"I'm sorry if that came out a little sharp," he said.

"That's okay," she said. "I suppose it needs to be a little tense right now." Was she crying? Barry leaned into the phone, tried to see past her lips to her eyes and cheeks. He couldn't tell.

Patricia, I'm an asshole. I'm a total and complete asshole. I dream about other women. I stare at their bodies and imagine running my tongue over every part of their skin. I don't know what to do. Not a day goes by that I don't dream of doing some lady in the backside...I just had some random lady from the Gaslight come up and ask me for a date. Please, for both our sakes, just pack up what you want and leave. Go to Montana or Wisconsin and start your life for real. Don't you want that? Don't you want a real life?

"You okay?" she said.

"Yeah," he answered. "I am. Just thinking about things."

"What kind of things?" she said, her voice lowered, intimate, like now that the truth was out between them, they could be honest again.

Barry stood up and looked across the showroom. A new couple had just entered the lot. Stan stared at him, pointed out at the couple.

"I, um, I gotta go. My turn just came up."

"Can you stop at Whole Foods? We need almond milk, and I could use some more green Superfood. Get the one by Odwalla, one of the large ones."

"Sure," he said, shifting his weight again. "Y'know, that thing you mentioned this morning. If you want to do that, I'll understand. I don't want you to, but if that's what you need to do..." his voice trailed off.

"I know. Thanks for that," she said before hanging up.

The couple turned out to be a hoax. They were in sales down the street at Buerge, wanted to see the latest prices on the Rav-4's. That and if Westside Toyota was hiring, which Barry assured them they weren't.

He headed back through the waiting room. He needed to pee in the worst way.

"Barry, my man, how's it hanging?"

Barry turned towards the voice, saw George the fix-it-part man slouched in one of the blue plastic chairs. George was tall and lanky; he had dark skin and was one of Barry's favorites at the dealership. They had a standing date for chimichangas every Friday whenever Barry made a sale. No sale, no chimi's. Barry smiled and watched as George lifted a customer-reserved chocolate éclair out of the pink box and sank his teeth into it. He smiled, his mouth full of pastry, yellow icing pushing out of the corners of his mouth.

"Hey, George. How are you?" Barry said as he passed.

"I'm good. I'm good. You might need me sometime. Don't you forget that. All right? You with me, Barry?"

"Yeah, I'm with you, George. Don't eat all of the donuts."

Barry made it into the bathroom. He thought about trying to figure out how all this had happened with Patricia, but instead closed his eyes and leaned against the tiled wall. He was tired. Bone tired.

Stan came in, took up the urinal next to him.

Shit. He'd forgotten about Chad.

"You talked to Chad?" Stan asked, right on cue.

"Just about to," Barry said, finishing up and going over to wash his hands.

"I'm serious about this," Stan said, giving himself an extra shake before zipping up. Barry tried not to look. It was awkward, the social rules in the men's room. Eye contact only. You drop your gaze south of the border and you were asking for trouble. Especially with your boss.

"Anything else?" Barry asked, looking in the mirror, feathering his hair back a bit.

"Nope. That's it. I want him gone by the time I get back from lunch." Stan was in a piss-poor mood and Barry wondered if Marge had moved out yet.

He was about to ask him, but thought better of it, nodding before going out, crossing back through the waiting room and onto the slick linoleum of the showroom.

"Paulino, you seen the kid?"

Paulino shook his head, continued to talk on the phone.

Barry scouted around, made his way up front to the receptionist's desk.

"Hey, April."

"Hey, Barry. What's happening?" She smiled as she spoke. Up close, Barry could see her nostrils, her pale brown eyes. She was gorgeous. Her soft blonde hair lifted back from her tan face, and she had a body that fashion models would be jealous of. But there was something he detected, a sadness, maybe. A neediness. He imagined being with her and realized he'd rather be with Patricia. Patricia with her pale, freckled skin and moody disposition. Patricia who sat at home reading other people's blogs and talking to her mother. Patricia who'd had two miscarriages trying to get pregnant for him. For them.

He'd rather be with Patricia than with gorgeous April.

Good. Good for them.

Barry realizes he loves his girlfriend. Film at eleven.

Barry smiled at the sarcasm then rejoined the conversation with April. "Oh, a whole lot of this and not much of that. Will you page the kid for me?"

April's voice crackled over the loudspeaker. "Chad, paging Chad Matthews. Please come to the front desk. Chad, this is your mother calling."

Barry scanned the lot. No sign. He looked back inside. Maybe he didn't have to do this right now. *No fucking way.* He wasn't going to carry this another minute if he didn't have to.

Barry drummed his fingers on the formica counter; he imagined breaking them off one by one and seeing them spill over the shiny floor.

"Here he comes," April said, nodding towards the cars.

Chad continued to glad-hand one of the customers, handing him another business card which the customer didn't know what to do with. Barry watched through the showroom window, interested in how bad a salesman someone could be. Chad gave the customer one more hand pump then excused himself and jogged towards the salesroom.

Barry braced himself.

Chad came in through the double doors. "Yeah, hey April, hey Barry. What's up?"

Marie Callendar's served mediocre food and lots of it. Barry had been coming here regularly for the past seven years. He knew every server, every addition or subtraction on the menu, and he and the manager, Brad, had gotten to be friends.

"What's good?" Chad asked, glancing over the menu.

They were in a booth back in the corner. Dark fake leather lined the dining room. From his seat, Barry could watch the servers come out of their station and still see the traffic passing by on Lincoln. The servers were mostly middle-aged women with large hips and names like Roseanne, Darcy, Peggy, although a couple stick-thin teenagers had just been hired and Barry was trying not to stare.

Barry smiled. "Everything except the soup. They actually throw in jugs of water later in the day when the pots start running thin."

"You're kidding me. They should come work for us." Chad laughed. Barry didn't crack a smile. "That was a joke, Barry."

"I know, Chad. I'm just not in one of my smiley days."

"How come, the girlfriend not giving it to you?"

Barry paused, not moving his eyes off Chad's face.

"Shit, Barry, what is going on here today? First Stan and now you," Chad said, this time with a little more sting.

Barry closed his menu. "I came here to let you go, Chad. Things just aren't working out."

"You're what?" Chad's menu hit the corner of the table with a snap. "You've got to be fucking kidding me! I've been here six weeks! How many sales am I supposed to have made in six weeks?" He said this leaning forward, his mouth open. Barry could see the dark lines between his teeth.

"That's not it, kid. It's that…" How much could he say? "Stan doesn't think this is a good fit, for you as much as us."

"What would Stan know? He has his head so far up April's ass, all he's seeing is stars."

Barry chuckled. He knew a good line when he heard one.

And that's when it happened.

Chad closed his eyes and started to cry. Slow, long tears that evolved into deep, mournful sobbing. Loud enough to echo throughout the entire restaurant.

Oh my God, thought Barry, looking around at the other booths, the customers slowly turning their heads to get a look at the lovers' spat.

"Chad, what are you doing?" Barry whispered, handing him a napkin. "Stop it. Cut it out. Get it together, kid."

"You get it together. I just got fired from the first job I've liked in twelve years. Do you know how many restaurants I've worked at? Do you? Well, I'll tell you: fifteen. Fifteen restaurants! Fifteen fucking menus to memorize. Fifteen different uniforms and specials and my girlfriend Tammy is pregnant and now I'm going to have to go work in some shithole like

103

this which serves lousy food to ungrateful people just so the whole thing can keep spinning."

"What whole thing?" Barry asked, genuinely confused.

"You know, the whole American thing. The system, the machine. Without food the whole thing breaks down." Big, wracking tears pouring down his cheeks. "People would have to go back to working near home. It's true. Restaurants are the key to our whole modern way of life." Chad blew his nose; ringing it like a bell across the restaurant.

"Your girlfriend's pregnant?"

"Two months. We just had our first midwife appointment. We're going for a home birth. I'll tell you all about it, that is, unless you fire me."

Barry cupped his hands and blew. Shit. Shit. Shit. *Why does Stan give me all the thankless jobs? Because he's the boss. Duh.*

"Let me talk to Stan." Barry heard the words come out, didn't realize he was saying them.

Chad looked up through red, wet eyes. "Really?"

"Yeah," Barry sighed. "I can't make any promises, but maybe I'll take you under my wing or something, on a provisional basis."

"You would do that?"

"Your girlfriend's pregnant. There's got to be some decency in the world." Barry knew what he was doing, going directly against Stan-the-Man, but he felt sick to his stomach leaving it like this. No one should get fired with their girlfriend two months pregnant, not even a terrible salesman like Chad.

They ordered their food, sat and ate like it was a normal meal. Chad told a couple jokes, Barry tried to laugh. His mind was whirring. Maybe he was feeling guilty. Maybe he hated places like Westside Toyota who made snap judgments about people, although in the seven years he'd been there, Stan's snap judgments had never been wrong. Salesman were born, not taught. Good ones as well as bad ones.

But maybe it was deeper than that. Maybe Barry could imagine being in Chad's shoes, his wife or girlfriend two months pregnant, clinging onto the job with everything he had. Barry could imagine that. The fear and the terrible powerlessness a man feels when his wife is pregnant and possibly losing the baby every single day and there's not a goddamned thing he can do about it. Barry tried to choke back tears. He watched Chad eat his turkey sandwich and fought to keep control. He could be in Chad's place. If he and Patricia could get their stuff worked out long enough for that gorgeous bump to form again in her belly, and day by day went by and nothing bad happened except she got a little nauseous and Barry stopped going to the Gaslight and stopped having strange women named Colleen show up at the dealership asking for pineapples and vodkas, then maybe the baby would keep growing instead of dying.

If all that happened, if he and Patricia decided to love each other and talk to each other and get back into that sacred space they had before college ended when everything was new and opening and exciting, if all that really happened, then he could definitely imagine them bringing a baby into the world.

They walked back in through the double doors. Chad raced off to the bathroom; Barry went to his cubicle and thought about how to face Stan. He picked up the phone.

"April."

"Yes, Barry."

"Is Stan around?"

"Why are we whispering?" April asked.

"Because we're on the phone and I don't want people to know that I'm too lazy to walk up to your desk."

"Oh, in that case," she said, dropping her voice into a barely audible whisper, "Yes, he's in The Back."

The Back. That's all anyone called it. I'll see you in the Back. Meet you in the Back. What time's the poker game? Seven o'clock *in the Back.*

The Back was nothing more than a converted bathroom with a set of cool pine double doors, an extra wall knocked down, cheap green carpeting and a coat of tan paint thrown in for a clean appearance. Someone had graffitied: 'For a good time, call your mother' in nasty purple scrawl; someone else had put up a picture of Howard Stern and written underneath: 'Your Mother.' But Stan had added two nice card tables, one with a round poker-top, and an electric putting green so the guys could practice their stroke.

That's what Stan was doing now. Up and back, up and back.

Barry watched a minute before clearing his throat.

"You're using too much of your hands," he said.

"You sound like my golf coach," Stan answered as he knocked one off the putting surface. It rolled under the table. Stan bent down into the corner, straining hard to reach it. When he came back, his face was red as a beet. "You do what I ask?"

"Not exactly."

"What is this, a Hertz commercial?"

"I tried. Honest. I had him over at Marie Callendar's and just told him straight. Before the food arrived."

Stan smiled. "You told him before the food arrived? That's cold."

"I don't like holding secrets. Anyway, I told him. First, he got mad. Then he started to bawl."

"You're kidding me."

"No, honest, like a giant seven year-old who just lost his best toy. I mean loud, gasping sobs. People were turning their heads. I told him I'd talk to you, maybe take him under my wing for a little while."

"How long is a little while?" Stan lined up a putt, hit it dead center.

"Give me a month. If I can't help him in a month, he can't be helped."

Stan eyed another one, hit it just off the lip of the cup. "Okay, you've got a month." His boss then stopped his putting, looked Barry dead in the eye with that crazy off-kilter look he'd been having the last couple days.

Barry blinked, returned the stare. *What do you do when you realize your boss is coming unhinged?*

Stan was sizing him up; for what, he wasn't sure. "But if he doesn't work out, then you're gone, too." Stan returned to his putting, missed one just to the right.

What did he just say? Barry had known this man for more than seven years, had sold probably eight hundred cars for him, if not more, during that time. He had come in early, stayed late, been the best damn employee anyone could think of, and now, just like that, if he doesn't perform miracles with Chad-the-wonder-dud, a walking anemia if he'd ever seen one, he's gone, too?

"What did you say?" Barry asked, still in shock.

"You heard me," Stan returned.

"That's not fair," was the best Barry could muster.

"Fair? You want fair? How about you do something when I ask you to do it?" Stan's face was turning beet red again. "How's that for fair? How about my wife doesn't haul off and have an affair with our pool guy, who's this young fucking punk with an ass the size of my palm? It was a simple request, Barry. Let him go means let him go, not let him hang around and pollute our dealership." Barry wondered then how close Stan was to having a heart attack, with his wife cheating and now talking about leaving, his secretive Jameson and coffee's every afternoon that were starting to come closer and closer to noon each day, the alcohol often on his breath when he was negotiating any deal after two in the afternoon.

Too bad he ran three miles every morning.

"I tried," Barry said. He could hear how weak he was sounding.

"Well, try harder. Try real hard this next month. When I ask you to do something, I expect it done." And with that, Stan turned his full attention to his putting and Barry realized they were done.

He backed out through the double doors, letting them slam, not trying to hide his displeasure.

14

B arry shifted weight, thought about it, then said, *What the heck?* Alex was a part-timer at Westside; he sold cars during the summer and went skiing up at Tahoe all winter. He always seemed to have some lady in the picture. Barry thought maybe he'd know a thing or two.

He gave Alex the low-down on him and Patricia.

"Ah, what can you do?" Alex stared at him, his leathery face talking all by itself.

What goes on inside Alex's brain? Barry imagined the inside of Alex's head; all he got was a large, floating joint.

"What do you mean?" Barry asked.

"I mean, and don't take this the wrong way, but when a woman talks about leaving, there's nothing you can do. That's it. It's over. Might as well pack your bags and figure out who's couch you're going to sleep on, which by the way, I'd let you stay on mine, but Bernice has her kids in town, so, y'know."

Barry looked at him. *Did he know what he was talking about?* Alex took a bite of his tuna sandwich, gnashing it with his teeth.

"Let me ask you something, Alex, if you don't mind."

"Shoot."

"How many divorces have you had?" Barry asked.

"Three. And all three of them started this exact way. First it was, I'm not happy about this. I'm not happy about that. But then this whole other tone came in, I'm talking like different, and it wasn't specific things they were unhappy about, it was the whole thing. Like this whole global, spherical thing about our relationship that wasn't working." Alex moved his hands in big circles, like the problem was bigger than even Barry knew. "Man, when they start hitting you with that, head for the hills, Barry. I mean that from the bottom of my heart. Run. Fast."

"Thanks, Alex. I'll take it into consideration."

Barry made his way out of the donut-and-soap-opera waiting room and headed back towards the front. *Jesus Christ,* he thought as he watched his shiny black shoes dance along the white linoleum, *why did I ever seek relationship counsel from that guy?*

He went to his desk, listened to his messages, and started flipping through his rolodex. It was time to sell some cars.

Patricia turned over in bed and smiled. *Had she really said all those things last night? Montana? Where did she get that one?* She couldn't remember the last time she'd been so honest with someone, especially if that someone was her live-in boyfriend.

What was going to happen?

She didn't know, and somehow the thought thrilled her.

She padded down the hall into the kitchen, her faded yellow tennis socks dusting along the hardwood floor. Light sprang from the windows, forming strange trapezoids on the floor beside her toes. Montana. Colorado. She wiggled her toes, watched them dance in the light. Big open skies and mountains, roads that led to places she'd never been. She felt herself start to dream some of her dreams from college: living in a small redwood cabin on the side of a hill in Montana or Colorado or even Idaho, strong coffee on the wood-burning stove, novel half-done on her computer, nothing in the air but beautiful and silent quiet. The overpowering fragrance of fresh mountain air. Dreams she'd put on the back burner the day she and Barry decided to go for pizza.

Back then, she'd been watching him for months, knew that he and his roommates were following her and launching an all-out assault to get Barry into her inner circle. She also knew, after spending two weeks laughing, questioning and challenging each other, that the day she lifted her sweater up over her head and showed him her sweet body, that he would never leave her. He would be faithful til his dying day.

Men talk a good game, but in the end, most of them are just like dogs: loyal through and through.

The question was: would she be faithful to him? Was he enough for her? And what about her dreams of living as a solo author in the middle of a winter wonderland? Didn't she get lonely in this picture? She could only write for two, maybe three hours a day; what did she do with the rest of her time? Did she ever want kids? She could feel some thread on the edge of the day-dream, some burly-armed man with a long beard wearing a red-and-black lumberjack shirt, with a name like Jack or Henry or Tobin.

Tobin.

Ooh, he had big arms.

Patricia pulled her mocha latte out of the microwave, reached across the table and grabbed the Travel section of the Times. She glanced at her watch; she still had four hours til she had to be at *Le Michele Boutique.* It was time to find some-where to go.

❧

"Hello, this is Barry."

Nothing but silence.

"Hello, Barry here…is there someone on the line? Hello, hello."

Barry waited a minute. He could hear the breathing, shallow, barely noticeable, almost like someone had a cloth over the receiver so they couldn't be heard.

Barry started talking then. He didn't even know where the words came from. He just opened his mouth and out they came.

"Look, whoever it is, I know you might feel like you know me, like I was nice to you once. If you're wondering if I'll be nice to you again, the truth is I'm living with someone. I may not be with them for too much longer, but at the moment, I am definitely taken. Please forgive me for whatever horrible promises or come-on's I made. It was a lie, okay? I was just trying to get in your pants, and the truth is, I wasn't even trying to do that. I was just trying to see if I could get in your pants. I'm actually completely whipped by my girlfriend, and she doesn't like me very much right now, so you see, the whole thing was kind of a mind-job from the start. There. Does that make you feel better? I'm off the market, okay? Please, for both our sakes, don't ever call this number again, unless you want to buy a car, and even then, I'll refer you over to Alex. You'll love him. He never wants to get married again."

"You bastard," the female voice said and hung up.

Barry stared at the phone. *Did he just do what he thought he did?* He wiped a bead of sweat off his forehead and kept staring at the phone, like the phone itself could tell him.

Oh my, Barry thought, *I've never done anything like that in my life. I'm either on the verge of a breakthrough here...or a total nervous breakdown.*

He looked back at the phone. Doors clicked and opened inside his mind.

How many bad things could happen in one week? For once, though, Barry didn't take it as the Universe being unfair to him. He had done this completely to himself. He thought about his secret phone calls to Brenda, the pineapple-and-vodka lady from the Gaslight, this crazy skank from who-knows-where, his decision to go against Stan and not fire Chad, the look on Patricia's face when he first walked in the door yesterday...and slowly, very slowly, he could feel the threads of his life coming undone. How bad a guy was he? Did he deserve to die alone with no one by his side? He was only thirty-two years old, but suddenly he was fifty-nine, lying in a bed like his father's hospital bed, gripping his son's hand and telling him he had to find a way out of this.

I need to make a change. If I want to stay with Patricia, and not have her move to Montana and never speak to me again, I need to do something. Quickly.

Oh my God, why didn't I think of this earlier?

There was only one thing to do.

He had to go see Taylor.

15

Taylor lived on a large hill overlooking the Marina. From his house, you could see the boats swaying back and forth in the tide, the tiny dots of houses as they spread out through Westchester and Baldwin Hills, and then, if you looked far enough with binoculars, you could see the hook of land down by Palos Verdes that rounded out the peninsula before dropping off towards San Diego and Tijuana.

Taylor Holmes. Barry and Taylor had known each other since they were five, Taylor's family growing up around the corner from Barry's cul-de-sac house in the Palisades. They'd gone to junior high school together, where Barry had gone from fat to thin and Taylor from short to tall, then to high school, where Barry had gone from extrovert to introvert and back again and Taylor had started spending large gulps of time smoking pot with his English teacher. He told everyone it was purely platonic, that they just got stoned and stared at the webbing between their fingers and explored the nature of polemical relationships in the 1800's. But several years later, when Barry had caught up with Taylor at a college party or bar

– Barry honestly couldn't remember where – Taylor had con-
fided in him that he and his English teacher had also started
exploring each other's entire bodies along with the webbing
between their fingers, that it had become a rocking-good sexual liberation for both of them, and it had almost led to her
divorce.

Senior year of high school, Taylor started spending most of
his time alone, the only one of their clique not to be on either
a sports team, school council, or something to look good on a
college application. Taylor was different than that. He never
seemed to care what other people thought. Barry had never
asked him this directly, but most of Taylor's life, he seemed
to be listening inside of himself. It was the oddest thing. It
had, in fact, gotten more pronounced with age, to the point
now where the last time they'd seen each other, Taylor actually tilted his head and waited for an answer to come. Barry
chalked it up to Taylor's either being brilliant or crazy, and
probably a little bit of both.

They had lost track of each other over the past five years,
as can happen with friends once high school and college is
done, but last Barry heard, Taylor had finished college at
Loyola Marymount, gotten his MA in Psychology from UCLA
and his therapist's license, and then started some eclectic spiritual path called Sufism. Barry had never heard of it, but if
Taylor was doing it, you knew it had to be out there.

Barry drove his Mustang up the dirt path leading to
Taylor's house. Potholes and rocks bounced the car like a
puppet on strings, with Barry actually hitting his head on the
Mustang's soft convertible roof until he decided to listen to
the speed signs and slow down to the interminable speed of
five miles per hour.

Barry took his time, thinking about Patricia and the questions he wanted to ask Taylor. Somehow, Taylor had become a spiritual counselor, a little bit of a guru actually, and as Barry crested the top of the hill and made the small descent towards the home, he wasn't surprised to see ten or twelve cars parked out front.

Taylor Holmes, his neighborhood friend, turning into a modern-day Jesus Christ right here in west Los Angeles.

The two-story house stood like a head on the shoulders of the bluffs. It was painted a faded white, but a nice faded white, like time had aged it gently rather than severely. There were nicks and scrapes as with any house, but there was also fresh paint in places, making it obvious that someone had cared for the building. Barry knew he was getting way too woo-woo, but the house actually felt happy to him. *Could houses feel happy?*

Thirty or forty plants lived on the front porch and a basketball hoop sat off to the side of the dirt driveway. An elderly woman with stringy gray hair and several teeth missing sat in a rocking chair at the far end of the porch. She was staring off into the distance and rocking back and forth very gently; she didn't notice Barry as he arrived.

Barry strode deliberately towards the house. What did all these people come for? Probably the same reason he was here, for help.

Taylor's wife, Wanda, greeted Barry on the porch. She was vibrant and slender with flowing blonde hair and the softest eyes Barry had ever seen. She and Taylor had fallen in love the last semester of senior year when Taylor used to spend all his time sitting in the middle of the ivy hill overlooking the baseball field. He had ended his "friendship" with the groovy English teacher and was now celebrating celibacy as a potential life-path, until two months before graduation when Wanda Baker, all eighty-seven pounds of her, had climbed up there and sat beside him and never come down. Barry had gone to their wedding on the bluffs the following summer. He remembered looking into the burnt orange sun while they recited their vows and actually made a little prayer inside his heart that he be as lucky as them.

Funny, he thought as he and Wanda embraced and she led him inside, who did I say that prayer to? Not God. The Universe, maybe? The Universal goodness that he usually felt when Taylor was around. That was the funny thing. Barry had never heard of someone like Taylor, someone who people came to for spiritual counseling, except great religious figures like Jesus, the Buddha, maybe the Dalai Lama. Barry figured the rest were mostly cranks and crack pots. The funny thing, though, is he really did feel different when Taylor was around, almost like there was a universal goodness, and in that sphere of influence, he sometimes believed that anything was possible.

At least for a short time.

"Barry, it's good to see you!" Wanda said, leaning in and hugging him. "How are you? How's Patricia?"

"I'm okay," Barry said quickly. Wanda had always made him nervous, like she could see right through him, her soft eyes penetrating past any of the defensive walls that Barry liked to believe about himself. "Patricia, too."

"We'd love to have you up for dinner some time."

"That would be great," Barry said. "Or maybe we'll have you over."

"I'm sure Taylor would like that. He's just finishing up with another client. He sent me down here to meet you, said he'd be just another minute or two."

Barry studied her face, noticed how little she'd changed since high school. "You look just as beautiful as you did in high school."

"Thanks, Barry. That's sweet. It's fun knowing each other all these years."

"How is he?"

Wanda looked surprised. "Taylor? The same. Overworked, happy, stressed. He spends too much time helping people." She whispered this last part, like she was confiding in a friend who wasn't there for help as well. "But our kids are great, so I have no complaints."

"Should I go?" Barry asked, suddenly not wanting to add to his longtime friend's load.

"Leave? Of course not. You're one of his oldest friends. But you can't believe how things have grown. He's talking to one, maybe two hundred people a week, everybody with someone sick or dying, or their son in a coma. It's heartbreaking, really. No one comes for simple problems anymore."

"Maybe life's not that simple anymore," Barry said.

"Or maybe it is and we're just trying to make it hard," Wanda said softly, and Barry realized she might have just as much wisdom as Taylor. Wanda closed her eyes for a moment, and in that space of two or three seconds, Barry imagined leaning forward and kissing her. It wasn't even a sexual act as much as a way of communing with her, thanking her. She had always held a safe space for Barry and he was grateful. Then Wanda's eyes were open and the moment had passed. "He's done with his other client. You can go up now."

"How do you know?" Barry asked.

"Clairvoyance. Taylor and I hardly even talk anymore." Barry's jaw dropped. "I'm kidding. See that little green light? Right there below the stairs? That's to let the next client know when the coast is clear."

"Is that what I am, the next client?"

She smiled. "You're here for help, right?"

"Right," Barry said, giving her shoulder a slight squeeze and heading towards the stairs.

♌

Barry climbed the stairs one at a time, nervous beyond anything he could imagine feeling. What was the big deal? It was a guy in a room. *Yeah, but a guy who can see into me and tell me all the places where I'm fucked up. Why didn't I go to a normal therapist, where we could stay on the surface for two or three years before getting into anything heavy?* Taylor had this amazing way of getting to the heart of the matter within a few minutes. It was unnerving, actually, almost like the gravitational pull he induced just pulled the truth out of you.

You had no choice.

Barry took the last of the steps, the words *'No choice'* ringing in his thoughts.

He swung open the heavy brown door and stepped inside.

"Barry," Taylor called out. He was sitting behind his desk, his legs extended onto the desk top. He looked like any executive in America, except...except what?

The light in his eyes, Barry thought.

"Hello, Taylor," Barry said, his own voice sounding deeper and more distinct than usual. Taylor stood up and came toward him. Barry took a moment, noticing all the details of Taylor's new office: the dark mahogany desk, brown leather couch, signed picture of Abdul-Kareem on the wall. Nice. There were also a couple of tall plants, pictures of friends and well-wishers, and a large Nerf basketball hoop jutting out from the corner. The man knew how to live well, that's for sure. All this on talking to a couple hundred strangers per week? I talk to that many people, except it's about leather interiors, not the interior of their heart or spirit.

"It's good to see you," Taylor said, bending down and giving Barry a hug. "How are you? How's Patricia? What's happening?"

Barry returned the hug, his head reaching just about to Taylor's shoulder. Barry had forgotten how tall Taylor was, coming in at just over 6'6" with a red, scruffy beard and a wide, genuine smile. "How long has it been?"

"Two years, I believe," Taylor said, motioning for Barry to sit on the couch. "Want some water?"

"I'd love some," Barry said, relieved. "I can't believe how thirsty I am. Nice view."

Taylor strode over to the plate glass window behind his desk. "Yep, it's just what I wanted. Wanda made me wait six years to build this office. I kept seeing people in an office in town, and then on the porch behind our kitchen. It was kinda weird." He poured Barry a large glass of water and handed him the blue glass. "You look well."

"Do I?" Barry responded. "I'm not."

"Tell me," Taylor said, sitting in a recliner opposite the couch.

"This is what you do, huh? Listen to people's problems all day long?"

"All day," Taylor said. "It gets kind of boring."

"You're kidding?"

"Actually, I'm not. After a while, the problems all seem to run together, like we're all one big family and there are only so many problems we can have."

"That's not a very Jesus-like thing to say," Barry quipped.

Taylor smiled. "I'm not a very Jesus-like guy, am I? You know me. Would you say I'm like Jesus?"

Now it was Barry's turn to smile. "You did spend a lot of time up there in that ivy...well, that and in your teacher's bed!"

"Mrs. Smith! She was awesome!" Taylor bellowed, laughing in spite of himself.

"Yeah, that's not what her husband thought," Barry said, grinning from ear to ear as well.

"Okay, now that we're all caught up, what's going on? What brings you to my humble door?"

"I'm fucked up, Taylor. Patricia is thinking about leaving me."

"Oh, I'm sorry to hear that," Taylor said.

"You are?" Barry said. "I'm surprised. Aren't we supposed to be okay no matter what the Universe throws our way?"

"Where'd you get that crap? Spirituality 101?" Taylor smiled. "Of course, I'm sad to hear about you and Patricia. You guys really loved each other once."

"We did, didn't we? I don't know what happened. It's like the love got up and left or something. I know that's not very poetic, but it's kind of true."

"Do you have any idea why she's thinking about leaving?" Taylor asked.

Barry sighed. "It's so many things. It's me leaving early, coming home late, not caring for her in a million little ways.

But I used to, things used to be really good between us, and then all of a sudden they weren't."

"What caused it?"

"What caused what?" Barry asked.

"The change in feeling."

Barry gulped. He knew exactly what caused it – and he didn't want to talk about it. "I don't know," he said weakly.

"I think you do," Taylor responded, his eyes narrowing.

Barry looked up at his friend. Taylor was leaning back in his recliner, his tall frame relaxed and poised at the same time. Downstairs his wife was probably making them something to eat, his calendar was booked full for the next four weeks, and his kids would be home from school in a few hours and they would have a *Little House on the Prairie* happy family scene.

Barry felt a sudden urge to punch his friend in the face.

"What is it, Barry? What's going on?"

"I don't want to talk about it."

"You don't want to talk about what?" Taylor asked.

"What caused things to get the way they are," Barry said.

Taylor took a deep breath, closed his eyes for a sec. "You came here for help, Barry. Trust me on this. If you want things to get better, then we have to talk about it."

"No," Barry said tartly, "we don't."

And with that, Barry was up and off the sofa, his glass of water spraying across the office, Barry himself flying back down the stairs, looking hurriedly at Wanda's surprised face as he bounced out the front door, sprinting by the wild-haired stringy lady, running for his life towards the car, Barry both aware and shocked that tears were streaming down his face. *What was wrong with him? Why couldn't he just face what happened and save his relationship and become the man that his father had never been able to become? Why did Barry resent every good thing that happened to other people and why did life have to be so hard in the first fucking place?*

Barry opened the door to his Mustang and jammed the key in the ignition, his engine roaring to life. He thought for a moment about swallowing his pride and heading back in there, knowing for sure that Taylor was still sitting in that same dumb-ass chair waiting for him, and if Barry was willing to spill his guts and cry and emote all over his perfect-little office, then Taylor would welcome him back with open arms.

"Fuck that!" Barry said out loud to no one in particular, cranking his car into gear before bouncing down the pot-holed drive at thirty miles an hour, dust flying everywhere, giving a big middle finger to the 5mph sign as he sped away.

Inside his office, Taylor turned towards the vista and exhaled. *I blew that one,* he thought. *Why did I push him so hard? Maybe because he's an old friend. Maybe because he's in such obvious denial.*

Taylor went and stood by the window. Sailboats appeared as far-away toys and listed in the afternoon wind, moving back and forth across the sea. For a moment, Taylor longed to be out among them instead of trapped in his office listening to people's problems all day.

Not where God puts me, he thought.

With that, he bent down onto the floor, making a kneeling prostration, pushing his forehead into the carpet. He closed his eyes and waited, letting go of his personal reactions until a calm feeling came into his heart, letting his forehead sink deeper and deeper into the carpeted floor.

16

Patricia stretched out like a cat, letting the sun wash over her bare skin. She moved her hand back and forth, putting it in and out of the light trapezoid on the carpeting, and thought about what had been happening. *I have no right to do this,* she thought. *I should be working a real job, a real career; bringing in my half. Barry's working, every day almost. He pays the bills, the mortgage, buys the food. What do I do, besides sit here and think about leaving?*

That's not true. You do a lot more than that.

Like what?

Like try and have babies. Like put up with all his macho-ego bullshit and let him prance around town like an idiot while people give you eye-rolls behind his back.

I'm in a negative space, she realized soberly. *I'm not thinking clearly. I am running around through the same mental loops and not making progress.* She pictured a tiger jumping through the same hoop over and over and over, his four legs landing on a treadmill that keeps him in the same place, but also not knowing that's what it was doing.

She thought about Dr. Anderson, his pale white skin, his long gaunt frame, the meds he had given her after the second miscarriage.

"This one's for stress, dear. And this one for depression and anxiety. Just in case," he had said, patting her hand. She had taken them, of course, feeling pasty and bloated and numb all at the same time. She had stopped taking them just recently, choosing instead to feel something, anything, besides the blah that characterizes those little blue bastards.

What do I need? What could pop me out of this frame of mind?

The mountains. Snow. Colorado!

Okay, think smaller, start small. A thousand mile journey begins with one step.

How about the beach? The beach always has something good for me.

🍥

Patricia drove through the Palisades, hit Chautauqua, purposely went left at PCH and up into Santa Monica, by-passing Will Rogers beach, the more upscale, volleyball one, choosing instead to drive ten minutes to their first stomping ground on the corner of Santa Monica and Venice. She turned right down Washington, found a spot open near the smaller part of Lincoln, parked, and started the two block walk to the beach. The beach. San Diego, Pacific Palisades, Santa Monica, Malibu. All of it was incredible. Expanses of blue upon blue that started at your toes and ended up in Hong Kong. The people playing in the surf and splashing around and acting silly for no apparent reason except that the sun was out and

California was a gift from the gods and everyone here seemed able to forget their problems for a little while.

They did have problems, right?

Patricia crossed the last street and broke into a little jog. *I just need to get my toes in the sand.*

Barry's dealership was only ten minutes away. She could go see him.

Are you kidding me? We're finally here at the beach, no way.

She stepped out of the last bit of concrete and onto the sand. There. Unstrapping her shoes, she glanced around, noticed how empty the beach was this morning. *Where is everybody? Working, I guess. Or taking their babies for walks, mommy and me classes, anything to make the time go.*

She thought about her mother, her crazy, now semi-happy mother, running around after her teenage twins in Cheviot Hills. Patricia looked out at the ocean. *I really do have a hard time enjoying myself, don't I? Here I am at the beach, the beautiful blue water and sky stretching out before me, and all I keep doing is thinking about other people...*

Hmm. Food for thought.

She strode down to a crest of sand just before the edge of the water and plopped down. Then she pulled out her diary and began to write:

> *March 12*
>
> *Had a fight with Barry last night. Not really a fight, what then? A stand-off, which I, of course, lost. But something shifted. I talked about Montana, brought my mother's crazy little plan out into the open to see what would happen. Will I ever leave? I don't know. Maybe you know, diary. How does someone*

choose to pick up and start over? How do you know when the time is right for change? You just know, people say. But those same people also encourage you to give up, like losing a marriage is no big deal. Not like losing a baby, or two babies. Now that's something we could talk about. Losing babies. Why does God make it that some babies live and some babies die? And what happens to the women and people who have to go on living after the babies don't? What happens to those marriages? They never show you in the films, that's just where the movie ends. The woman is pregnant, everybody's happy, and then suddenly she's not. No one's happy. The film ends. Tragic, yes, but honest, poignant. Babies do die. I've seen it happen, felt it happen, inside my own body. Twice.

Patricia stared at the page.

Twice.

That was the hardest part. Once could happen to anybody, did happen to lots of women, but not twice.

Twice meant a problem. Twice meant you shouldn't ever try again, you should adopt or instead move to the remote parts of the great open range and disappear into the hills, become a hermit or a loner and let everybody forget that you were the woman who couldn't bear children.

Patricia squeezed back a tear. *This was supposed to be my happy day. A day at the beach. Not a day to cry or feel depressed.* She took a deep breath, closed the mouth of her diary, and tried to sleep.

Several hours passed. The sun moved gently across the sky, beach-goers came and went, their suntan lotion and beach balls leaving a trail of debris that cluttered the sand

and eventually built a small wall around her. She continued to sleep. And sleep. And sleep.

Like a person emerging from a drug-induced coma, she woke and walked the quarter mile back to her car. *Where am I? Who am I?* She didn't readily know the answer to either question. She walked across the concrete, staring at the small homes that dotted either side of the side street, then got in her car and drove towards the alphabet streets and home.

17

Barry drove hard and fast down the dirt road, his Mustang leaping from the dirt to pavement, from the pavement to highway, from the highway back down to pavement, ending up in the Gaslight parking lot. An afternoon haze was just starting to settle across the city and gray clouds formed overhead, threatening rain.

This time I'm going to do it, Barry thought. *Just like that. I'll do it. I'll show him. I'll show her. I'll show all of them. This is my life, goddammit, and if I want to fuck it up, none of them are going to stop me.*

Once inside, Barry gave himself a minute for his eyes to adjust. The good old Gaslight. Santa Monica's finest. Black floor, red vinyl booths, bottles of liquor stretched in three even shelves around the entire bar. His kind of place.

"Hey, Barry, what's shaking?"

Barry looked up at the bartender. "Not much, Jake. Certainly not me."

"We can fix that, can't we?" the barrel-chested bartender said, smiling. Jake weighed about 220, could bench press until you got bored watching, and had a long blonde pony-tail that hung down to the middle of his back. Welcome to Santa Monica, California, home of nuts, butts, and coconuts.

"Regular or tall?" Jake asked.

"Make it a double," Barry moaned with a half-smile. "My shrink was hard on me today."

"A double for Mr. Barry-the-Car-Salesman, straight out of Toyota selling school. Coming up."

Jake poured the rum into two large shot glasses, backed it up with a Coke and a wedge of lime. Barry set down a ten-dollar bill, but Jake waved him off.

"Nope, it's on me today. My ex is getting married." Jake held up a shot of his own and smiled. The smile gave Barry shivers, but he held up his drink and downed it.

The rum burned his throat, burned it all the way down past his tonsils. Barry shook his head, bit down on the lime and downed some of the coke to kill the burn. That was better.

"Someone's looking for you," Jake said.

"Who's that?" Barry asked.

"Look for yourself. She's coming this way."

Barry turned, just in time to dodge a kiss from a tall, off-kilter blonde woman, the same chick who'd visited him at the dealership last week.

"Whoa, Colleen, how are you?" Barry said, slipping to the side.

"I'm drunk, Barry. How are you?"

"Sober. Very sober," Barry said. "But looking to get drunk."

The woman tried to look at him, her eyes going in and out of focus. "You want to party?"

"No, not tonight, Colleen. I have a date."

"You have a date? I thought you had a girlfriend. You told me you had a girlfriend or otherwise you and me could have a good time," she said, swaying a bit and grabbing the bar rail to steady herself.

"That's who my date is with, my girlfriend. She should be here any moment. In fact, I better go look for her. Talk to Jake."

"Jake who?" Colleen slurred.

"Jake the bartender. He's right here, right to your left. No, your other left. There you go. Atta, girl."

Barry turned and winked at Jake, who smiled and steadied the woman by her arm.

"There you go, beautiful. Now how about some coffee?"

Barry moved through the bar, hoping to see someone he knew. No luck. He passed the red table tops, the vinyl booths, even peered into the back corner to see two women pressed together, making out with slobbery, wet kisses.

He came back to the bar front and thought of his options. He could call home. Medium-to-bad option. He was in self-destruct mode and he knew it. He could call Taylor. Worse option. He could sit down and cry and try to remember where things had gone so wrong. Not really the option he was looking for.

Barry pulled out his cell phone: the face was black. He'd forgotten to charge it last night and now it was dead. What a fucking day! Barry stomped down the darkened hallway behind the bar, then fished in his pocket for a quarter and slid it into the pay phone.

"Please deposit fifty cents," the annoying recording said.

Barry searched for another quarter. Again, no luck.

"Jake, can I get change for a dollar?" Barry asked, coming back into the main room. "Jake? Where's Jake?"

A woman turned on her stool. "That broad, the blonde one, she started puking on the bar. Jake took her to the ladies' room."

Barry reached behind the bar and grabbed Jake's tip jar. He dropped a dollar bill in and took out four quarters.

Dialing the numbers, he could feel the wrongness of what he was about to do. *I am crossing a line,* Barry thought, *some line I'm not supposed to cross. You get mad. You even pout for a while. But you don't do what I'm about to do.*

"Helloooooo…" the voice was warm, sultry.

"Brenda."

"Why, it's my favorite naughty car salesman," she said. "Where are you, sweetheart?"

"It's Barry," he said.

"I know, honey. Where are you? Brenda feels like she might actually get to see you this time. You want to come over? I'm all alone."

Barry checked his watch: it was four-thirty. Patricia might be at home, she might not. He sighed.

"I can't, Brenda. Next time, maybe."

Barry hung up, went to the bathroom where he read the Santa Monica daily sports page while he peed into a disgustingly brown urinal, then walked outside.

He could feel himself spinning out of control. *Had he really stormed out of Taylor's office? Were things that bad between him and Patricia? Had he really called Brenda and said he'd see her next time?*

Barry took a deep breath, thought about his dad's affairs, the look on his mom's face each time his dad would come home late or not come home at all, and realized he didn't want to be this kind of man. Not at all. He slid behind the wheel of his Mustang, popped in a mint tic-tac, hoped he wasn't took drunk from his double rum, and started the fifteen-minute drive towards home.

18

They arrived home at nearly the same time, Barry pulling his Mustang into the driveway thirty seconds before Patricia pulled her little white Mazda up to the curb. Their driveway was only big enough for one.

"You made it," he said, getting out and stretching.

"You, too," she added as she lifted her towel and bag. She felt different, like something had been taken from her on the beach. *What was it? Grief? Confusion?* She didn't know. She walked towards him, and all she knew was that for the first time in a long time, she wasn't thinking about Montana or Idaho or any mountainous region far away from southern California.

"Hi," she said, leaning in towards him.

"Hi back," he replied, kissing her gently and sweetly on the lips.

Inside, he poured them both a glass of chardonnay and headed out onto their small, wooden deck. She sat by the small wicker table, her knees tucked up under her chin, reminiscing about the time they fell in love. *Am I crazy?* She wondered.

One moment, I'm thinking about leaving, the next I'm back in love. Weird. Very weird. *What would my mother say about this? That I truly am bi-polar?* She thought about her mom's voice, that little demonic presence that sat right above her right shoulder tucked in under her ear, in fact could hear it calling to her and just beginning to talk -- *wait a minute, I'm finally feeling good, I don't need to feel miserable.* She turned her head away from her shoulder, literally breaking the connection to the nasty, wicked little creature.

"I went to see Taylor," Barry said, handing her the wine.

"Thanks. You did? What for?"

"For us," he said and looked straight at her. "I took what you said seriously."

"You should. I mean it seriously," Patricia said, letting the moment register with both of them. Then she smiled, breaking the tension. "What was the swami's remedy?"

"I don't know. I ran out before we could finish," he said, looking down at the wooden slats of the deck.

"That bad?" Patricia asked.

"Worse," Barry responded, looking like he was about to cry. Barry exhaled and looked out over the backyard. Their backyard was small, pushed up against a crooked wooden fence that had neighbors on every side. The alphabet streets used to be throw-aways, the Palisades refuge for wanna-be actors and their families. But it had gotten hot in the last fifty years, highlighting with President Reagan buying a home in the Riviera section. The alphabet streets were about ten minutes west and still a poor cousin to the glitz and glam of the Riviera, but their unfinished two-bedroom on a tiny plot was still worth over half a million. Crazy.

"Did he say anything worth mentioning?" she asked.

"I didn't give him a chance. We'd just gotten started, and he wanted me to talk about...to explain my feelings around... y'know how Taylor has always had that laser beam that just zeroes in on the one thing you don't want to talk about?"

"I've never met him, honey," she answered.

"Well, trust me, he does. And I needed some more time in the shallow end of the pool, y'know, get used to the water a little bit, maybe splash around a little, and he had us diving in down at the deep end within like thirty seconds."

"How much does he charge?" Patricia asked, pinching her lip with her forefingers, making it squishy and soft.

"A hundred bucks," Barry said.

"Will you try again?" she asked.

"You think it will help?"

"It certainly couldn't hurt. I'm glad you're seeing him, shows me you care about what's happening between us." Patricia took a sip of wine, looked over at the fading sun. "There's something I want to talk to you about."

"What's that?" Barry asked.

"You've asked me what's wrong with our sex life," she said.

"Yes," Barry replied, nervous where this was going.

"Well, come here. There's something I need to show you," she said, taking his hand.

꙳

She led him into the bedroom, lowered the blinds to block out the afternoon sun, then stripped down naked in front of him. Barry looked at the curves and lines of her body; he was still mesmerized by her beauty. She had a freckle just below her right rib cage; Barry realized that he might be one of the few people in the world who knew about that and smiled.

"But I thought…" Barry began.

"Don't ask," she said. "Just follow."

She closed her eyes and reached her hand up and lowered his eyes as well. She then leaned towards him. "If you're still seeing my body, you're not seeing me," she whispered. Then she began moving his hands over her body, letting him feel her again as if for the first time, the first time for both of them, when they were young and innocent and making love for the very first time in her college apartment the weekend before her roommate came back.

Barry couldn't stand how slow it was. He wanted to push, wanted to stop this touching and exploring and get her on the bed and mount her. He bucked his thighs up against her. He didn't know how to go slow. Patricia stopped him, backed him up, went back to the slow touching.

Barry started to go crazy inside.

"I don't know what to do, Patricia," he admitted, his voice dropping a notch. He felt lost, confused, intently aware that he was going to make a mistake.

"Follow me," she whispered in his ear, feeling more like her true self, so glad she had followed her instincts and gone to the beach. Something truly had been taken from her while she slept on the sand.

"I can't," he said. "You don't understand."

"What don't I understand?" she said back. She was inside his mind, reading his thoughts. He began to feel nervous, deeply, deeply nervous.

She's going to find out, any second.

Barry fidgeted with his hands, shifted weight. *I've got to get out of here,* a voice screamed inside his head.

Then another voice: *She's going to find out...find out what?*

He didn't even know.

Patricia leaned forward again, speaking gently into his ear. "What's there to understand? You love me, right? It's a Thursday afternoon, neither of us have work, we are living together, there's no one else around...just be with me, don't worry about getting somewhere."

Barry thought about the first time he saw her, the whiteness, the purity, the tingles he had running through his body. *Paradise,* he had thought, *falling into that lovely girl would be paradise.* Yet, here he was, naked with her in his bedroom, their bedroom, their grown-up bedroom where they were allowed to have consensual adult sex.

And he had never felt more alone.

Afterwards, after she had asked him again to go slow, Barry pushing back with his anxiety and nervousness and just wanting to get it over with, Patricia climbed on top of him and gave him what he wanted: going fast, not kissing, not even making eye contact, until the moment when he began to climax and she leaned down and put her mouth on his and for one fleeting moment they were together, until he bucked and spasmed and then it was over.

"I love you," he said, his breath coming in gasps, small beads of sweat appearing on his brow.

"I know," she said, rolling away from him and moving towards the bathroom.

A few minutes passed. Patricia came back to the bed and lay down. Neither of them moved much. Barry looked away and out the window, thought about Cherry Garcia ice cream even though it was still the afternoon. Then he thought about the Tiki Hut, whether scar-face would be back there again. *What was wrong with him? Was he incapable of being happy?*

"What's the matter?" she asked finally.

"How honest do you want me to be?" he said.

"Very," she answered. She felt like a volcano was about to erupt inside her, possibly spraying molten lava all over him and melting him into the floor.

He picked her hand up and sighed. "Do you know how my dad taught me about sex? Magazines. He kept them under my bed, in a big, huge cardboard box. Playboy, Hustler, XXX. I knew all of them. 'Here, read these,' he'd said in a gruff voice. That was his sex talk. So when you want me to do this touchy-feely stuff, I start to go insane."

Patricia stroked his shoulder. She really did love him. Her mom was wrong: he was not a creep or a bad man. He was, in fact, a really, really good man; he was just confused.

"I know where to take us," Patricia said, turning towards him, looking him full in the face. "If you'll go slow, and follow me, we can both have orgasms…and the most wonderful intimacy imaginable. But you have to trust me." She leaned over, kissing him softly on the cheek. "And if that happens, I won't even think about Colorado or Montana, unless you want to go fly-fishing there with me."

Barry appreciated the intimacy, liked her being close. "But we already have orgasms. Why does it have to be more?"

"Truth?" she asked.

He nodded.

"I've only had one orgasm with you, that very first time at my apartment in college."

"Bullshit!" he said, sitting up sharply in the bed. He wrung his hands and huffed. "Just last night. You had an orgasm last night."

"I didn't, Barry. I've been faking it for years." She didn't cry, she didn't even look sad. She just looked...quiet.

"Really?"

Now it was her turn to nod.

"And that's why you've been thinking about Montana?" he asked, lying back down beside her. He couldn't believe what he was hearing; no wonder she was thinking about leaving.

"That's just part of it," she began. "It's a lot of things. I've lost myself. I sit around and think about everything too much. This house has gotten very small, very fucking small." Barry liked to swear, but somehow, coming from her, it stung a bit. "Our lives have gotten small. At least mine has." She picked up his hand, turned it over, began studying the tiny lines on it. "You have nice hands, Barry. Honest hands. I need to go find something to do, something real, more than just selling crap at *Le Michele Boutique*."

Barry nodded. "I would love for you to go back to work."

"Does that mean you don't think we'll have a baby?" she asked.

"That's not what I'm saying. Maybe if you get busy again, feel productive again, who knows…maybe you'll get pregnant right away. That's what happened for Amanda and Brian."

"Yeah, I know," she sighed. She felt so…defeated.

They lay there for a minute, neither one talking, naked and enjoying each other's nakedness without the pressure of turning it into more.

"I have something to tell you, Patricia," Barry began, a lump forming in his throat.

"What's that?" she asked.

"I flirt a lot," he said, his voice dropping an octave.

She took a deep breath, let it out slowly. "I know. I've seen it. It's awful, sort of like a mobile home flipping over in slow motion."

"Is it that bad?" he asked.

"Pretty bad," she answered, pausing a sec. "Have you ever acted on it?"

"Nope. I don't really want to. I've had chances. I don't know. The whole thing is stupid," he admitted.

"Just want to see if you still got it, huh?" she smiled. "Well, why don't you come over here for Round Two and show me if you still got it."

They made love a second time, this time Barry on top, leaning into her, through her, driving her shoulders back into the bed with his force and his passion. She enjoyed it this time, opening to receive him, letting go of her mother's objections, her mother's criticisms, her mother's everything.

Talking truthfully and honestly opened something between them, something that had been closed for months if not years, and even though it wasn't everything for Patricia, at least she didn't fake anything this time. She didn't moan or shudder or lay huddled in a ball like the earth had moved inside her. She was simply present, and engaged, allowing him to take a tiny, small, fraction-of-an-inch step towards her.

She could see it in his eyes, his guard was coming down, his pupils looking more of a true brown to her. His admitting about his incessant flirting – was that all it was?? – lifted a skeleton from one of his closets and he was now more present with her as well.

They did love each other, and it was nice to feel it again.

When it was over, Barry gave her a kiss and went to take a shower. Patricia lay in the bed, happy, or at least happier. She still wasn't getting what she wanted, what she needed, but at least it was a move in the right direction.

There were no books for where she wanted to go. Higher sex. Spiritual sex. Not tantra, not raising energy. She wanted to merge, to disappear, to fly together into the heavens and reach something beyond this Earth.

Maybe she was crazy.

Maybe she wanted too much.

Maybe she should take a lover.

Patricia thought about what was possible for them, the higher worlds of light that she knew existed, places she knew they could travel while making love, that they were in fact spiritual beings and not just physical beings, and that when she compared that to the stark reality of how Barry liked to have sex: fast, physical, devoid of any true connection between them...she felt like she was going to explode, implode, or scream.

Several months later, as she lay beside someone other than Barry, she realized she didn't even need the higher worlds of light, she just needed a heart connection, something that let her know she was more than just a giant blow-up doll for someone to get their rocks off. She thought about the magazines, the way Barry described sex and women, and for a moment felt compassion for the kind of upbringing he'd had, that even though things looked good on the outside, he'd received some of the worst advice and modelling she'd ever heard of. Who stuck a box of porno mags under their son's bed? Who had sex with three women in one day and then bragged about it to their kid, especially when one of the women was the kid's mom? Barry's dad; that's who. David Lemming. The gift to all women. Patricia felt the battle rage inside her: one moment hating Barry for his backwards, Neanderthal ways, the next feeling empathy and compassion for him and wanting to snuggle up beside him.

She knew their relationship was going to blow up. She didn't know how or when, but like a tremor in the earth that foretells a big quake, she could feel her earth moving, and for the first time in over a decade, she wasn't sure Barry was on the same side of the fault line.

19

The week passed. Barry spent time at the dealership, time at home, time back at the dealership helping the new kid try not to be a schmuck to customers even though it seemed to be his nature.

"I don't understand," Chad said as the disgruntled customers drove away empty-handed, cursing silently under their breath.

"Let's go through it again," Barry explained. "Why do you want to be a car salesman?"

Chad smiled. "To make the bucks, like you. That and I hate waiting tables. Oh, and my girlfriend is pregnant. You gotta make some dough to have a kid."

"You're pathetic, you know that?" Barry blurted out. "Not really. You remind me of when I started, that's all. I had $100,000 imprinted on my brain from an ad I saw on television. No one respects car salesmen, that's one of the things you need to know. Not our bosses. Shit, they need us but they don't respect us. Not our friends. Can you imagine telling your closest family and friends that you're deciding to spend your life selling cars? It'll never wash. And, lastly, certainly not the customers. Most people have been lied to, pushed, convinced, pressured, everything in the book by the time they get here to you. You're job, Mr. Chad, is to be a nice guy. Be their friend. Help them get what they want. What they want is a new car. They want to feel what it's like to drive a new car, sit in a new car, listen to their favorite Eric Clapton cd in a new car. Emphasis on new. Something their friends will admire. Big, shiny, expensive. Now they feel guilty because they already owe twenty thou on their credit cards, they're barely making their mortgage each month, their boss has just threatened lay-offs and they're sitting here thinking about pinching pennies on groceries but laying down fifteen grand on a new Toyota. Can you see the dilemma? You add one more ounce of pressure to that scenario and you're going to lose people just like you lost that last couple. Understand? Let's try it from the top. Why do you want to be a car salesman?"

Chad thought about it a sec. "To help people get what they want."

"Good. Glad you were listening. I want you to write that on a piece of masking tape and put it three places you see everyday: your bathroom mirror, your refrigerator, and whatever you look at when you're sitting on the can."

"You're kidding me?" Chad laughed.

Barry grimaced, his eyes narrowing in focus. "You think I'm kidding. Did I tell you that Stan's going to fire us both if you don't shape up within a month?"

Barry leaned back on the couch, ice cold beer in his hand. He'd had a rotten day. Chad was quite possibly the worst car salesman he'd ever been around. Most people who try car sales have some sense of self-preservation. Not Chad. He expects customers to just roll over and give it to him, like he deserves it or is entitled to it, or maybe it's just that he needs it and he doesn't want to go back to waiting tables. *The Universe, dear Chad, doesn't respond to need. It responds to worth. Are you worthy of selling a car? Worthy of paying your rent? Worthy of your girlfriend's admiration?* Barry took a sip and pressed the cold, metal can to his forehead. *Jesus fucking Christ, what was I thinking? Maybe I can go to Stan, get a reprieve, bury the kid and all will be forgiven.*

Barry took another long swig and sighed. He had his own problems besides Chad. *One fucking orgasm?! Are you kidding me?? In ten years? I'd leave, too,* Barry thought to himself. *All those times...what the fuck is wrong with me? I'm out pretending to be this big, sexy stud-muffin of a man, and meanwhile my Patricia, the woman I love and cherish, is closing her eyes and faking.* He thought about his dad then, that awful big box of porno mags and the fact that his dad stored them under his bed – whoever heard of someone doing something like that?? – but more than that, Barry thought about Patricia trying to go slow and how crazy that made him, like he was truly going to bash his eyes in if it went on for one more second. Was there something actually wrong with him? Like maybe he was a mental case and didn't know it. This was unfamiliar territory to Barry: none of his friends talked about it, his dad sure as shit never talked about it, he didn't see books on the shelves where men were talking about giving women what they wanted emotionally. Maybe it was talked about inside those relationship books, but Barry had never opened them, never knew he needed to. In fact, he only knew one person who might be qualified to talk with him about this, and Barry had unfortunately stormed out of his office the last time they met.

Barry set down his beer and realized he was going to have to go see Taylor again. He felt like he was going to be sick.

But rather than stay in the nausea, rather than sit there with anxiety and trepidation and feeling like the walls of their small house were closing in, he did something he knew he shouldn't do, knowing full well that it might have consequences beyond his control: he picked up the phone, punched in the digits, and waited for Brenda's sultry voice to answer.

20

Things grew cold between them. He wasn't sure how, it seemed to happen minutely, small glances here, unfinished sentences there, Barry leaving early for the gym or Patricia meeting Lynn for dinner instead of waiting for Barry at home.

Six weeks later, they were sleeping on opposite sides of the bed and barely speaking. Patricia was furious, blaming Barry for her lack of sexual satisfaction and feeling like she was nothing more than a human blow-up doll for his pleasure and relief. She became pouty, then angry, then cold and distant until even she didn't recognize the emotions and behaviors coming out of her.

Barry didn't know what to do. He had always been the peacemaker in their relationship: he was usually the one who messed up and also usually the one to close the gap between them. But not this time. This time, he knew he hadn't done anything wrong. So he waited, and waited, and waited.

She didn't budge, going instead to have dinner with her mom and talk about alternative options, even her new step-dad chiming in that he hadn't seen her and Barry happy in quite a while.

When she got home, she purposely let Barry languish in the living room watching sports highlights until he got droopy enough to go to bed. Patricia knew how to play the game, freezing him out until he became sullen and depressed. She didn't care. This was about her: her needs, her wants, what she wasn't getting out of life. If he wouldn't give her a ring and give her another shot at babies, then fuck him, she was moving on.

And so, at the end of the next week, when Paulino invited Barry for Happy Hour tacos on Friday night, you bet Barry said yes and climbed aboard leathery-faced Paulino's Honda Red Wing motorcycle, the two of them screaming down Lincoln towards Santa Monica's Oar House, with fit-in-your-hand crumbly tacos, 99 cent beers, and as many gorgeous co-eds as could fit in one wood-paneled room.

Patricia sat at home, counting the hours and minutes. She knew change was coming. She didn't know what it would look like, but both she and Barry knew that nature abhors a vac-uum, and that was exactly what had grown between them, a gigantic, obnoxious, life-sucking vacuum.

They were in trouble.

21

Le Michele Boutique was on Santa Monica Blvd just below 26th, in the hippest, coolest part of Santa Monica. The owner, Michele, was a forty year-old hairdresser who had lost eighty-five pounds, moved to Paris, married a rich Parisian man, and come back home wealthy, gorgeous, and incredibly over-the-top snobbish.

Patricia had been working at the boutique for three years: every Tuesday, Friday and Saturday from 11am – 5pm. She ran the register, set out the trinkets that arrived from all over the world, like the little glass frogs that were hand-blown in Kiev and sold for $49.95 apiece. She swept the front walkway from leaves, stood on the small purple step-ladder and dusted, and basically did everything Michele asked for 18 hours per week.

Here was the kicker: *Le Michele Boutique* was making it hand-over-fist.

Michele's husband, Roger – pronounced Ro-jer – paid the managing editor for the Santa Monica Daily News ten thousand dollars to feature the boutique on the cover of their annual magazine and run subsequent articles every week in the throw-away. It worked. People flocked to the boutique and bought every magnificent little piece that Michele picked out: glass frogs from Kiev, stained glass from Barcelona, ceramic napkin holders from vintage artists down in Venice Beach, and everything at triple the price because this was, after all, southern California.

Patricia was bored to tears. She'd stand in the back of the store, pretending not to hear the chimes of the front door opening, continuing her puppet play between a gourmet lobster pot holder and a sexy corn-on-the-cob holder that looked suspiciously like Vanna White.

"Oh, Vanna," the lobster pot holder began, "I must have you!"

"Not today you mustn't, dear lobster head," Vanna replied.

"But Vanna!"

Patricia, completely lost in her reverie, did not see Michele approaching from behind.

"Patricia! Patricia!" Michele hissed, her formerly big hips swaying to and fro, "What am I paying you for if not to greet people when they come in the door?!"

Patricia jerked her head up like a marionette, simultaneously saw Michele scowling behind her and the Texan-looking couple now inside the door checking out the avocado grippers that Michele had just flown in from south Florida.

"Hey, how are you folks doing?" Patricia called, lobbing the pot holder and Vanna back into the corner.

"Howdy," the man began. He had large, red saggy cheeks and looked like he was about to sneeze.

"Looking for anything in particular?" Patricia asked.

"Wellllllllll—" the woman extolled, "we are visiting from Ft. Worth and we read about your little shop on the airplane magazine, so cute, so cute indeed, and they mentioned something about some mango salsa that had won some kind of award?" the woman clucked her tongue as she spoke and Patricia had this image of the woman's head transforming into that of a giant chicken, her mouth becoming a sharp yellow beak as she spoke.

"Yes, the salsa is fabulous and it's right over here," Patricia led them down an aisle, smirking to herself and saying slowly inside her head, *I love my job, I love my job...*

꙳

Three hours later, Patricia waved goodbye as Michele and her good Parisian husband sauntered off to happy hour down at the pier. She jotted down a note in the log book and was just about to return to her lobster puppet show, when a large, handsome blonde man came in through the front door.

"Hi, welcome to *Le Michele Boutique*," Patricia began, "looking for anything in particular?"

"I'm not sure," the man said, "it's my first time here."

Patricia looked up and they locked eyes. She knew him from somewhere...Greg! Greg and Barry knew each other from somewhere: they'd fallen into a weekly coffee-house routine that had grown to include five or six different couples before falling away several years ago. Good-looking, hunky Greg, Patricia commented inwardly, wondering where his other half was: gorgeous, perfect-all-around girlfriend, Melanie.

"Greg," Patricia said.

"Patricia!" Greg said, smiling and taking a step towards her. "I didn't know you worked here."

"It's not something I exactly brag about," she confessed. "How are you?"

"I'm okay," Greg said, kind of on the quiet side for him.

Patricia studied him for a second: he had large blue eyes, dimples, and the body of an Olympic swimmer with large, masculine hands. He was wearing faded blue jeans and a white cable-knit sweater and any woman in her right mind would want to lie down with him right there on the cold boutique floor. Patricia shook her head to banish the image.

He looked up and caught her staring at him.

"I'll let you look around," she said, blushing and retreating behind the register.

Twenty minutes later, after he had told a few jokes and she had laughed at all the appropriate places, she placed his glass frogs and purple eggplant holder into a recycled-paper bag and handed him his trinkets.

"It was great to see you," he said, smiling.

"You, too, Greg. Take care," she said, wanting to say more but biting her tongue. And with that, he was gone, and Patricia had two more hours to kill before Le Michele came back to lock up.

Maybe I should take a lover.

The thought was still fresh in Patricia's mind several days later as she parked and made her way into the Barnes & Noble. A windy gust kicked up, circling around her ears and forcing her to turn up the sides of her coat as she hurried through the Santa Monica alley way, through the outdoor mall, and finally inside the large, wonderful bookstore.

Barnes & Noble. Patricia loved bookstores. Border's was her favorite, but since that lumbering giant went under, what real choice did she have? She'd heard the whisperings...that B&N was also destined to fail, that since people discovered used books at half the price on Amazon, Barnes & Noble was falling further and further behind. Patricia didn't care. She loved big, giant, get-lost-in bookstores. She gladly paid $100 a trip for three or four books and an afternoon spent among super-high ceilings, fresh brewing coffee and some of the greatest minds publishing today.

She walked down the aisles slowly, letting her fingers graze the tops of different books. It was as if she was coming out of a fog, a long, drawn out fog comprised of nothing but her and Barry, Barry and her: their struggle, her miscarriages, and the ten-year gulf between the love she wanted and the love she actually received.

I can't do it anymore, she thought, shaking her head. *Not the way it is. Do I want to leave him? Do I want to go to Montana? Not really. What I want is some way to compensate, some way to not only get even, but some way to get what I need. What do you do when you're faced with an impossible situation where you're not allowed to leave, but within that situation you also cannot get what you need? How many women feel this way?* Patricia didn't know, but imagined thousands of lonely housewives searching the aisles of Barnes & Noble's looking for the answer to the very same question: what do I do when they lock me up and throw away the key?

And why am I not allowed to leave?

Patricia went through the best sellers, made it over to finance, housekeeping, gardening, fortune telling, then settled down in the literature section which reminded her of her college days.

Maybe it's me, she thought, flipping the pages of a Hemingway novel. *Maybe I'm the one with the problem. No one else I know complains about not getting what they need. Wait a minute, that's a bunch of crap. Everyone I know complains about it. In fact, do I know anyone with a satisfying sex life?*

Two people: Greg and Melanie. That's it. And they seem like crazy rabbits who almost never come out in public, except when they do they are both happy, radiant, with a warm, pink glow emanating from their cheeks.

"What is their secret?" Patricia had once asked a mutual friend.

"Good sex," the friend replied.

"What do you mean, good sex? Good sex is why they're always happy?"

The friend had turned at that point and looked Patricia right in the face. "Are things that bad between you and Barry?"

And that was…how many years ago? Three? Four? Patricia wondered if Greg and Melanie were still together, if good sex was enough to keep a couple satisfied. It's more than that, though, she realized, drifting out of the literature section and over into romance. It's communication, it's sharing. It's giving, is what it is.

That's what I need from my husband, and that's what I'm not getting.

And he's not my husband. At least not on paper.

She pulled a couple Zora Neal Hurston novels off the shelves and sank down into the floor. Maybe I'm obsessed, she thought, opening to the first page of *Their Eyes Were Watching God* and starting to read.

Suddenly, she had the distinct feeling she was being watched. *I'm paranoid,* the thought. *I'm here in Santa Monica, at one of the biggest book stores in North America, my boyfriend is out at the dealership working, who could possibly be watching me?* Still, there was something, so she stood up and glanced around. *Nothing down that way, nothing in the middle rows, nothing over... wait a minute, back up, there, who's that? Oh my God, it's Greg! And he's looking this way? What should I do?*

Greg parked his Honda in the parking structure and turned off the engine. *Things do end,* he thought. *Doesn't mean it has to be anybody's fault...oh, right, okay, that's a bunch of crap right there, we know whose fault it is, okay? Let's not pretend to know otherwise.* Greg thought of the different images of Melanie: coming home from work, looking over her shoulder to smile at him and maybe even kiss him while cooking asparagus for dinner. Most of all, though, he thought about their love making. There was a giving there, he recognized, something that wasn't present the rest of the time. Was it him? Her? He still wasn't sure. But they were able to touch something deeply emotional and satisfying while lying down with their clothes off, almost as if their clothes held all of the anger and pain between them. It started with a nod, or a slight brush of her hand against his shoulder. They might be in the living room, the dining room, and they would both feel it, a shift in the energy, and one of them would touch the other, then she'd take him by the hand and lead him down the long stairway, Greg getting harder with each step because he knew what was coming. They'd walk through their bedroom doorway, shut the door even though they were the only ones home, then fly to each other, pressing up against the door, the cabinet, the floor. Tearing at each other's clothes as if they couldn't get them off fast enough. Those damn clothes! It wasn't just the clothes; it was the world, the trimmings of the world, all the faces people made when you did something wrong. But here, in their bedroom, tearing at their clothes, they could make it different. They could make it right. And they did. Over and over and over. Something emerged between them that startled both of them. More than just orgasms. Greg closed his eyes, remembering it. Love, I guess. Or what we call love. More than that, though. A shared energy between them that passed from his heart to hers and drove both of them crazy, hurtling them onwards until they crashed again and again.

When did it change? Slowly. Fewer shared looks in the living room, fewer trips down the long stairway. Shorter impassioned moments and more cold ones as the heat of their exchanges became memories and something to talk about in reminiscing tones instead of experiencing them on a daily basis.

And then it was over.

He came home and saw her bags packed, saw the note on the kitchen table, and, worst of all, saw her scrambling around trying to get out before he came home. He hated to admit it, but that was when he knew. Actually, he knew weeks before, he'd just been in denial, hoping it wasn't happening. Breaking up a long-term relationship is like feeling the weight of a continent moving away. The direction doesn't even matter. It's the movement that feels unavoidable, like an earthquake or a rainstorm or some force of nature that's beyond your control. Like Melanie packing her bags. She hadn't even said anything. That part hurts. Greg had come home from a long day at the office to find his sexual and romantic partner of seven years running around their home, frantic in her attempt to be gone before his coming home. Had it gotten that bad? So bad they couldn't even talk? He'd walked in, seen the bags and the note, and just kind of slumped into a chair. She was dressed in black, all black, and she ran into the dining room and then screamed when she saw him sitting there.

"You don't have to go," he had said softly.

She started to talk, but tears and phlegm and other things started coming out instead of words. Standing there a moment, her hand trying to suppress the tears, Melanie had finally turned and faced him.

"I do," she said, her eyes turned down.

"Why?"

"I don't know," she said, starting to cry again. "It's this crazy dream."

Greg moved towards her. She let him hold her, rested her head against his chest.

"I still love you," he said.

She nodded, as if to say she did, too, but she didn't say that. She didn't say anything. She patted his chest, took her purse off the table, picked up one of her suitcases, and walked down the other long hallway towards the front door.

Greg stood there, helpless, his life flashing before him: baseball games, his parents' marriage, the day his sister was born, and now Melanie, his love of seven years but his best friend for twenty, turning her back and heading out the front door.

"Don't. Don't go," he wanted to say, except he didn't.

He didn't say anything.

Click went the door lock, and then she was gone.

Six weeks, Greg thought, tucking his keys into his pocket and heading towards the bookstore. *Six weeks and it's all I've thought of every single day. I need to get out. I need excitement. I need something to get my mind off that fucking woman.* She hadn't even called; had never really given him a full explanation. *Excitement? Well, at least something to make me stop thinking of killing myself.*

He wasn't serious about that. He had a good job, a good home. He had loved and could still love. He knew that to be true. But he felt sideways. People say upside-down; that wasn't his experience. It was more like the world had tilted sideways and Greg now saw everything with his head cocked to the side. What used to be funny was now sad. What used to be sad was now tragic. *There is a cloud over my head,* he thought, crossing the alleyway and heading into the bookstore. *What can you do about that?*

Patricia looked back at him, the two of them staring at each other from forty feet away. She felt heat turn on inside of her. My God how long had it been since she felt that! She took in every ounce of his Ivy League looks, his blonde hair, the shape and definition of his chest. *Patricia,* she thought, *you are flirting. He is forty feet away but you are definitely flirting.*

Good. Good for me for flirting.

Besides, I am not flirting. I am noticing. Just because I'm living with someone doesn't mean I have to be dead. I didn't start pushing up daisies the day I moved in with Barry. And besides, just because you're on a diet doesn't mean you can't look at the menu.

Even if it was a helluva menu.

She'd heard all the one-liners, thought they were all sad justifications for people doing what they wanted. But this was different. This was a potential get-out-of-jail-free card. Hmmm.

"Hi, Greg," she said, crossing the distance between them and sidling up beside him. She was a good half foot shorter than him, but she used it to her advantage: letting her hair fall just so against her shoulder, revealing her breasts inside her sweater.

"Hi, Patricia! Twice in one week! What are you doing here? I've been coming here for five years and I've never seen you here." Greg noticed her chest, tried not to stare, Patricia watching his eyes with every move.

Jesus Christ, Greg thought. *Patricia, Patricia. Living with Barry, the car salesman. Short, funny, gorgeous. Was she always this gorgeous? And where do they live? Alphabet streets in the Palisades. Right.*

"How's Melanie? I meant to ask about her at the boutique. I haven't seen her in ages," Patricia asked, shifting her weight and biting her lip.

"Melanie is fine," he said, debating. "What the hell. We broke up, but I hear she's doing okay."

Patricia took a step back. "You broke up? But I thought you two were happy. You were the one couple I knew who had good sex." They both laughed. "Sorry, I shouldn't have said that."

Greg looked at her. "That's what you thought?"

"It's what everybody thought. You two were the talk of the town."

"It wasn't really the sex," Greg said after a long pause. They were in a small Mexican place on Lincoln, Patricia twirling her hair and forgetting all about the fact that she was already in a relationship. Well, not completely. Every fifteen minutes a thought would pass through her head: *Aren't I supposed to be somewhere? Isn't there something I'm supposed to be doing?* And then nothing, so she'd go back to the conversation.

"I know exactly what you mean," she said.

"You do?" he asked.

The waiter came over, refilled their water glasses.

"Tell me," Greg said.

"You first."

Greg looked around, fearing that Melanie's spirit might come popping in at any moment. "There was a giving there, something we didn't have in the rest of our relationship. It was like the words and the clothes and the stuff of the day – all the normal stuff of living – that's what got in the way. And we'd bypass it or transcend it by taking it all off, literally. And then it was really good. She gave a tremendous amount."

"And you?" Patricia said.

"What about me?"

"Did you give?" she asked with just a hint of a smile.

Greg looked at her. It had been a long time since a woman had looked at him like that, such openness, friendliness, even playfulness. He imagined her naked, her breasts and her hips and the snow-white color of her skin. He wanted to take one of his tortilla chips and scoop her up right there in the restaurant.

She's with someone, he thought. *Be careful.*

Fuck being careful. It's all I've been for the last seven years and look where it got me.

He took her hand with his, covered and held it right there at the table.

"Yes," he said, "I gave, too. Quite a lot, actually."

Tingles ran down her spine when he said that. *Oh, Jesus Christ, where are you heading, Patricia? How many sins are you trying to commit in one night? First, you go out to a bookstore when you know Barry's going to be home any minute. Then you meet and flirt with the one man you know who could give you good sex. Now you're at dinner with him five minutes from your house, at a place Barry could walk in any minute, and now he's holding your hand. And you know the worst part: you're really liking it. You're actually hoping Barry will walk in at any minute so he can see what he's been missing.*

What would my mother say now?

Go for it. Barry's a selfish bastard who deserves to rot in hell.

Thank you, Mom. Thanks for piping in. A little strong, but I get your point.

She turned her attention back to Greg, to his angular face, warm smile, incredibly ripped body under his maroon cardigan.

God, his hands are nice. It has been so long since I have felt held. That is really all I want. Yes, I want to travel. Yes, I want Barry to take me places. But more than anything, I want to feel held. Safe. Secure.

Patricia gave Greg's hand a little squeeze, then took her hand back, started eating her veggie fajitas again. Looking down, she could feel Greg's eyes on her.

"Did I do something wrong?" he asked in a low voice.

"No," she said. "You did something very right. That's the problem."

Greg smiled. It had been a long time since he'd made someone nervous. *God, this is so much fun, all these little nuances of dating, getting to know someone. Why have I been cooped up in my house these past six weeks? Hmmm, six weeks, that's not very long. Long enough to know I need to get out more.*

"Tell me about Barry."

Patricia coughed on her food, choking on a grilled onion, her eyes watering as she reached for her drink, Greg patting her on the back to help the spasm stop.

"You okay?" he asked.

"I will be," she responded, downing half a glass of ginger ale. "There, that's better. What did you say?"

"Barry. Tell me about him."

Patricia shook her head. "I'd rather not."

"How come? We're friends. How is he?" he insisted.

She leaned forward a bit on the table, just enough to get him to lean forward as well. "Greg, I'm going to be real straight with you. Are you thinking at all about what I'm thinking about?"

"Yes," he said, looking right at her.

"Then let's not talk about Barry."

"Okay," he said, nodding.

They walked out to their cars, parked one behind the other in the alley way besides the restaurant. Greg even let his hand sway against hers and she took it, feeling the rough skin and calluses.

"You have calluses on your hand?"

"Woodworking," Greg responded. "It's a hobby."

Funny how comfortable I feel with him, she thought. *Maybe it's just denial. Or maybe it's just a lack of tension. God, thank God for lack of tension.*

"So what now?" he asked as they made it to her car door.

"What would you like?" she said, smiling.

"I think I would like to see you again."

"And you know that I'm living with someone?"

Greg smiled. "Yes, I do know that."

"So you know what we're talking about?" she asked, feeling the palm of his hand and pressing against it.

"What are we talking about?"

She pulled him close and whispered in his ear, making him redden and lean in against her.

"Now?" he said, complete putty in her hands.

"Not now," she said, opening her car door and whisking away from him. "But soon. Very, very soon."

22

Driving home, Patricia was elated. She opened the windows, turned on the radio, and yelled at the top of her lungs. She drove past Lincoln, past Washington, through the PCH tunnel and up Chautauqua, bouncing along Billy Joel's *Piano Man* before reaching the alphabet streets. *You're going to get it now, Mr. Barry-Cum-Quickly. Ouch, she thought, I'm zinging him tonight.* She thought about Barry, about when they were falling in love, meeting each other in college and spending time together in an easy, almost casual way, and then realized that that time felt very, very far away.

23

Barry sat in the dark of their living room, thinking. The bottle of rum was almost gone and he had a sour feeling in his stomach...usually the one that came right before he either puked or passed out. But tonight was different. Tonight he had a certain level of clarity, like seeing things for the first time. He had no idea where Patricia was; she was normally home waiting for him, a glass of chardonnay and simple dinner nearby. But tonight, Barry sat alone, thinking over the past few months, then past few years of their relationship, and he came up with one big glaring realization:

He and Patricia no longer had an intimate, romantic relationship.

They had a co-existence.

They lived near each other.

He worked, and chased women, and came home and lied about meetings and functions when all the time he was trying to see if he could stick his penis in someone other than his girlfriend.

He hated being so straight about it, but something about the last phone call to Brenda and how desperate he was to have sex with a woman he'd never even met rang true inside him, like:

How did I get to this point in my life?

How did I get here?

What wrong turn(s) did I make that led me to this?

And why am I not married, with kids, with a career I can be proud of?

And then the one single devastating question that he had no answer to:

What the fuck is wrong with me?

He'd spent the last two hours tracing back, all of the choices, all the left's instead of right's, beginning with the mistaken belief that he and Patricia could be happy together. College was a lie. The whole thing was a big fucked up lie. And then add on the fact that she wasn't even here, that he didn't even know where she was, and it just made for one dinger of a headache.

He knew he was drunk, and not happy drunk. Mean drunk.

Barry threw open the front door and staggered out towards his car, trying to decide what to do.

Okay, I know I shouldn't go to Brenda's. What's there is sex, forbidden sex, but it's going to open up other things as well. *But fuck, when do I get what I want? When do I get to turn a woman over and say whatever the fuck I want while I give it to her? Like how you like me now, bitch?*

He stumbled and fell on the grass, smashing his head and face on the damp sod, then opened his car door and slid behind the wheel. *Why does sex with Patricia have to be gentle, honest, sincere? Why can't it just be fucking? I mean plain, in-the-light-of-day, humping. We used to do that. Me and her. That used to be enough. And then you had to go start watching Oprah and reading books like* <u>*Women are from Venus, Men are from Mars*</u>, *and all of a sudden it was like I became the wrong species, embarrassed by the fact that I have a penis and it likes to do things. Yes, I admit it, your honor, I do, in fact, have a penis. And yes, it does like to do things.*

What kind of things, Mr. Lemming?

You know, go places, take trips, get outside for a stroll or something.

Sounds like a dog, he could hear Patricia say.

He smiled in spite of himself, turned the ignition key in his souped-up Mustang with the V8 engine, tried to put it into reverse and instead slammed it into drive as he stamped down hard on the pedal, crashing into their garage door and cracking it right down the center with a giant, loud thunder clap!

The two sides of the garage door swung on their hinges, falling away from his car like the parting of the Red Sea.

Barry laughed, then he began to cry.

Patricia turned the last right onto Oleander, made it past their neighbor's house, and pulled up to the curb. Was that Barry's Mustang? No way, that car's in the middle of our garage door. Our garage door! He's cracked it down the middle!

"Barry, are you okay?" she yelled, running forwards.

"I'm okay. The fucking garage door got in my way."

"You're drunk," she said.

"So what? You weren't even here. I bet you were out getting laid," he slurred, still sitting in the driver's seat.

"Come on, Barry, let's go inside," she tugged on his arm, but he waved her off.

"No, we are not going inside. Not until we figure this out."

"Figure what out?" she asked.

"This. Us. You and me. Why aren't we happy together, Patricia? What happened? We used to be happy, you know. It wasn't a lie. But now it's like we don't even know each other. Who are you? Who am I? Hi, Patricia, I'm Barry. I sell cars, work out at the gym, and try to fuck women I don't even know."

They looked at each other.

"I didn't mean the last part. Shit."

Patricia let her eyes fall. "Is that true?" she asked.

"Sometimes." He rubbed the top of his steering wheel.

"Have you?"

He sighed. "No. I just take it as close as I can, but no, I never have."

"Well, guess where I was tonight," she said.

"I have no idea. The league of stay-at-home-mom's."

"Don't get mean, Barry."

"I'm not trying to, Patricia. It's just all fucked up right now. Where were you? Seeing a movie with Lynn?"

"No, actually. I was meeting a friend."

"What kind of friend?" he asked.

"The kind you wouldn't like," she replied.

"You were what?" Barry tried to stand up, forgot he was in the car, and rammed his head into the roof.

Patricia turned on her heels and strode towards her own car.

Barry scrambled out of his car and lumbered towards her. "Wait a sec! Just hold it right there!" He was running as fast as he could, but the ground kept tilting, causing Barry to fall and smash his face into the grass once more.

"C'mon, Barry, you can't even stand up straight," Patricia said.

"What do you mean, a friend I wouldn't like? What's wrong with us, Patricia? Why haven't we said boo to each other in like six weeks? Don't you still love me?" He was up off the grass now, only to fall back down once again.

"Barry, sober up. Get your shit together. I'll be at Lynn's for a little while. Call me when you're ready to talk." And with that, Patricia slipped her car into gear and drove away.

Barry watched her drive away down their street. He knew this day was coming, knew it from the first moment they met that he would eventually fuck it up. He punched the grass as hard as he could, three or four times, until the underside of his hand began to ache. He then looked over his shoulder at the cracked garage door, the one that somehow now looked like the sad smile of a clown, and bowed his head and wept.

24

"Marlboro Lights, please," Patricia said to the Indian man behind the counter. She looked out through the window of the 7-11; traffic passed by on Wilshire in both directions.

"Would you like a bag for the beer?" the man asked, his accent suddenly pleasing to her.

"Yes, please. Thank you."

She paid for the things and went out to her car. *Shit. Shit, shit, shit. I don't have a nightgown, my toothbrush. I don't have anything.*

She whipped out her cell phone and dialed Lynn's number, thinking about Greg's face and smiling. He was nice. Maybe he would cushion the blow.

"Hello," a female's voice answered. "Patricia, is that you? You sound awful."

"Lynn, can I come over? I just walked out on Barry."

Patricia drove down Wilshire to the coast, heading up PCH towards Malibu. Lynn had been her best friend since high school, when they'd both been cheerleaders and on senior council together. Whatever it took to look good for college.

Not a very likely pair, Lynn was tall and thin and dated jocks. Patricia? Well, Patricia had really only dated Barry.

We always think of ourselves in terms of the men we're attracted to, the men we've dated, the men we might marry. *Who am I apart from men, apart from Barry? If Barry were to die tomorrow, what would I do?*

You mean, like would I celebrate?

No, for money, for work, what would I do?

I'd probably go back to school and get a Master's degree. But in what? Psychology? I could be somebody's therapist. Maybe I should do that anyway.

She drove another fifteen minutes in the dark, passing Pepperdine University and its thin orange street lamps lighting up the gorgeous hill of rolling green grass. Lynn's house was tucked just into the shadow of the school, behind a small hill that gave them almost complete privacy and isolation, but still with an unobstructed view of the beach and the Pacific Ocean. It was heaven.

Patricia parked and walked up the long steps to Lynn's house. Lynn had moved up from San Diego first, met her husband John at a function her first week out. They'd been married now for twelve years.

John was a lawyer, a good one, and he answered the door after two knocks. He gave her a hug.

"Sorry to hear about you and Barry."

"Yeah, me, too. It's been coming for a while," she said. "Thanks, John. Thanks for letting me stay here for a little bit."

"Stay as long as you want. Mi casa es su casa. I'll go get Lynn."

He walked off down the hall. *What a nice guy? Why can't I find a nice guy like that?* Wait a minute, I have a nice guy.

Barry's a nice guy, when he's not being a complete asshole. It hit her then, what he'd said. That asshole! How dare he lie to me about all those meetings. She couldn't picture it, Barry trying to pick up on other women. Oh, yes, she could. She'd seen him one day at work, leaning over the secretary's partition when he didn't know she was there. He had this look in his eye, this want-to-come-have-fun? look which drove some women crazy and other women insane.

"Look at you, you poor thing," Lynn began, taking her by the shoulders and hugging her. "What did he do this time?"

Patricia didn't know what to say. She just stared at her.

"Are you okay?" Lynn said in a half-whisper, leading Patricia through the front door and onto the landing by the stairs.

"Can I ask you something?" Patricia asked.

"Yeah, sure, anything. You want something to drink?"

"In a sec. Did Barry ever try and hit on you?"

"Patricia...I know things are tough right now, but..." Lynn stammered.

Patricia waved her off. "Yes, they are tough right now, but I just need to know. Did he?"

Lynn looked past her to the kitchen, where John was humming and making himself a sandwich. She lowered her voice to a full whisper. "Yes, he did."

"Why didn't you tell me?" Patricia asked.

"I don't know. I didn't know how to talk about it."

Patricia just stared at her. She could feel her life unspooling inside her.

Lynn fumbled around for a sec, averted her eyes. "I was embarrassed. Actually, if you want to know the truth, I liked the attention, okay? John and I were going through a rough spell, and Barry probably sensed that, he's always been sensitive to that, and he just showed up here one night after work."

"You're kidding me! My Barry showed up here one night after work?"

Lynn smiled. "See, this is why I didn't tell you. Nothing happened. I didn't want to upset you."

"How long ago?   And what do you mean, nothing happened?"

"Jesus, Patricia, I'm your best friend. Calm down."

"I'm a little upset right now, Lynn," Patricia snapped, shifting her weight and thinking about bolting for her and a cheap motel room somewhere in Santa Monica.

"I know, I know. C'mon in, sit on the couch, I'll fix you a drink and tell you everything that happened. Did you bring any things?"

Patricia shook her head, looking like she was about to cry, and headed over to the couch. "I'll go back and get them tomorrow, when Barry's at work."

Lynn poured her a vodka tonic with a slice of lime and joined her. Patricia took a long, strong sip and shook her head.

"Barry drove his car through the middle of our garage door."

"Was he drunk?" Lynn asked.

Patricia nodded, looking somber and ashen before downing the rest of the vodka and tonic. "Make me another?"

Lynn fixed her another drink and brought back some pretzels.

"Don't down it this time," Lynn said.

"So, tell me, tell me the whole sordid story of Barry Lemming putting the moves on his wife's best friend," Patricia said, taking half the drink in two gulps and then stopping, more for Lynn than herself. She didn't even realize what she'd said.

"That's part of the problem, isn't it?" Lynn said, her voice dropping.

"What? Oh, did I refer to myself as his wife? I do it all the time...Yes, it is," Patricia explained. "What happened between you two?"

"There isn't that much to tell," Lynn began.

"Then why do you keep looking towards the kitchen?" Patricia asked.

"Because John doesn't know," Lynn hissed through closed teeth. "Look, I'm sorry you're having trouble, but, c'mon, Patricia, be sensible." Lynn looked again towards the kitchen, and when John went the other direction into the study to watch a ballgame, Lynn visibly relaxed. "Sorry. I've been wanting to tell John, but haven't quite known how. You know some of the things we go through as women...we bought our car from Barry. You're my best friend. I didn't want to mess things up."

"You should tell him," Patricia said.

"You think so?" Lynn asked.

"Yep. I think it's time for all of us to stop covering for Barry's ass -- whether I go back to him or not. Are you going to tell me or not?"

"Is there more you want to tell me first?" Lynn asked. "Wait a minute, I'll be right back."

Lynn walked down to the kitchen. Patricia looked around their home. It always felt nice, lived in, down-to-earth even though it was a multi-million dollar property. From meeting either one of them, you'd have no idea how much money they had. Lynn also had had two miscarriages. It was something they laughed about, cried about. It had almost torn Lynn and John apart, but unlike other couples, in the end, they just accepted it. Lynn took up golf and crochet; John racquetball and investing. Boom, that was it. No kids, no craziness or all of the things that come with a family.

"Do you miss it?" Patricia had asked her once.

"Children?" Lynn had thought for a moment. "Yes and no. No when I'm just living my life, free to do as I please. Yes when I talk to my girlfriends who have kids. Even in the midst of all that craziness, there's something there, isn't there? A warmth. A belonging. Something."

Lynn came padding back from the kitchen. She looked better, almost like she'd drawn strength from talking to her husband.

"Okay, John's heading downstairs and settling in for the night. I'm all yours."

"Did you tell him?" Patricia asked.

"About Barry? In forty-five seconds? No, I'm going to wait on that just a minute. I shot a seventy-five at Hillcrest today."

Patricia smiled. "You shot a seventy-five? Lynn, that's good enough to go pro. And that's a helluva course."

"Yeah, I wish. I'm playing in a tournament next week. We'll see if I fold under the pressure. Okay, where do we start: more alcohol, some marijuana, or just pretzels and girl-talk?"

Patricia snuggled in against her shoulder. "Men are assholes."

"Some men."

"Okay, some men are assholes. Most men," Patricia said, smiling.

They talked for hours, laughing back about high school, the different things they'd done to get boys to like them, coming back around to marriage and infidelity and the pressure of making a relationship work.

"Okay," Patricia began, "now that we're all comfy and relaxed, tell me the truth."

"It wasn't that much, Patricia. He came over one day after work. John was on a business trip on the East Coast and I was doing some painting and working on one of my projects. He looked kind of – I don't know what the word is – lost. He looked lost. Like something had been taken from him and he wanted me to help him find it."

"Did he say that?" Patricia asked.

"No, of course not. He came in, I made him a drink, he stayed for a little bit and then he left."

"That's it? No big proposal, no tense words?"

"Well, he asked if I wanted to fuck."

Patricia sprayed her pretzels and drink out across the table. "Get out of here!"

"Not in so many words. But you know when that's what someone is thinking," Lynn explained.

"What did he say exactly?" Patricia asked, sitting upright on the couch.

"Exactly? This was two years ago," Lynn continued.

"I don't care. Be as exact as you can."

"I think his exact words were: 'We could be good friends, Lynn.' And I said, 'We are good friends, Barry.' And he said, 'No, better friends than that.' And I said, 'Barry, Patricia is my best friend and I think it's time you went home to her.'"

"That was it?"

"That was it. Not all that exciting."

Patricia let her eyes soften their focus. She pretended the room was spinning, which it sort of was. *How many vodka tonics had she had?* "I wonder how many of my friends he's propositioned."

"You should ask him. Might as well get the truth out. You don't have anything to lose."

"Can I ask you something?" Patricia asked. "If you weren't my best friend, would you have slept with him?"

Lynn thought about it a sec. "No."

"How come? Because of you and John."

"Partly that. Mostly that. It's more than that, though. Barry is attractive, you know I've always thought that. But there's something, like a hunger or a neediness. I wouldn't know what to do with that." Lynn smiled, almost apologizing before carrying their glasses into the kitchen.

I don't know what to do with that, either, Patricia thought, turning onto her tummy and letting her face fall into the couch. She pictured Barry in his needy pose, the way his eyes said *'Please, help me! I don't know what to do with myself!'* She wondered what he was doing at that moment, figured he was drunk and still sitting in the car, then smiled that she'd actually left. *I never thought I'd have the courage to do that. Life comes down to a few, short moments, and I just had one.* She smiled a drunk, dreamy smile, then her mouth slacked open, she began to snore gently, and for the next few hours she did nothing but enjoy her sleep.

25

The sun crept over the horizon, spreading east across the ocean and onto the mainland. Southern California slept fitful dreams, content in their place in the world, except for those who wanted to move ahead. For them, the sleep was not so fitful, but more of a break from the mad rush to succeed. For them, sleep never brought contentment, only a pause in the action.

Barry slept face down on the couch, full beer still in his hand. He had gotten off of the wet grass of the front yard around 2 a.m., staggered into the kitchen, grabbed a beer, then tripped over his feet and passed out on the couch.

The sun came in over the hedges in the backyard, spread along the deck, gradually poured into the living room. Barry woke with a start, more a product of his dream than anything else: he was on the beach, sunning and enjoying himself. But then it shifted and everybody from his childhood was there, dumping sand on top of him. His friends from school, his parents, his neighbors Hugo and Andy who were always weird and sometimes mean. The sand came in his eyes, his ears, filled his nostrils and hair. Then Patricia was there, dumping sand right down his throat, and when he woke, he gagged and spit and took several minutes to stop thrashing about on the couch.

"Where am I? Patricia? What the fuck is going on here?!" He shouted. Then it started coming back to him, what had happened, what he'd said in a drunken stupor that he should have said a long time ago. He remembered smashing the garage door and having a drunken, stupid fight with her; her shoes clicking away from him last night, and in a bizarre way, he felt oddly free, as if telling the truth had lifted some great weight from his neck and shoulders.

She's gone, though, you idiot.

Yeah, but at least she knows.

Knows what? That you try and fuck women? Big deal, everybody does that.

Not everybody.

Not Taylor.

And it still doesn't make it right.

Oh, shut up, you dumb s.o.b.

Walking into the bathroom, he glanced up in the mirror while he peed. He'd seen worse. But then he took a deeper look, into his eyes, the bloodshot exhaustion causing red lines and streaks to fill the whites of his eyes, and there, staring at himself in the mirror at 6:30 in the morning the day after Patricia walked out, he finally realized he was in real trouble.

Men have a funny way of realizing they're in the situation they're in. They rarely know it when it is happening, i.e. during a fight, during an argument, sometime when they could still do something positive about it. It's only later, in the absence of women and everybody else for that matter, that men start to feel pain. Without the nurturing, without the love, they honestly begin to feel what is happening inside them. It's not pretty. In fact, it can be downright ugly. But even then, with no one else around, it comes across as a dull ache that gets blamed on overexertion instead of accurately assessing what is really going on.

Does it work? Not really. That's why most men need to find another woman. Fast.

Barry went and sat on the bed, thinking over his options:

I could call Taylor.

Yeah, right. I'd rather stick a fork in my eye.

I could start calling our friends, one by one, until I find her.

And then do what?

Hi, Patricia, I didn't mean it, it was a lie?

I could go hang out at my uncle's house – his dad's only brother and a bachelor his entire fifty-seven years – Chris would pop a beer and say, *Congrats, the ball-and-chain is gone!*

Barry didn't even know if Patricia was gone for good. She was just gone right now. And Barry had a slamming, pounding headache.

Barry went back into the bathroom, lowered his shorts, and masturbated over the toilet, thinking of the different positions he and Patricia had had sex in: Patricia on top, Patricia giving him oral sex as they drove home from a Bowie concert in college, Patricia opening her legs and making love to him, holding him while he came. He sprayed cum over the toilet, missing the mark but hitting several different parts of the enamel, not bothering to wipe it up, but instead lowering the lid, noticing the different spots he had hit. He went to the frig, got a cold beer, then popped through the front door into the cold morning air.

He was on automatic pilot, and he didn't give a fuck.

Barry fired up the Mustang and within minutes had a twelve-pack in the passenger seat, a new cold one in his hand, and was on his way down Lincoln to the Toyota dealership.

The dealership. That asshole, Stan, who barked and gave orders to his own private army. The Turn, meaning no customer left the lot without being "touched" by at least two salesmen. He felt like a prick, saying, "Excuse me, can you hold on just a sec?" and then going to find Orzo or some other loser in a suit, knowing eyes were on him, whispers going like *He blew another one*, and then the look in the customer's eye as they see him returning with one of his counter-parts, ganging up on them now, the customers sitting, the salesmen standing, all of it about power, us over you. No wonder people hated car salesmen. But it wasn't the salesmen, it was the people behind them. And the people behind them. And finally the institutions behind them.

Well, sometimes, he had to admit, it was the salesmen. Like the time Paulino rolled a couple from San Bernardino into a $600 per month lease, making a sweet $1200 on the deal, all because he offered them a price on the car, the lady looked at the paper and said 'Yes!' and boom, there you go. Six hundred bucks a month for the next three years, when it could have been, should have been, no more than four. Don't ever say yes to a car salesman. Just keep saying no until you get what you want. Even then keep saying no. That was Barry's motto.

I lot of good it's done you with your wife.

He finished his beer and popped another. The lot was open, hundreds of shiny new cars sitting in the early morning light. Barry parked right next to the dealership office, kitty-corner like, the mouth of his car facing out towards the street. He tasted the beer in his mouth, visualized the cold, wheat-colored liquid as it slid down his throat, and felt the wheels coming off his wagon. One by one.

Patricia has left me.

I could go talk to Taylor.

I could call all our friends, one-by-one. And then say what? Patricia, I didn't mean it?

Barry remembered something his father had said before he'd died.

They were on the 405, held up on the side of the road with traffic whizzing by, his dad having convulsing fits because his lungs weren't working. Barry stood next to him, not sure what to do, holding his dad's weakened shoulders and ribs, the bones pushing up through the skin, two years of chemo having taken its toll.

"Make it important," his dad had said.

"Make what important?" Barry had asked.

"All of it," his dad whispered, nodding his head over this way and that, pointing to everything going on around them. "Because whatever you think it is, however important you think you are, it's going to be gone before you know it."

Barry finished his beer, crumpled the can and tossed it into the back, then reached over to the glove compartment and brought the gun onto his lap. It felt good, holding it, like it brought with it the doors of possibility.

He sat that way for a half-hour, maybe more. Guys started showing up to the dealership: Latino workers from the back, the guys that cleaned and shampooed the cars. Barry nodded his head at Manny, an old-timer who'd been there since '73. Manny decided to come over.

Shit, Barry thought, *do I always have to be so friendly? Even on this day, I have to smile like I'm running for mayor?*

"You okay, gringo?" Manny declared.

Barry slid his hand off of his lap, revealing the gun and the half-empty beer.

"Oh, man, what happened to you? C'mon, Barry, you've always been sane, dude. Your lady leave you or something?"

Barry nodded, feeling out of time. He slid his forefinger into the gun. Manny started backing away, keeping his eyes on Barry, just like he would a dog that had suddenly gone rabid.

The red demon appeared on his right shoulder then. It was about six inches high and could talk into Barry's right ear.

Barry looked over, noticed it, went back to fingering the gun.

It's time to go inside, the demon said.

"And do what?" Barry said inside his brain.

You know, the demon answered before disappearing.

"Fuck it," Barry said, opening the car door and heading towards the showroom. He stashed the gun in his rear waist-line, feeling the cool metal as he walked. Barry felt powerful, strong, and completely out of control.

"Morning, Barry," April said, half-turned as she organized papers on her desk.

"Have you seen Stan?" Barry asked, hearing his voice from outside himself.

"He's golfing," April said, barely above a whisper. "Hey, are you okay? You don't look like yourself."

"I'm fine," Barry responded. "Golfing where?"

April stopped what she was doing and looked at him, really watching him. "Barry, honey, go home. You don't need to be here til two o'clock. It's Wednesday, swing-shift day. Go enjoy the day."

It worked. Barry snapped out of his trance and saw her, almost for the first time. "You're right. It's Wednesday. Thanks, April. I'll see you in a couple of hours."

Barry made it back to his Mustang and peeled away from the lot. He bounced onto Lincoln, turned left on a small connector road before hitting PCH and opening the Mustang up, going almost ninety with the top down and his gun still in his lap, the safety on but not for long. The ocean and the sand flew by on his left, and Barry had music on the radio but for the life of him couldn't name the song. He didn't care.

Where to go?

What to do?

He felt strangely elated.

I am breaking every rule I know.

I smashed my garage door last night because I put a gear shift in the wrong hole. The wrong hole! My life is all about wrong holes.

He laughed, then spit up, beer vomiting out from his mouth and dripping onto the floor of the car. Gross, he thought. My last day here on Earth and this is how I'm spending it? Nasty.

He pulled into a beachside parking lot, tilted his seat back away from the rising sun, and closed his eyes. *Maybe I just need some sleep. Sleep has always worked wonders for me.*

He woke several hours later. Spit had dried on the side of his mouth and he had a terrible, warm-beer taste when he woke.

What time is it? What's going on?

Then he felt the gun, remembered what had happened and what was still happening. He wondered where Patricia was, but realized that this wasn't about Patricia. This was about him, Barry, and what he needed to do. He knew, somehow deep inside him, that he would always end up at this point. He'd been avoiding it, dancing around it, trying to pretend it wasn't coming. But wasn't he the one that wrote the short story *One Against the World* in eighth grade? Hadn't he always been different, not sure how to fit in, not wanting to fit in, so even when Hugo and Andy called him big-nose and Jew-nose and hook nose and ugly nose, he had to agree with them. Barry Lemming. Huh. He was doing a real good job of making everything important.

He looked at his watch: ten o'clock in the morning. He'd been asleep for almost two hours. He started the ignition and drove the four miles to Brenda's house, having no idea if she'd be home, not caring really. He was in full destruct mode and he knew it. So when he got out of the car and actually knocked on her door this time, it was no surprise when she opened up and invited him in.

She was short, shorter than he'd imagined on the phone, with large blonde curls and breasts that seemed to swell as they talked. Barry offered her a beer, and when they crashed on the couch, he wasn't surprised when she slid her hand over and started massaging him. He moved towards her, sliding a hand on her breast and then down into her shorts. And within minutes, they were naked on the couch, touching each other, feeling each other, Brenda climbing on top of him, riding him bronco style and Barry arching his back and ejaculating inside of her. *I don't care. I don't care. I don't care.* he heard himself saying, ignoring the fact that he'd finally crossed the line, finally done what he'd wanted to but sworn he wouldn't all of his adult life, and when they finished she crossed into the kitchen, brought out some ice cubes and started rubbing them on his nipples. He loved the sensation, brought his hand back down to the dark hair between her legs, and they had sex one more time before falling asleep in each other's arms.

26

Patricia didn't know what to do. It was three-thirty in the morning, she was in Lynn's guest apartment, and she was having an anxiety attack. *What did I do? Why did I leave? I love him. I need him.* She watched her chest heave in and out; she got up, flicked on the light, and looked at herself in the mirror. She looked awful: tired, painful eyes, like someone who'd been through a prizefight except she couldn't remember any punches being thrown. But then she looked back, watched her chest heave and tremble, and finally she sat down on the bed and began to cry.

She cried for a long time, and when Lynn gently knocked on the door at quarter past four, Patricia turned the knob, let her in, then sobbed in her arms for a good forty-five minutes.

Morning didn't bring much relief. The sun was out and Patricia had no idea what time it was. She looked over at the clock: eleven fifteen. *Don't I need to be somewhere? Where?*

She glanced around the room Lynn had decorated in bright yellows and greens. *She always knows how to brighten things up,* Patricia thought, then wondered again where Barry was and why he hadn't called.

Except I don't want him to call. I don't want to speak to him. I don't want to be near him. That lying, motherfucking bastard.

Patricia grabbed the pack of cigarettes she'd bought at the 7-11, tapped one out, then fired it up, realizing she didn't smoke, had only smoked two cigarettes in her entire life and both of them before she was sixteen. She inhaled, then coughed like there was no tomorrow, finally drowning the stick out in the bathroom sink. *Fuck, I can't even do that right.*

Walking upstairs, she realized that she could do anything she wanted. She could go to Florida, she could go back to Ohio and live near her hundred cousins. The world was her oyster. Then why did she feel so crappy?

"Well, look what the dog brought in," John said, smiling over his sports page.

"That bad?" Patricia asked, squinting in the light.

"I was only joking. Sorry, kind of a bad one. I'm not good at uncomfortable situations."

"Don't worry. It would only be uncomfortable if you put your hand on my leg," Patricia commented, plopping down in a chair next to him.

They looked at each other. John smiled and lifted his arms in a 'hands off' signal.

"Where's Lynn? Early golf game?" Patricia grabbed half a bagel off the table. "Man, I'm starving!"

"Yep. She should be home around one. Make yourself at home, grab a shower, watch a movie, do anything you want."

"No work for you today?" she asked.

John glanced at his watch. "Today's my late day. I go in about an hour." And with that, he went back to reading about the USC football game.

Patricia smiled. Lynn had found herself a good man. There weren't that many, at least not from what she'd seen. She took another bite of her bagel, whipped some cream cheese on top, then suddenly found herself thinking about Greg and smiling. Was he a good man? She didn't know. Was he sexy and available? Definitely sexy. Available? He seemed pretty available. How long had it been since his breakup? Shit, she was so tired of worrying about every little thing.

"I just decided something," she said.

"What's that?" John asked.

"From this moment on, I am officially going to let people take care of themselves. I did it for Barry for ten years and look where it got me. That's it. I'm done."

She walked back to her room, shut the door, then fumbled getting the piece of paper out of her wallet. Eleven-fifteen on a weekday. He'll never be there. I'll call and just leave a message, tell him I enjoyed seeing him again. Nothing provocative. Just nice and slow.

"Hello," a man's voice answered.

"Oh, hello, is Greg there?" Patricia squeaked.

"Yes, this is Greg."

"Greg, this is Patricia. We, um, hung out a little bit at the bookstore yesterday."

"I know who you are, Patricia," he said in a deep, soulful voice.

She stood near the door, pacing. Maybe she was making a mistake. *Maybe she should go back to Barry and beg him to take her back. No! She deserved better. Every woman did. Men like to fool around, and the minute we stand our ground, look what happens. My live-in boyfriend out chasing every friend I have. The fucking nerve.*

Greg wound his way through the hills, his gray Nissan Turbo moving like a metal shark through the expensive, finely-manicured homes. He came to the end of Lynn's street, looked out at the large expanse of ocean blue, then pulled up in front of the house.

Patricia came bounding out, then caught herself half-way down the stairs and slowed to a sultry walk. She carried a tan purse which matched her beige blouse and sweater – all of it loaned to her by Lynn -- and she looked better to Greg with every step she took.

"Hi," he said, getting out and coming around to her side of the car. "You look great."

"Hi," she said, a little shy, but still leaning up and kissing him on the cheek.

They held each other a moment, and Patricia felt something open inside her chest. *Maybe he'll be the one*, she thought, then smiled deep inside at her optimism.

"Where should we go?" he half-said, half-whispered.

"Anywhere. Let's just go."

They drove out towards Malibu, the lines of Pacific Coast Highway blurring besides them. Patricia didn't say much, instead she leaned her seat back and smiled as Greg slipped in a Blind Faith cd. She felt completely content to forget everything and just let Greg drive and drive.

He drove for hours, passing through the Malibu hills, into Oxnard, then Ventura, then touching the base of Santa Barbara before they stopped and had lunch at a small Mexican place only the locals know about. Warm corn tortillas stuffed with fresh lobster and melted butter; homemade coleslaw that Greg dripped into the burritos and licked off the ends of his finger tips. *He was so sexy!* Patricia felt almost guilty being there, like it was too much given where she was coming from.

"You okay?" Greg asked at one point.

"Just getting used to this, that's all. This is a big change from what I had with Barry."

Greg smiled. "You want to tell me?"

"Nope," she replied, stuffing a fingerful of lobster into her mouth. "Not yet."

Then they were back in the car, the sexual tension between them suddenly palpable. Would he lean forward and kiss her? Would she? They smiled, easing back into their reclined positions and heading back down through the coastal towns, Route One all the way until Malibu came and went and somehow, as if through a time machine, Greg's car was idling back in front of Lynn's house, five hours to the minute past when they'd left.

"Here we are," Greg said. "I told you I'd get you home safe."

Patricia looked at the front door to Lynn's house, then back at Greg, then back towards the door. She could feel the pang of loneliness she had waiting for her in there.

It's best not to make decisions out of loneliness, she could hear her mother say. *Loneliness and fear are a woman's two biggest obstacles.*

Forget you, Mom, she thought, then touched his hand.

"Let's go to your place," she said quietly.

Greg nodded and slipped the car into gear.

27

Barry woke with a start. *Where am I?* He looked at Brenda, at the strange room he'd come into hours earlier, then suddenly the pieces started falling back into place. *Jesus Christ,* he thought, *my last day on Earth and this is how I'm spending it?* He looked at Brenda's naked body, at her breasts and stomach which now seemed flat and flaccid. *What was the appeal? What was the lure here? The unknown? The forbidden fruit?* Now that he'd eaten...he didn't know...it just wasn't the same.

He stood up, collected his clothes and belongings, went and rinsed his mouth out in the sink, then placed sixty dollars on her dresser and went out into the afternoon light. It was chilly, colder than he'd expect for a fall day in Los Angeles, but still he knew what he had to do. What he'd been destined to do. He went back to the car, took the gun out of the glove compartment, and laid it in his lap as he started the engine.

Barry drove through Santa Monica towards the ocean, down Wilshire, past the Gap and Q's, down past Santa Monica Place, turning right on Ocean Avenue where old ladies walked their poodles and tourists took postcard photos against the wooden rail with the pier and ferris-wheel in the background. He turned right, heading down into the canyon, passing a gray Nissan Turbo he had no idea held his wife in the passenger seat, then came out the other side of the canyon and turned right up into the Palisades.

The Palisades. Home of the wealthy and famous. It had been his dream to live there one day, to have a home and children and make his life something fantastic. Instead, he hugged the gun closer to his groin and passed the million-dollar homes at a frenetic pace.

He turned left onto Sunset, wound his way past the smaller streets, could have turned right towards his home and safety, but instead turned left to go past the car wash and the library and the park, heading again past more homes, now doing forty in a twenty-five mile per hour zone until the seven or eight blocks ended out at the bluffs.

The Bluffs. Nothing but ocean for as far as the eye could see. The wind blew in large gusts out here. Two small trees swayed to the right and left. Barry pulled his car over to the side and parked.

He sat for a moment, thinking about what he was about to do. I don't have a choice. *Patricia knows the truth, there is no hope for us or me with anyone else, not with what I have.* He pictured a red demon coming off of his right shoulder to sit in the passenger seat beside him, large and red with bumpy horns and a foaming mouth. This demon was the single greatest fantastical character Barry had ever seen. What he was doing in his car, talking to him, instructing him on what to do, Barry had no idea. He didn't have time to contemplate or wonder; he only had time to listen. The demon laid out the plan step-by-step. Barry listened to the demon's words, not feeling scared or nervous, but ironically feeling calm, very very calm, for the first time in a long time, as if making the choice, losing the battle and the war, was finally going to bring him peace. Barry listened to the end of the demon's instructions, then deep in his own heart he bowed to what the demon was saying and began to load bullets into the gun.

28

Patricia laughed at Greg's joke. It was a silly one, where a priest and a shuttle driver both die and go to heaven.

After a little while, the priest complains to St. Peter, saying it's not fair that the shuttle driver has a big mansion and a fancy swimming pool, while the priest is stuck in a one-bedroom shack with no backyard and no windows.

Well, St. Peter replies, all the time you were preaching, the people in the church were sleeping. But all the time the shuttle driver was driving, all the passengers were praying.

She laughed again.

"I love your laugh," Greg commented, smiling and taking another sip of his beer.

They were on his couch, her beer half-finished on the coffee table. It was just past five and the sun was turning into an orange glow above the horizon.

"It feels nice here," she said, not sure how she got here. "How did I get here again?"

"You went to the bookstore. You saw some gorgeous guy. End of story." Greg kissed her hand, then went into the kitchen.

Patricia leaned back on the couch, hearing the pops of her vertebrae as she stretched. How different life could be! It had been years since someone other than Barry had shown an interest in her. She bathed in the attention. Could it stay like this? Could it last? Then her thoughts turned to Barry, where he was, what he was doing. A small, dark cloud came and hovered near her head.

"Uh-oh," Greg said, coming back in with baby carrots, cucumber slices and ranch dressing. "Those aren't happy thoughts."

"Tell me about your wife," Patricia said.

"We never married," Greg answered as he picked up a cucumber slice. "It was like we were married, though. Seven years and then one day, boom, it was over. I knew it was over, but I didn't, if you know what I mean. Tell me about that dark cloud."

Patricia tried to smile. "I was just thinking about Barry. I stormed out eighteen hours ago and already I'm here with you, having a great time. Shouldn't I feel bad about that?"

"Do you feel bad about that?" he asked, munching on a cucumber.

"No. Yes and no. I don't know." She covered her head with her hands and sunk down on the couch.

"Y'know," Greg said, prying through her hands, "You're allowed to have fun. It's in the rulebook."

"Where?" she asked.

"Page twenty-seven. I underlined it twice. All humans are definitely allowed to have fun." Greg picked up a magazine, pretending. "There. Right there. Page twenty-seven"

Patricia looked at the magazine cover. "That's a Sports Illustrated. And it's talking about Kirby Puckett."

Greg looked directly at her. "He hurt you, didn't he?"

"Yes," she responded. "You have no idea."

"Physically?"

"No, it wasn't like that with Barry. It was more neglect. Physical and emotional neglect. Like he had me, so he didn't have to care for me."

Later, several hours later, Patricia lay beside Greg on his bed, stroking the hairs on his chest. She should feel guilty. She should feel bad. She was, after all, still living with someone.

Or am I? she thought. *Did I storm out for a couple nights because I couldn't stand his drinking anymore...or did I actually leave for good without realizing it?* She looked into Greg's face and his closed eyes as he lay there on the bed.

I deserve to be happy, she thought. *Everybody does.*

To be free from the weight of a relationship that isn't working is like being let out of jail.

She exhaled, realizing the truth of that statement.

Greg said nothing, allowing her to process through her different emotions. He watched her, though, imagining he must be going through a similar process, remembering his beautiful Melanie, what she had looked like when he'd first met her, how they'd built their home together, what it had been like raising their pair of Great Pyrenees, and then, finally, that last day, when she'd walked out without saying why.

That day still hurt. It had been six weeks, but the sting was fresh as ever.

"You never know where you'll end up, do you?" Patricia whispered.

Greg shook his head. "No, you don't. What do they say: man proposes and God disposes?"

Patricia smiled. Neither of them were in a laugh-out-loud kind of mood.

"You think it's easier to leave or be left?" Greg asked.

"I don't know," Patricia answered. "I think both are hard. Are we ready to stop talking?"

Greg nodded, enjoying Patricia but still focused squarely on Melanie.

Patricia pictured Barry, wondered where he was, then pushed him out of her mind and leaned over on the bed, kissing Greg first on one eye, then the other, then she smiled shyly and lifted her shirt over her head.

29

Barry finished loading the bullets into the gun and waited.

Not here, the demon said, *Out on the bluff.*

Barry nodded and obeyed. He was on automatic pilot. Everything in the last two months had led him to this moment. Shit, everything in the last thirty-two years had led him here. But still, at the moment of decision, the moment of reckoning, it was still his body obeying commands and doing what he was told. The good boy down to his final minutes on Earth.

Even in this, he thought as he closed the door to the car and made his way onto the bluff, a slight breeze buffeting against his face, *even in this, I don't have a choice.*

He'd put three bullets into the chamber of the gun before spinning it round and round.

I like my chances, he thought, smiling.

"What now?" he asked inside his head.

Put the gun to your head and pull the trigger, the demon said, the words forming clearly in Barry's brain.

Barry wanted to turn around, wanted to look at this big demon and ask *Why? Why me? Why now?* But he was tired. He'd been fighting for so long. First, his parents, and then Patricia, and his drinking and his womanizing, and all of it had taken everything, and now it was just time for rest.

He was thirty-two years old, he had no children, and it was time for his story to be over.

He put the gun to his temple, closed his eyes, and pulled the trigger.

Click.

He took a deep breath and felt his legs go out from under him.

He fell, hitting the ground hard.

Get up, the demon said.

Barry stood back up, his hand shaking now, the gun gesticulating back and forth in front of him.

Steady yourself, Barry, the demon said. *You need to do this. It's the only way you'll feel better.*

Barry nodded and crossed his left hand onto his right, trying desperately to steady the gun. This time he brought the gun into his mouth, tasting the cold steel and not believing he was about to do this.

Don't do this! some part of him screamed.

The whole thing felt too surreal...like he wasn't really standing on the Bluffs in the Palisades, looking out over the gorgeous Pacific Ocean, listening to a big red giant demon with a gun in his mouth about to end his life.

I don't want to do this, he thought. *I don't want to go out this way. I can make it. Things are tough, but I know I can make it out.* He thought of Patricia, their first few dates back in college, making love in the afternoon to Van Morrison's *Tupelo Honey* and skipping class to go out to the Reservoir and drink Coors Light cold from the can.

The gun shook in his mouth, until he felt a force come and steady it, the demon's hand reaching around his face and holding the gun in perfect suspension aimed right at his tonsils, and then Barry was squeezing the trigger, barely able to contain the suspense of what was about to happen.

Click.

Jesus Christ, he thought, *enough already. No more. I can't take any more.*

He turned from the bluff and started heading back to the car.

You fucking wimp! the demon yelled. *You've never finished anything in your life. You're not a winner. You're a loser. A fucking, wimpy loser.*

Oh yeah, Barry thought, taking the bait. *You want to see what a winner I am? You want to see?*

Barry raised the gun and fired.

The bullet exited the chamber, heading at the speed of light towards his brain.

30

Patricia put a hand to her stomach, like someone had just punched her in the gut. *What was that?* Something was wrong, something was terribly wrong. She looked over at the clock, but she knew that time was not the problem nor the answer. Closing her eyes, she tried to ignore the sinking feeling in the pit of her stomach, like someone or some thing had just blown a candle out.

No luck. *There has definitely been a disturbance in the force.*

"Did you feel something?" Patricia asked.

Greg mumbled something and went back to sleep.

She pulled on sweats and padding out to the living room. She called her house, where the phone rang and rang. She then called Barry's cell phone; it went straight to voicemail.

I hope it's not him, she thought, realizing for the first time the full implication of what she'd done. What they'd done.

She sat on Greg's couch, knowing something was terribly wrong, and, equally painfully, knowing there was not a single thing she could do about it.

31

It was the flash of light he'd remember most. And then the traveling...the beautiful, beautiful traveling.

He had been walking quickly back from the plateau of the bluffs, making it to stand near the front left tire of the car. That much he remembered clearly.

He was arguing with the demon, challenging him, trying to prove to him that he wasn't a wimp.

Stupid, yes, but that's what had been happening at the moment.

He'd fired a third time. He remembers the recoil in his hand as the gun shook. And this time a bullet definitely came out.

But he wasn't dead. Or was he?

Where was he?

There was silence. Unbelievable silence.

You never knew how loud the world was until you heard silence like this.

Barry closed his eyes. What are the facts?

I'm cold.

I'm lying down.

I'm dead.

I must be dead.

Then why am I thinking? Can I move my fingers?

Shit, I can't move anything. And I can't see anything. But my mind is still alive. I don't believe it. I killed myself and never even got a chance to say goodbye to Patricia, to tell her how deeply sorry I am, what I fool I was, how I took the goodness and beauty we had and just flushed it down the toilet, and for what? To listen to a stupid red demon? Really, Barry Lemming? That's how you went out: drunk, with a gun in your hand, trying to prove your manhood to a giant red demon??

This must be where someone gets me ready for the funeral so everyone can come and say goodbye.

But then why am I still lying down? Why am I trapped inside my body with my mind still alive? If I were dead, wouldn't I be like a ghost or a spirit watching the whole thing from the corner of the room?

Isn't there someone who can tell me what is going on??

32

Patricia didn't know what to do. It was six-thirty in the morning; she'd been up since 3 a.m.: pacing, drinking coffee, not wanting to wake Greg but feeling horribly out of sorts. Where was she? What had she done? *And what is that terrible feeling in my gut? Something is wrong. Something is terribly wrong.*

"What are you doing?" Greg asked, slipping up beside her and causing her to scream.

"You scared me. Don't do that," she said.

"Whoa, you're jumpy. Did you see a ghost?"

"Something is wrong, Greg. Can you take me home? I need to go home."

Greg sighed. "You're feeling guilty. I thought it was too fast. It was my mistake. We should have gone slower."

"That's not it," she said, putting a hand on his robe. "Last night was wonderful. Better than that. It's just—I don't know how to explain it. Something is terribly wrong."

"You think it's Barry?" he asked.

"I don't know," she replied. "I'm just really nervous all of a sudden."

She ran and got dressed. He slipped on an overcoat and met her at the door.

They drove in silence, barely any traffic out at this early hour. "Which home is home?" he asked.

"Lynn and John's up in Malibu, if you don't mind. My car is there."

"Can I just offer something?" Greg asked, shifting his Audi into fourth and heading out onto PCH. There was an early morning breeze and a few lone surfers had their pick of gorgeous waves.

"Sure," she said.

"Something might really be wrong. I have no idea. But we also just slept together for the first time, and you and Barry haven't even broken up yet, at least not officially. You might just be feeling confused. It's only been six weeks since Melanie left and I know I'm feeling a little confused."

Patricia smiled. "I appreciate that, Greg, I really do. But this is something else, trust me. As soon as I find out that all of my close people are alive and no one's tried to kill themselves, I'll be fine. And last night was terrific, it really was... this is not me shrugging you off. I promise. I just...I know something has happened."

They drove the rest of the way in silence, Patricia giving him a peck on the cheek before jumping out and speeding away in her car.

33

The lights seemed to be flickering.

Should they flicker before you go into the tunnel? Is that how this goes?

Barry couldn't decide where he was. He knew he was dead; that much was obvious. But as to where he was...that was another story.

He could hear things. Muffled things. Scary things. He tried to think back on his life, to all of the mistakes he'd made, realizing now that he would do things so differently if only... if only he could have more time...if only he could heal his addiction...if only he and Patricia could get another shot...if only...if only...those two words might haunt him for the rest of eternity.

Then all of a sudden...POW! Bright lights, talking doctors, faster-talking nurses telling him to do this, do that.

"Mr. Lemming, Mr. Lemming...Barry Lemming! Right here, I'm talking to you right here. Can you see me? Can you open your eyes?"

"Am I dead?" Barry croaked, his mouth incredibly dry.

"No, Mr. Lemming. Not yet." This was a doctor with a deep, resounding male voice. "Although you gave it your best shot, that's for sure."

"We need you to take these." This was a softer, more feminine voice, probably a nurse. Barry still couldn't open his eyes properly. "Right now, Barry, c'mon, honey, you're not out of the woods yet."

He wasn't dead. He wasn't dead at all. He was alive! Half his ear was blown off and his vitals were going up and down like the stock market after a bomb scare, but he didn't care, he didn't care, he was alive, he was actually fucking alive.

34

Barry tried to talk to the nurse, the pretty young woman walking nearby, but she kept on moving, her clipboard tucked to her hip and her lips set straight. A giant male doctor's face came into close view.

"You've blown off half your ear," Barry could hear the doctor saying. *Half my ear. Half my ear. How does one do that? I was firing at the demon, I wasn't even in the picture.*

That's not true. I was firing at me. I was trying to prove to the demon I could do it. That I was not a wimp.

Jesus, what a pissing contest to try and win.

Hey, what are you doing, Lemming? Oh nothing, just messing around with some giant red demon and a loaded gun in my hand.

Shit.

Who would believe him?

He went back to the moment, to the whole surreal afternoon which focalized into his telling the demon *I'm not a loser* and then raising the gun and firing. That's when the bright light came. He saw it from the left, rushing towards him, a bright, blinding flash of white light that knocked his hand with the gun just slightly away from his face and towards his ear, the bullet missing his precious brain and swallowing the bottom half of his right ear before traveling over the cliff and onto the beach below.

Later on, when he and Taylor would dissect this scene over and over, Barry would come to believe that it was an angel who had saved him. But at the moment, he couldn't fathom why a bright light would come and knock his hand off-course. He couldn't fathom why he was still alive, why the demon had not won, or what he was even doing in a Santa Monica hospital instead of the morgue.

But he was alive.

And that was all that mattered.

Barry opened his mouth and sucked some more water through the straw. Hazy sunlight drifted in through the slats against the windows. Cars honked below on Wilshire and the Los Angeles smog moved gently among the high rises.

"You're a lucky man," the doctor said, making notes on his clipboard. "Most people don't miss from that range."

Barry nodded and kept looking out the window. "I never was a very good shot."

"Now tell me again about that bright light," the doctor began.

"Why? You're not going to believe me," Barry replied.

"Try me," the doc said.

"Are there forces of good and evil in the world?" Barry asked. "Is it possible that a demon was telling me to shoot myself, and some kind of bright light came and saved me? Tell me, Doc. Is that possible?"

Barry looked at the doctor. He was a middle-aged man, red eyes and sagging skin beneath them. But he was also a kind man, one who knew in his heart of hearts that this young man should be dead.

"For all accounts and purposes, you should be dead, Barry. You went out there under the influence of alcohol, with murderous intent, a loaded weapon, and the will power to do yourself in. Why you're still here, I don't really know." The doc paused. "I'm not a particularly religious man. Maybe we should get you a priest or a rabbi. I've never heard of something like this. You really don't want to harm yourself anymore?"

Barry chuckled and went back to sipping his water.

"It's standard procedure to give you these," the doctor said, handing him three little green pills in a plastic tray.

"What are they?" Barry asked.

"They're to ensure you won't try and hurt yourself again."

Barry slid the tray back towards the doc. "Thanks, but no thanks. Look at me, Doc. I've just had some kind of religious experience. I don't even think I'm going to drink alcohol again. The last thing I want to do is harm myself. What I want to do is find my girlfriend and apologize for all the crap I've put her through."

The doctor looked at him, then back at his chart. "You're putting me in an awkward position. If I let you go without the meds and you do something, it's my ass on the line."

"Doc, do I look like a man who's about to do harm to myself?"

The doc sized him up, shook his head, jotted down a note on his clipboard. "I'll give you one day's reprieve. We'll check in again tomorrow. You want to see the priest?"

"I want to see Patricia," Barry said. "Can you call her for me?"

"You know that's not my department, right?" the doc said, smiling. "But I'll see what I can do."

35

Patricia sprinted up the driveway and into the house. The front door was unlocked. "Barry! Barry!" She moved from room to room, past the sunken living room, the unpacked cardboard boxes, the giant poster of Magic Johnson on the wall. "C'mon, Barry, where are you?"

She made it into their bedroom: the bed was a mess, but that didn't mean anything. It could have been unmade for days; Barry was famous for "not seeing" things like this. She looked in the bathroom, the study, the back deck – *where was he?*

She went back out to the garage, peered in through the cracked garage door; his car was not in the driveway or the garage. She looked at her watch: 7:30am. *Where in God's name was he?*

Then her cell phone rang.

Patricia tore through traffic, ignoring the slower moving cars, weaving in and out until she pulled into the underground parking lot of St. John's hospital and rode up seven flights in the large, institutional elevator.

"Hi, Barry Lemming please," she said to the large nurse at the seventh floor station. "I'm Patricia Meyer, his girlfriend."

"He's sleeping right now," the nurse said. "But I'm Janice. Would you like to go in and wait for him?"

Patricia entered the room: the blinds were turned down and there was just a shard of light entering the room. It was horribly quiet. Barry looked awful. His right ear was hidden behind a large, white bandage, the color of his skin was yellow and sickly, and his eyes – she'd never seen his eyes look like that. He's been through a prize fight, she realized, small tears sliding down her cheeks.

"Hey," he said weakly, stirring in the bed.

"Hey yourself," she said, leaning over the bed and kissing him on the cheek. "What happened?"

He nodded without opening his eyes. "I've been through some shit."

"We are such idiots," she said, sitting on the edge of the bed next to him.

"Speak for yourself," Barry said, trying to smile, his eyes slivers as they half opened. "I'm Einstein and I know it."

"We have to fix this," Patricia said, suddenly feeling very serious and dramatic. She looked over her shoulder, making sure they were alone.

"Not we," Barry whispered. It actually hurt his throat to talk. *Had he been yelling at a demon out on the bluffs?* "Me. I have to fix this. You are perfect just the way you are."

Patricia didn't know what to say. Barry had never spoken to her like this.

"What are you talking about? I'm far from perfect."

"You're perfect for me," he said, taking her hand and resting for a moment before propping himself higher on the bed. He knew what he needed to say, but took a moment to gather his thoughts. This is 'the speech' that he'd been needing to tell her for years, the words right there on the edge of his heart, driven back by fear and the potential intimacy that might follow. Could he let someone close to him? Would he hurt them? Would they hurt him? Ten years of living with Patricia and still he'd kept her at arms' length. But now, having faced death and survived, he was finally no longer afraid. He knew exactly what he needed to say and knew exactly what her heart needed to hear.

"I'm the idiot, Patricia. I'm the one who tried to blow half my face off. I'm the one who can't let you near me. I'm the one who still drinks and chases skirts and is just fucking up in general. But I'm different now, Patricia. I swear. God or the Universe or whatever is "Up There" has given me another chance, and I intend to make the most of it." He looked away out the window, blinking back tears. "I have loved you from the first moment I saw you, when you were coming across the quad by yourself out at UCR. I remember thinking, 'Who is that person? She is spectacular! Why is she by herself? If she were with me, I'd never let her be alone.' I just…have a funny way of showing it sometimes."

She took a deep breath and looked at him, really looked. He was a good man. He was trying to become a better man. Barry Lemming. The love and curse of her life. *Could she see a future with him? Spend the rest of her life with him?*

"We have to talk about some things. I think we've both done some stuff we're not proud of," she said, taking his hand.

"I broke the garage," he said.

She smiled. "You broke more than that, Barry Lemming."

He reached over for his hospital-approved, putrid-yellow drinking cup and took a long sip of water. "I promise you, Patricia, I will never drink alcohol again."

"I've heard that before, Barry."

"This time it's different. I almost died. I'll tell you the whole story, every little part, but first can we take a nap? I can't believe how tired I am."

"Here? Now?" she asked.

"You can use the recliner. I'd love for you to come lie next to me, but I still have these iv's and tubes and things. You'd think I was fighting for my life or something."

"Can I ask you one thing?" she asked.

Barry nodded.

"What happened? The doctor told me you almost died, but he didn't give me any of the details."

He nodded. If they were going to have a relationship, a real relationship, it would have to be based on truth, on telling the honest truth to each other. Barry had never had that; he was used to secrets, to the space they gave him. Could he trust another human being? Could he let someone into his weird little world? He had seen the pain in her eyes from being shut out, from living alone at some level. Is that why there were still unpacked boxes filling half the living room? Was she just as afraid to make a commitment, maybe because she didn't trust him back? Maybe she had her own trust issues, but right now, he was so focused on himself, on how he needed to grow and his ability and willingness to be honest, that he didn't give a rats' ass what she did or didn't do. He made the conscious decision to let her in, and that began now.

He squeezed her hand, looked her full in the face.

"When you left, when I didn't think you were coming back, I got my gun and I got drunk and, I don't know how else to say this, I had a giant red demon telling me what to do. It was the weirdest thing I've ever been through. Totally surreal. I don't know where it came from or how it got there, but it told me to drive out to the Bluffs and shoot myself. I put three bullets in the chamber; the first two clicks came up empty. And then I sort of woke up, realized what the hell was going on, told the demon to go to hell and starting walking back to my car. And then – this part was so weird – the demon started calling me a loser, that I'd never finished anything in my life, and I pulled the trigger that last time just to show the demon that I wasn't a loser. Can you believe that?"

"So why are you still here? What happened?" Patricia asked.

"You ready for this? I knew the bullet was coming for me; I could feel it. And then out of the corner of my eye, there was this flash of light, this gorgeous, brilliant white flash of light and it knocked my shooting hand two inches to the right, and the bullet hit my ear instead of my brain. That's why I'm still here."

"That was an angel," Patricia said.

"I thought you didn't believe in angels and heaven and all that stuff," Barry remarked.

"I do now," she replied.

They sat for a minute in silence, letting the gravity of the events sink in.

"I promise you, Patricia, from the bottom of my heart, that I will set up weekly sessions with Taylor until I figure this out. I mean it this time."

She held his hand and smiled, taking in what he said. She knew it was always a possibility with him, the way his moods ran high and low. "Do you promise about the weekly sessions and never drinking again?"

"I do," he said.

"And you're not just saying that post-near-death-experience? Trying to get me back and all?"

"Patricia, look, I love you. I have always loved you. And I've been a crappy boyfriend and made a ton of mistakes, but it all changes now. I'm not saying I'm going to be perfect, but I need to do this for me, for my life. I promise you I will never drink alcohol again, period. It makes me too crazy; it's just not worth it."

Patricia smiled and leaned over and hugged him. They held each other for a good, long time.

"Okay, yes, Barry, for now, I'll say yes to taking a nap. We'll figure everything else out."

And with that, Patricia climbed up into the bed, being careful to avoid the i.v.'s and different tubes coming in and out of his arms, then curled up next to him in the bed and fell fast asleep. Barry watched her for a few minutes, then closed his eyes and slept as well.

36

They dreamt different dreams. Barry slept like a baby, dreaming of clouds and rainbows and the first time his dad taught him to ride a bike. Barry had been five and could feel the wind blowing through his hair before he'd crashed and skinned his right elbow on the concrete.

Barry smiled when he woke. He'd been through a dark tunnel and was now on the other side, enjoying the fruits of his survival.

Patricia, however, was moving through a house, somebody else's house, and there was something she'd lost: a trinket, or some kind of small object from her mother. Patricia was suddenly searching frantically through every room, unable to find the object, when suddenly the house disappeared and she was standing on the edge of a huge gorge, the dark black swirling down below. Both Greg and Barry were standing beside her. A bird circled overhead, a bird of prey.

She woke with a start.

"You're awake," Barry said.

"You're alive," Patricia responded, covering her mouth with her hand.

"Why do you do that?" Barry asked. "Cover your mouth with your hand? You have a good mouth; you should show it more."

Patricia didn't know what to do. She stood up and stretched her legs, then lay back down and wrapped her arms around him.

"You okay?" he asked.

She shook her head, still thinking about the dream, not sure what to make of it.

"You want to talk?" he asked.

She shook her head again. "Let's just lie here for a while." They moved the iv and tubes, Patricia snaking her body to curl next to his.

She closed her eyes. Several minutes passed. Last night with Greg seemed a million miles away.

"Why'd you do it?" she asked, running a finger over the light brown hair on his forearm.

He sighed. "This isn't going to make a lot of sense. You were gone; I could feel it. I woke up drunk, went and bought a twelve-pak and was downing beers as I drove to the dealership. The question is: why did I bring my gun? Why do I even own a gun? I'm, like, the most peaceful person I know."

Patricia rolled her eyes.

Barry smiled and continued. "Seriously, though, I was standing out there on the bluff. My dad is gone. I hardly see my mom or sister. You're it. I hate to put that on you, but it's true. I have work, but I don't have any real friends, not the guys from the dealership that I hang out with sometime. So

I stood there, looking out at the ocean and the sky and it's like…it wasn't even me. It's like I was outside myself watching myself go through these motions. The worst part of me, maybe, but not the real me." He swallowed, looking up above her head then back down. "I want to tell you something, but I don't know how."

She smiled, touched his arm. "You might as well go ahead. We have nothing to hide at this point, Barry. Even if we don't stay together, at least let's separate for the right reasons. I'll make you a deal: I'll tell you all my secrets if you tell me all yours. Then we can see what's what."

"You have secrets?" Barry asked.

"A few," she said, smiling. "Probably not as many as you. Okay, you first."

"All those times…" His voice caught a bit. "Fuck, this is hard…I've been lying for so long, telling the truth feels really different, kind of like skiing without a seatbelt." He took a breath and relaxed. She loved his corny jokes like that. "All those times I was chasing women, I didn't really want to do anything. That's the weird part. It was like some sick game: I just wanted to see if I could, you know? See if I still had it. Like I was back in high school trying to prove something."

Patricia didn't say anything.

"Who was I trying to prove it to? That's the question," he said.

"Maybe you're afraid of death," Patricia said.

"And that's why I was chasing other women? Maybe. Like committing to you meant the end of my life? Yeah, maybe. But I know what death tastes like now."

"How does it taste?" she asked.

"Bitter," Barry said. "At least death by a handgun with a giant red demon standing over you. Remember on Passover when you dip the greens in salt water to remind you of the bitterness of being slaves in Egypt? Death is a hundred times worse. But I'm avoiding what I have to say: yesterday, when everything got crazy between us, I did it. I fucking went and did it."

"Did what?" Patricia asked.

He didn't say anything.

"C'mon, Barry. We've been through too much now. Just tell me."

"I went and slept with somebody. During the day, after you left."

Patricia sucked her breath in sharply. She hadn't expected that.

"Do you love her?" Patricia asked.

"Love her? I paid her, Patricia. Okay? That's the level of love we're talking about."

Patricia got up off the bed and walked over to the window. She ran a hand through her hair and looked down at the people passing by on the street. *Shit, now I have to tell him about Greg.* She came back over and pulled a chair up to the edge of the bed; she then took Barry's hand, turned it over, looked at the life-line running down towards the right edge. There was a blip in the line.

"I think you just survived the blip," she said quietly. "See right here? That was you out on the Bluffs."

Barry looked at his hand. *Were they really sitting here together like this?* It had been so long. He felt like they were back in college, staying up late pretending to study. Barry held her fingers and kissed them.

"That's it. That's everything. There's nothing else I have to tell you. Oh, and I've hit on every friend you've ever had."

"Yeah, I know about that, you asshole. Lynn? Really? While she and John were having problems?"

"We never did anything," Barry tried to explain.

"Yeah, because she said no!" Patricia snapped.

"No, Patricia, that's the thing. I had women throwing themselves at me left and right, but I never did anything til yesterday when I thought you'd left."

"So you're saying that even if my best friend Lynn had said yes, you still would not have had an affair with her?" she folded her arms, waiting for an answer.

"I...I don't know," Barry said, shrugging. "Lynn's pretty hot!"

"Asshole Jerkface!" Patricia laughed and smacked him with a pillow.

"Truth?" he asked

"Always," she said.

"You know this already, so it won't come as some huge revelation, but I'm bad at sex. I'm a pervert and a hound-dog because I don't get it. I don't get how you women are wired, and I am terrified. Deeply terrified of something. I just don't know what."

"Going slow kind of terrified?" she asked.

He nodded. This was where they needed to go, what they needed to talk about and explore, and he knew it, even if he was scared.

"Would you like my help?" she asked quietly.

Again, he nodded. "Yours and Taylors. You can be my team of advisors."

"How do I know you won't do it again? We've been at this for, what, ten years? That's a long time for things to not change, Barry. A really long time."

Barry spoke softly. "It's different now. I realize how messed up I am. I almost shot myself for chrissakes, Patricia. How much lower can I go?"

"Oh, I don't know, fucking a whore while you're living with your girlfriend is pretty low."

Barry's face tensed.

"I didn't mean that," Patricia said.

"Yes, you did. And it's okay. I deserve it."

Barry picked up her hand again. "Fresh start? For both of us?"

"Not so fast. There's something I have to tell you first."

"Sure, anything," he said.

Patricia looked out the window, gathered her thoughts.

He closed his eyes and waited for her, grateful to be alive and to be having this time with her. He remembered the very first time he saw her, staring at her from across the school quad, wondering who that gorgeous, freckled, snow-white girl was.

Patricia took another moment, then turned and looked right at him. "I also slept with somebody."

Barry blinked. He must have misheard.

"You what?"

"I slept with someone. Last night, in fact."

"No way. You're pulling my chain," he said.

"I'm not. I wish I was," she responded.

Barry sat up in the hospital bed. "Who? How? When?"

"Someone I met last week. He's an old friend."

"An old friend? Who?" Barry demanded.

Patricia took a breath. No reason to keep secrets. "It's Greg. Greg Murdock."

"Greg Murdock?! Greg Murdock is *my* friend! I introduced you. Does he know we're living together? I'll beat the living shit out of him."

"Barry, calm down. You've just tried to kill yourself after screwing a prostitute and attempting to have sex with hundreds of other women, including my best friends. So chill out a little bit. You have some karma coming back your way."

Barry bit his lip. Again, she was right.

"Do you want to see him again?" he asked.

"Well, I did," Patricia began. "I didn't expect this."

"Expect what?"

"To be talking with you like this. We haven't talked like this in years. When I left the other night, I left. That was it," she explained.

"And now?" Barry asked.

"Just give me a minute. It's a lot to process."

Patricia closed her eyes. She could feel Barry's gaze upon her, but she didn't care: she pictured Greg's face, his large, round shoulders, his naked, gorgeous body and the way he'd held her.

"Was it over me?" she asked, her eyes still closed. Greg's naked body wasn't quite out of her mind's eye yet.

"Was what over you?" Barry asked.

"Trying to kill yourself. Was that on account of me?"

"I don't know," he said truthfully. "I think I was always capable of it. I just got to a really low place after you left. I'm sick, Patricia. I need help. I'm able to admit that now."

Patricia took another minute to look out the window. Barry studied her high white cheekbones and made a small promise to love her for as long as he could.

"I tell you what, Barry. If you promise to see Taylor week-ly and never drink alcohol again, I will move back into our house. I will love you and care for you and we will get through this together. But one slip up, and I mean one taste of rum or malt liquor or booze or whiskey or whatever when you think I'm not looking, and I find out about it, and that's it, I'm gone forever. You are an alcoholic and a sex addict and I am having a zero-tolerance policy with you. I realize that's kind of harsh, but that's how it has to be right now. Do you understand?"

Barry nodded. He knew better than to speak.

"And no more flirting or chasing women or going any-where near those God-awful bars or near that goddamned prostitute. That part of your life is over. Do you understand me?" Anger flashed in Patricia's eyes. "I want you to go down to the Gaslight and the Tiki Room and all your other hang-outs, have a club soda, say goodbye to everybody, and then come home a new man. That's what I want. Oh, and I would like to be able to see Greg socially, as a friend, for coffee and stuff," she said.

"No sex?" Barry asked.

"With Greg? No, no sex. Not unless you mess up. And then, yes, lots of sex with Greg," she said, a wicked smile com-ing across her lips.

"You drive a hard bargain, Meyer," Barry said, also smil-ing. "But yes, deal. I'm in. And I'll make it up to you, you'll see." He kissed her hand and smiled again, tears welling up in his eyes.

With her love and support and standing by him through this, he just might make it after all.

37

"Oh my God!" was all Taylor could say as Barry related the details to him: the cracked garage door, the loaded hand-gun, having sex with the prostitute, arguing with the demon out on the bluffs, and then finally, the screaming bullet, the flash of white light, and the large bandage covering what was left of Barry's right ear.

"Jesus Christ," Taylor said. "Excuse me for saying that. I've just never heard anything like this. How are you feeling?"

"Happy," Barry said. "It's weird. I don't know if I've ever felt happy before. Like some great weight, some awful angst, has been taken from me."

Taylor let out a low whistle, uncrossed his long, gangly legs and leaned forward in the chair. "Tell me again about the demon and the flash of light."

So Barry did, blow-by-blow, just like they were back in high school setting up a chemistry experiment in Mr. Layton's lab.

"It's a miracle," Taylor proclaimed.

"I know!" Barry exclaimed. "It really is! If it hadn't happened to me, I wouldn't believe a word of it."

"Do you still have your job?" Taylor asked.

"Oh yeah. I paid off the guy who saw the gun. He won't squeal, we've been friends for years. And as far as the dealership, I've been whoring and producing for them for almost eight years now. There's no way Stan's going to let me go."

"Do you want to keep selling cars?" Taylor asked.

"I don't know," Barry answered. "I know I'm not out of the woods. I'm not really a twelve-step kind of guy. What I want is to work with you, to take the next year and see you weekly and try to figure all of this out. Oh, and the best part: Patricia has moved back in. As long as I stay sober and continue to see you, she and I are going to give it a real go."

"That's amazing," was all Taylor could say, still shaking his head. "I've worked with a lot of people and I've heard a lot of stuff, but this just might take the cake, Barry."

"I know. I know how lucky I am to be alive. I feel incredibly grateful," he said softly.

"Amen to that," Taylor said, raising his glass of water. "So where do you want to start? What feels like the most important things to tackle right away?"

"You want to hear the list?" Barry asked, leaning forward a bit himself.

Taylor nodded, grabbed his notepad, and settled into his chair. He loved helping people, and it showed.

Barry pulled out a wrinkled, half-folded envelope from his back pocket. He'd scrawled a list of questions on the back in dark blue ink:

1. *Where did that demon come from?*
2. *What was that flash of light?*
3. *Does God really exist?*

4. *How can I hang onto this happiness?*
5. *Why did Patricia and I never get married.*
6. *Why am I still alive?*
7. *How can I forgive my parents?*
8. *Why am I bad at sex?*
9. *Am I crazy?*
10. *How can I stay sober and straight?*
11. *What do I need to do to make Patricia happy?*
12. *How can we finally start a family?*

And finally and most importantly:

13. *What is my real purpose in being here?*

Taylor smiled, paused a minute, let the questions sink in.

"What's funny?" Barry asked.

"You're just the kind of person I've been wanting to work with."

38

Barry walked out onto the back deck. He was carrying a tray with toasted English muffins, sunny-side up eggs, turkey bacon strips, and fresh honey-dew melon slices. Steaming mugs of licorice tea sent up little billows of steam as he walked.

"Breakfast is served, madam," Barry announced, smiling.

"Hey, that looks good. I'm starved," Patricia said, turning back from the fence and the view beyond.

"Ready to freak out a little bit?" Barry asked.

"About what?" she asked.

"Can we say a little prayer before we eat?" Barry continued.

"What? What kind of prayer?" she asked, the look of surprise on her face worth a thousand words.

"I don't know...God, the Universe, an angel...something up there saved me. I just want to say thanks."

"You're like a different person," Patricia exclaimed.

"Different bad?" he asked.

"No, you big goof! Not different bad. Different wonderful."

Barry smiled and closed his eyes. He took Patricia's hands and bowed his head slightly. "Dear God, or the Universe, or whatever you are up there, I thank you for this food, I thank you for bringing Patricia back home, and most of all, I thank you for saving my life. Amen."

"Amen," she said and opened her eyes.

"Let's dig in," he said.

She took a giant mouthful of English muffin and eggs, then said with her mouth mostly still full, "You're not going to become a Jesus freak are you?"

"I don't know," Barry said, smiling with his own mouthful of food. "Was Jesus that flash of light that saved me?"

He and Taylor set up a regular appointment for every Thursday at 11am -- Barry's day off. The glitz and the glamour of being alive began to wear off some during the week, especially as Barry went back to the dealership, back to mentoring Chad, back to some of the crap that led him to the Bluffs in the first place.

But the week went quickly enough, and before he knew it, Barry was back in Taylor's office, sitting on the couch and staring out the window at the sailboats listing in the breeze.

"It is so peaceful here," Barry commented.

Taylor was busy banging away on his calculator. "So a hundred bucks a session, fifty-two weeks in a year. Let's figure two weeks off for vacation. That'll be $5000, and that's payable up front. We take Visa or Mastercard."

"You're kidding!" Barry said.

"Yes, I'm totally kidding. You gotta watch out for me and Wanda; we love to kid around. I don't know exactly how much you make down at the dealership, but I'm thinking I'd like to offer you my 'hard-working-man-just-got-saved-by-a-flash-of-light' discount. How does eighty bucks a session sound? That's a bunch off my normal rate, but you know what, you're worth it. You can give Wanda your credit card on the way out and we'll keep it on file and just run it each week after we work together. How does that sound?"

"That sounds good," Barry answered. "Thanks for the discount; I appreciate it. So what do we actually do? I ran out so fast last time, I didn't quite get the gist of it."

"Well, every patient, every case is different. I actually let go of my therapist's license a few years back, so now I'm a hundred percent spiritual healer, totally free to do what feels right with each person."

"How many sessions do you do each week?" Barry asked.

"About thirty, give or take, plus group on Wednesday and Thursday nights."

"A hundred bucks a session, thirty sessions a week, that's about three grand per week. Take your family to the Bahamas twice a year…you're making about $150k a year?" Barry asked.

"A little bit north of that, but yeah, somewhere in that neighborhood," Taylor replied.

"Not bad for a spiritual healer!" Barry remarked.

Taylor chuckled. "I have a lot of mouths to feed. Can we get back to you now?"

"Sure," Barry said. "Where do we start?"

"Everybody is different, Barry. Everyone has their own unique make-up of voices and pictures. And I'll explain what those are in a minute, but the first concept to understand is there are rules for what we're about to do," Taylor explained.

"Rules? What kind of rules?" Barry asked.

"Not rules like get-in-trouble kind of rules. Maybe rules isn't the right word. How about 'governing principles'? And I violated one of those governing principles. Look, Barry, we're old friends, so I thought I could go faster than I normally do. I apologize. I was a little too quick that first time, and it resulted in you bolting out of my office. It was my fault and I'm sorry. I promise that will not happen again."

Barry took a slow breath, felt some space open up inside his chest. Maybe there was a reason that so many people came to Taylor for help.

"But you have to do your part as well," Taylor continued. "You have to be honest with me, as honest as you can. It's like we're detectives and we're on the case together. I don't consider myself some great healer, although I can do things that most people can't do – or don't know they can do – but that's only because I've been working on myself for thirty years. And humans are way more powerful than we realize. But you are the most important ingredient here. It's your subconscious we're trying to unlock. The answers to all of your questions are locked up right inside here," Taylor said, pointing at Barry's chest. "I can take you there, guide you there, help you open each of the doors, but ultimately, it's you who's going to have to walk through."

Barry felt a sharp twinge of fear, wondering what was on the other side of some of those doors.

"The good news is we can go much faster than traditional therapy. Traditional therapy can take years and years to go where we're trying to go. You ready?"

"Ready as I'll ever be," Barry said, rubbing his hands together and blowing on them.

"Okay, session #1," Taylor mumbled to himself, jotting down notes in a small notepad. "Barry Lemming, here for?"

Barry thought he was joking, didn't say anything.

"It's your turn to talk, Barry," Taylor said.

"Oh, sorry. What was the question?"

"What would you say you're here for?" Taylor asked.

Barry squinted, watched the room and Taylor get very small. *How to summarize the last six months of his life into a few sentences?*

"General fucked-upedness?" Barry joked.

Taylor smiled. "Not one of the categories. Try and tell me three concrete things you'd like to work on during the next year."

Barry took a deep breath. They were leaving the shallow end of the pool, but it was okay. He thought about the guys down at the showroom, one of them right this moment probably trying to talk someone into more car than they could afford. Orzo. Paulino. Stan. This is the last place on Earth they'd let themselves be: the couch of a spiritual healer!

"Three things? One, I want to work on my relationship with Patricia. I would like her to not leave again. Two, I want to work on some sexual stuff, which of course affects my relationship with Patricia. And three...is all of this in total confidence, Taylor?"

"Absolutely."

"Even if we do a couples' session with Patricia, you won't repeat anything I tell you?" Barry asked.

"Not without your permission," Taylor replied.

"Okay, here's the real deal: I am a total sex addict. I think about sex four hundred and ninety-seven times a day. I rub myself on inanimate objects when no one is looking. I ogle every woman's body who even comes near me. I am a walking horn-dog. I have been since I was, shit, like five years old. Never worked on it, never talked about it. Inherited it from my dad the way some kids inherit the family business. I know Patricia knows about it. And then, this is the part that doesn't make any sense, when she actually opens her heart and we are being intimate, I can't wait for it to be over. I hate every single second of it. And I mean hate. She's always wanting to go slower, to take our time, for me to connect with her, and I'm like, 'Aaah, I'm going to stick very sharp knives in my eyes if you don't stop saying that!' And I have no idea what any of it means. That's why I'm here. You help me figure that out, you'll have earned your money, big time."

Taylor looked at Barry for a moment, sizing him up. He was surprised, but then again, not really. People had said some pretty outrageous stuff on his couch.

"How old were you when you first masturbated?" Taylor asked.

"Seriously?" Barry chuckled.

"C'mon, Mr. Sex Addict, how are we going to fix it if we're not allowed to talk about it? Sex is a natural thing. It's okay to talk about."

"I was four. Four years old. My parents were fighting, my dad was getting ready to leave the house and he was screaming at my mom, and I ran up into my bedroom and locked the door and went under the covers and rubbed myself until it went dead."

Barry had a far-away look as he spoke, remembering the scene.

"Went dead?" Taylor asked.

"That's what we used to call it, me and my sis. I told her about my masturbating all the time. It was a way I could deal with our parents' fighting. I was so young that I don't think my body could orgasm, like literally nothing came out, but mine would shake and spasm and then go dead. I remember doing it so much that my skin turned this awful shade of burnt red and hurt like a mother f-er," Barry said.

"Mother f-er?" Taylor asked, raising his eyebrows.

"I'm trying to swear less," Barry explained.

"Ah, right. A little slow on the uptake. Did your parents end up getting a divorce?" Taylor asked.

"Yep, they sure did. My dad started having affairs when I was three, moved out when I was five, had girlfriends off and on, but my parents actually stayed married and separated until my sis and I were like eleven or twelve," Barry explained. "It was good because there was a chance they'd get back together; it was bad because we were always on our best behavior, thinking if we were just perfect, then maybe they'd give it another chance."

"And they never did?" Taylor asked.

"No, not even close. My dad moved in with an old girlfriend, someone he'd had an affair with when my sis and I were real young, and that was it. My mom lawyered up the next week," Barry explained.

"Okay, that's definitely a place we could spend some time," Taylor commented. "I'm going to ask a few more questions, if that's okay. How much were you drinking before the incident on the Bluffs last week?" Taylor asked.

"Who said anything about drinking?" Barry retorted.

Taylor didn't say a word, just waited for him to answer.

"Three, maybe four times a week," Barry responded.

"And how much each time you drank?" Taylor asked.

"What are you, my mother?" Barry snapped.

Again, Taylor didn't budge. He just sat, his pen poised above the notebook, and waited. Addicts have having their secrets exposed.

"A couple of drinks each time, just enough to take the edge off. And then I had a hip flask, usually filled with Johnny Walker Red. I would take a hit or two before work, sometimes do the same before coming home and walking in the front door."

"Did Patricia know?"

"Nope," Barry answered, staring straight ahead. "She knew something was off, but I covered my tracks pretty well. I was personally keeping tic-tac's in business."

"Have you had a drink since the Bluffs?" Taylor asked.

"No, sir. Not even close," Barry said, smiling.

"What is that now? Ten days sober?" Taylor asked.

"Just about. Today is nine," Barry said, smiling again.

"Good for you, Barry. Honestly. Most amazing story I've ever heard. Next question: do you ever think about joining AA?" Taylor asked.

"I'd really rather not. Is that okay? I've read the book. I know the steps. I just want to do it my own way," Barry said.

"The 'cold-turkey, argue-with-a-demon, get-saved-by-an-angel' kind of way?" Taylor asked, smirking.

"Something like that," Barry said.

"Works for me," Taylor continued. "Are there any other secrets I should know about, Barry? You're doing great by the way. This is the hardest part of the whole process, getting all the gunk out. There may be other times like this, when you feel like we're ripping an old band-aid off, but this, right now, this truth-telling session, this is when real breakthroughs happen," Taylor explained.

"When does the healing start?" Barry asked.

"It already has," Taylor said. "Think of it as letting light into a dark room. Our psyche, our being, is like a giant house filled with rooms. And some of these rooms we live in every day: they have light, fresh air, clean floors. Other rooms, some of the rooms we're looking at now, they haven't been opened in years. They are dark, dank, dusty; the problem is these rooms can make big problems for you because stuff – bad behavior, negative thinking, destructive forces -- can come out of these rooms if you ignore them and pretend they're not there. The demon you faced would be an example of that. This process, this blend of traditional therapy and spiritual healing, is all about bringing light, God's light, to the deepest, darkest parts of our personal cosmos. It's how you can heal your heart and change your life all at the same time."

Barry took a deep breath, blew into his hands again. He got up and walked around the office before sitting back on the edge of the couch. "Okay, here goes, Taylor. Letting light into the dark rooms, right? I can't believe I'm about to tell you this...I masturbate at work, in the bathroom stall, when things get stressful, probably 3-4 times a week. And I've done it in my car once, backed up at a red light on Santa Monica Blvd near the 405, but that was just one time." Barry looked up. Taylor wasn't moving, he was just nodding his head and listening. Barry physically gripped onto the couch to stop himself from running away. He wanted to puke but knew he needed to get this out. "There's one other thing, Taylor, and then I think that's it. That's all the secrets I know for now."

"What's that, Barry?" Taylor asked.

"You've got to swear to not tell anyone…professional licensure or courtesy or whatever you call it that won't let you tell anyone else. If this gets out, I could be finished in my relationship and my career."

"Go ahead. You have my word," Taylor said.

"I dream of punching women sometimes. Right in the face, as hard as I can. And it's not Patricia, I mean, sometimes it's Patricia, but it's more just random women, over and over and over. They're crying and bleeding and I'm like, 'Take that you stupid bitch!' It's usually after I finish watching porno's or when I'm at work and things aren't going well."

Barry's breaths were coming in shallow gasps and he looked around the office quickly, expecting it to explode. He'd never said these words to anyone.

"Have you ever?" Taylor inquired.

"Ever what?" Barry returned sharply.

"Punched a woman?" Taylor asked.

"No, of course not. I've never laid a hand on Patricia. Ever. But that's part of the problem. I have these urges, these feelings, and I don't know where they come from and I sure-as-shit don't know what to do with them. And I just wonder if…I wonder if Patricia can feel some of this and maybe that's why she doesn't feel safe with me."

"How do you know she doesn't feel safe with you?" Taylor asked.

"Well, in ten years of being together, she's only had one orgasm with me and that was our very first time, way back in college."

"You might be right about that," Taylor expressed.

"So what do you think? Am I a hopeless case?" Barry asked, still breathing unevenly. He was actually in shock he'd said these words out loud.

"Not at all," Taylor replied, twirling his pen and staring down at the pad, as if the words there could provide some answers. "You're honest and you're brave; those are two great assets. We've got some work to do, that's all."

Barry stretched out on the gray couch, his head resting on a small, purple pillow. "Okay, Therapy Session #1, Healing Section," Taylor said as much to himself as to Barry. "Are you comfortable?"

"Ready to fall asleep," Barry replied.

"Really?" Taylor asked.

"No, Taylor, of course not. I can't believe I told you all those things. I feel horrified and liberated at the same time."

Taylor got up out of the recliner and scooted a metal folding chair right next to the couch, his large frame looming over Barry for a sec. "Too close?"

"You're fine," Barry said, closing his eyes.

"Barry, I'm going to lead you on a guided journey. It'll be about your heart and about your past and about letting go of some of that stuff we talked about. But before we start, just to help me get the lay of the land...do you believe in God?"

"What do you mean?" Barry asked.

"Like do you believe there is a Higher Power, a supernatural force watching over everything?"

"I'm not sure. If you'd asked me a week ago, I would have said, 'Hell no!' But after what I've been through," Barry stammered for a sec. "Do I need to believe in God for this process to work?"

"It helps, I admit," Taylor said, "but no, it's not a requirement. You do need to believe or be open to something larger than yourself; that can be light, a waterfall, anything good that you can connect with."

"I actually have real issues with nature," Barry commented. "Sorry to be a kill-joy. It's always the ones who need a scholarship that give you the toughest fight," Barry said, turning towards Taylor and rising up on one arm. "I will tell you one thing, though: if there is a God, or someone or something up there watching over us, then I have some super hard questions for Him, like why the heck did all this happen to me? I've been through a lot of shit! Now some of it, I did to myself, I admit. But some of this stuff, like some of my early childhood stuff, jeez. So I guess my answer is: I'm not sure, but if there is a Higher Power or God, then I'm super pissed at Him."

Taylor smiled. He loved working with people like Barry because they could see such tremendous growth in just a short time. "Then that is where we shall start," Taylor said. "Is it okay if I place a hand on your leg just above your ankle?"

"Sure," Barry said, leaning back and closing his eyes again.

Taylor lay his right hand on Barry's lower shin. "Lean back, Barry, close your eyes, and just follow along with my words. Picture yourself in your childhood home. It's a Tuesday afternoon, say maybe four o'clock. Who's in the house?"

"My mom," Barry began, "and she's crying."

"How old are you?" Taylor asked.

"I'm four. My mom is running up the stairs and down the hall and slamming the door to her bedroom. She did that a lot," Barry said in a low voice.

"Okay, who else is in the house?" Taylor asked.

"My dad. He's in the kitchen and he's breaking things: glasses, a plate, just smashing them on the counter and walking around all mad-like."

"And your sister? Is she in the house?" Taylor asked.

"No, but she should be. If I was four, she'd be two. So she should be there and she should be screaming. But no, she's not in the picture at all. Maybe she was at Grandma's."

Taylor cleared his throat. "Barry, memories like this are what we call 'pictures.' A picture is a memory with mental or emotional charge. Now this happens to be a strong one, but we can approach them just like we approach anything else. The key is to not get too attached to the picture, or to believe that it will never change. Does that make sense?"

"I guess so," Barry said. "But how could a memory change? I mean, it happened, right?"

"You'll still have the memory; you'll always remember what happened. You just won't have the pain associated with it. It's like the emotions get washed or cleaned. In energetic or spiritual terms, the Higher or Divine light comes and lifts the pain out of the heart. It's a pretty amazing process," Taylor explained. "A lot of times these memories are buried. I mean who wants to remember this stuff? Yet, if it's in the heart, if it's making trouble in your current life, like much of what you've been experiencing, then we have to deal with it, right? So this spiritual healing process is a way of recovering old, buried memories, taking them out of storage, dusting them off, and then letting God or whatever your version of a Higher Power is come clean the pain hidden in the memory. It can be a life-saving process, to tell you the truth."

"And how is this different than traditional therapy?" Barry asked, his eyes still closed. "I'm not trying to fight you. I'm just trying to understand."

Taylor smiled. "Because we're about to turn this picture over to God's light and see what God's light will do with it. That's how it's different. Traditional therapy can be amazing at uncovering stuff, but depending on the practitioner, there's not always a proven way to release and transform stuff. So some people feel like they're just stirring the pot, but not really getting the gunk out. In my experience of thirty years as a healer, the minute someone becomes open to healing, God's light is right there, ready to help. It's amazing actually, the way God cares for His creation."

"Okay, that makes me want to gag," Barry commented.

"Well, go ahead and keep telling me about the memory and let's see what God has in store for you," Taylor said, crossing his arms for a second before smiling and placing his hand back on Barry's leg.

Barry leaned back into the couch, felt his shoulder blades press into the cushion. He closed his eyes, took a deep breath, and then he was back in his childhood home, and the memory was so vivid, it almost physically hurt. "My dad is mad, real mad, and he's stomping around and kicking the shards of the plate he broke, and now he's thumping past me up the stairs and I'm grabbing at his pants leg but I can't stop him. His face is red and mad and he's swearing and stuff. Now he's banging down the hall and I can hear my mom crying behind the door. And I'm running after him, but I can't stop him. I'm only four. And he's now opening up the door and going inside and I'm following him and my mom is face down on the bed, the right side of the bed, lying on top of the off-white comforter with the little clay-red swirls, and she's sobbing. And my dad is raising a hand to hit her but he's not swinging, he's just holding it there, and now he's turning to me and yelling at me and I'm running back out of the room, down the hall, back into my bedroom where I dive under the covers and I cry a little bit, and then I start to touch myself, and now I'm masturbating for all I'm worth, like two or three times until it's dead and I just lay there."

Adult Barry in present time was crying now, small, silent tears leaking out of both eyes. Taylor offered him a tissue but Barry didn't budge. He hadn't cried in years.

"You're doing great, Barry. A real champ. Can you see how sex might be getting mixed up with what might be one of the most painful memories of your life?"

"Yeah, I sure do," Barry croaked.

"Is there a chance that this might be why you're terrified of going slow when you're being intimate with Patricia? I think you said, 'You'd rather put sharp knives in your eyes then go at the pace she's suggesting.'"

Barry nodded. There was a big lump in his throat and he couldn't speak.

"Is there anything else to see with the picture?" Taylor asked.

"I don't think so," Barry said.

"Do you feel ready to do some healing?" Taylor asked.

Barry nodded. He was still lying in his childhood bed, writhing in pain and pleasure as his small, four year-old body lay still after masturbating. Down the hall, he could hear his dad yelling, drowning out his mom's scared sobs.

"Turn towards God..." Taylor began.

"I don't feel ready to turn to God. I'm mad at him," Barry said in a really small, four-year-old voice.

"That's okay, Barry. That's just fine. How about we don't use the word 'God,' but instead we just turn to the light and we're going to let the light help us out?"

"That's okay," Barry said.

"Picture your four year-old self, lying in bed...what's happening with your parents?" Taylor asked.

"They're shouting and yelling a little more, and then my dad is saying a nasty word and stomping down the stairs and out the front door."

"And what does your mom do?" Taylor asked.

"Nothing. She just lies in bed and cries."

"She doesn't come and comfort you or talk to you?" Taylor asked.

"No, not at all," Barry replied in a small voice. "I don't see her for days."

Taylor paused a sec. Barry was one of the most intriguing and challenging patients he'd worked with, and he wanted to be absolutely sure with his next step. *How do you bring someone to God's light if they don't believe in God? Or what if they actually do believe in God, but have a tremendous amount of unresolved anger towards their Creator?*

Taylor sat quietly for a minute, repeating a sacred phrase he'd learned from his spiritual teacher, until something came into his mind.

"Barry, I have an idea," he said.

"What's that?" Barry asked.

"I want you to picture an angel, a super big beautiful angel, and he's flying down into your room and he's protecting you. Can you picture that?"

Barry nodded.

"What does the angel look like?" Taylor asked.

"It's amazing. He's all white, and I can't really see his face, but he has these wings that stretch out like seven feet wide, and he's coming over to me and putting his wings over me and I'm crying but it's good tears, it's safe tears. And it's really good he's there because there was a nasty, dark thing over in the corner of the room and I think in real life that dark thing came over to me and I swallowed it by accident and it's been living inside me all these years. That might be why I drink alcohol, to try and get away from the dark thing. But with the angel here now…it's changing…the dark thing is lifting up out of me and going away. And I'm starting to feel better. I'm watching it lift and it's really nasty, like a big red-and-black snake that has three heads and spits venom and it's been living inside my belly all these years. The angel is amazing and it's folding its wings over me and singing a song, like a lullaby, and my four year-old self is smiling and going to sleep. I can't hear my dad yelling or my mom crying anymore. The angel is folding his wings over my ears so I can have peace."

"That is what we call spiritual healing," Taylor said softly. "A true healing. Keep letting the angel protect you and sing over you. Just take your time."

They sat, not moving or speaking, for a good five minutes. Barry felt a peace he had never known, like a deep quiet instead of all the turmoil of his parents' screaming. He smiled and sank even deeper into the couch.

Barry eventually opened his eyes and smiled. "Was that real? Was I making all that stuff up?"

Taylor smiled, a quiet grin that came from deep inside his heart. "That was the real deal, Barry. You couldn't make that stuff up if you tried. There are different classes of angels; God gives them missions or assignments. One class is assigned to protect the human race from the kind of ugly black thing that you said you swallowed, and the great thing about this healing work is there is no time or space when it comes to this stuff, so you sitting here now, watching that dark snake lift out of your belly…that is as real as if it had happened that very day. How do you feel?"

Barry grabbed a tissue, blew his nose loudly. It honked like a horn and both men laughed. "I feel great. Different. Tired, maybe, like I'm weak or something. Do you have any water or juice?"

"I do," Taylor said, "we can go downstairs and get some. But before we do, Barry, I want you to know that that was one of the greatest first-time healings I've ever seen. You have a real knack for this, and you're not even sure you believe in God!"

Both men laughed again.

"You did all the hard work," Barry said, getting up and stretching. "I just followed along."

"You know that's not true," Taylor said, patting Barry's ankle and grinning widely. "I can only go as fast and as far as your spirit is willing to let me."

Downstairs, Taylor poured them both a glass of apple juice and smiled.

"You might be a little tired later," Taylor advised.

"I'm already feeling it," Barry said, draining the last of his juice. He tore a check out of his checkbook and handed it over. "Here you go for today's session. I'll give you my credit card next week."

"You bet," Taylor said, surprised when Barry threw his arms around him and hugged him.

"Thank you, Taylor," Barry said. "I can't believe how different I feel. Thank God I survived that day on the Bluffs, and thank God I know you and could come see you."

"Thank God indeed," Taylor said, shaking his hand and showing him out the front door.

Barry stepped out into the sunshine. Everything looked different: the sun, the sky, the trees. Everything was in technicolor. He couldn't remember feeling this great...ever. He stepped off the front porch and headed towards his car. He wanted to find Patricia and give her a good, long hug, too, and tell her everything that happened in his session.

Could God actually exist?

"I don't know," Barry said out loud, smiling as he hustled towards his car.

39

They were in a park, sitting back to back, letting the sun wash over them. Barry closed his eyes and smiled. Patricia stretched out her legs, feeling the blades of grass press up against her snow-white skin.

"This is nice," she said.

"Super nice," Barry admitted, digging his toes into the grass and earth.

"Can we try something?" Patricia asked.

"Sure. Anything," he replied, cracking his fingers one by one.

"Okay. Stand up."

They stood and faced each other. Barry looked her up and down from head to toe, felt a tingle rush through him. He was still insanely attracted to her, maybe now more than ever.

"This is a trust-building exercise. It's something we learned at UCR for building trust with clients," she explained.

"What kind of clients?" he asked.

"Remember I took undergrad psychology? When I thought for five minutes about becoming a therapist?"

"You'd make a good therapist," Barry commented.

"Maybe. Anyway, let me explain this before the moment gets away from me." She placed her hands on his shoulders, turned him around so he was facing away from her.

"Oh, is this where I close my eyes and fall backwards and you're supposed to catch me?"

"Yep," she answered.

"I don't know if I can do it," he said, half-turning around. "We tried this in junior high and one of my friends, Jake Balfour, supposedly one of my good friends, let me fall all the way to the concrete. It hurt like hell."

"Well," Patricia countered, turning him back around, "I am not one of your good friends from junior high, we are not on concrete, and I'm not going to let you fall. Here, I'll take a step closer to you for the first one. It'll be like a half fall. Now cross your arms over your chest, close your eyes, and let yourself tilt backwards."

Patricia stood just a foot or two behind him, hands up and ready.

Barry took a deep breath, hemmed and hawed. "Patricia…"

"C'mon, big man," she said, lowering her voice, "How are we going to have those amazing simultaneous orgasms if we don't trust each other?"

"That's not fair," Barry said.

"Whoever said I play fair!" Patricia exclaimed. "You're wasting time. Let's go!" she said with a huge grin on her face.

Barry closed his eyes, tried to forget about the pain of smacking on the concrete when Jake-shaggy-hair-Balfour deliberately backed up and let him fall. Instead, he felt the sun on his skin, wiggled his toes in the grass, and tipped backwards.

Patricia caught him effortlessly. He'd only "fallen" a few feet.

Barry looked up at her, smiled.

"How was that?" she asked.

"That was good," he replied.

"Let's try it again, this time a little more."

They did it for over an hour, each of them taking turns until they could completely let go and actually feel the falling sensation before being caught by their partner. Patricia was super present, talking to him and joking the whole time. Barry, on his end, eventually began to ease up, to even expect Patricia to catch him. He could feel the tension leaving his neck and shoulders as the game progressed. *Was he always that wound up?*

Shadows began falling across the park. They picked up their things and left hand in hand, smiling.

Barry felt a warmth in his chest. He was as happy as he could remember.

40

B arry leaned back on the gray couch once again. He'd made two sales the day before and things were feeling good.

"How many days sober?" Taylor asked, reaching for his notebook and pen.

"Seventeen," Barry answered. "But who's counting?"

"Is it really true about one day at a time? I've never been a big drinker and I've never been to twelve-steps," Taylor commented.

"I used to think about it as a one-day battle, and every day was a battle. But since encountering that demon...I've been scared sober. Can we work on that demon today?" Barry asked, stretching his arms out in nervous anticipation.

"I think let's get a few more sessions under our belt before tackling that big guy. Okay with you?" Taylor said.

"You're the boss. Lead away," Barry said, leaning back and closing his eyes.

"This is Barry Lemming, Healing Session #2," Taylor said. The little audio recorder turned round and round on the side table. "Y'know, Barry, I totally forgot to ask you last session: is it okay that I record our sessions?"

"Making a little money on the side, huh?" Barry smirked. "Blackmail and stuff?"

"Yeah, y'know, just in case I ever need it," Taylor grinned as he spoke. "It's in case I ever write a book, and to teach young healers how to do what I do."

"You teach people how to become spiritual healers?" Barry asked.

"Every weekend," Taylor spoke. "Just like I learned from my teacher."

"You can learn this stuff? Yeah, it's fine," Barry said. "It'll be my contribution to science, or religion, or whatever the heck it is that you do. Can we get started now? We're on my dime last time I checked." Barry smiled to show he meant no harm.

Taylor smiled again. There was only one Barry.

"Okay, so take a deep breath, let go of the events of the day, of the week, just let yourself drift for a few moments." Taylor got up, turned down the blinds to darken the room; the mid-morning sun was glaring off the ocean and the boats. *There could be worse views,* Taylor thought. "Good, you're doing great, Barry. Now what is it you're feeling in your body?"

"What do you mean?" Barry asked.

Taylor scooted the metal chair over, leaned forward a bit and placed a hand on Barry's shin. "So as you drop inside, as you follow your breath down inside your lungs, inside your chest...name one physical sensation that you feel."

"Hmmm, I can feel my shoulder blades pressing down against the couch. You mean like that?" Barry asked.

"Exactly like that," Taylor continued. "Now take another breath, and tell me another physical sensation that you notice."

"My hips, there's some tension around my waistband."

"Good! You're doing great. Now see if you can go inside, into something you're feeling *inside* your body," Taylor guided.

"I don't really know what that means," Barry said.

"That's okay; I'm going to teach you. Bio-energetic or gestalt therapists use this technique all the time; it's a way to access emotions through the physical and energetic body. It's one of the techniques I use to help people access deeper or buried emotions. Ready to learn something new? Just follow my words and let's see if I can take you there...Take a nice deep breath, imagine the air moving in through your nose or mouth, going down your trachea, entering into your lungs, the oxygen then being dispersed throughout your entire body, going wherever it needs to go and replenishing each of your individual cells. Your body has its own innate wisdom; it knows how and where to use the oxygen. Good. Take another deep relaxing breath, dropping deeper inside this time, and now feel into the molecules and cells deep inside your body. Imagine the blood moving through your veins and your whole body working as one beautifully designed organism...Good, Barry. Now staying at that deep level, what's one sensation you're feeling inside your body?"

Barry didn't say a word. His eyes were closed, his breathing regular and slow.

"Barry? Barry, it's Taylor. Are you awake?"

"Huh?" Barry woke with a start. "Yeah, um, I just nodded off for a sec. That was really relaxing."

"That's okay," Taylor said, smiling. "Lots of people nod off. Let's go back inside, just follow my words and watch your breath…now what's one thing you notice?"

Barry closed his eyes and let himself relax again. He could feel his shoulder blades and trapezius muscles pressing down against the couch, his hips and backside pressing on the cushions; he could feel his right Achilles heel in a slight stretch as he lay there. *Were these the kinds of things Taylor was looking for?*

"I can feel different physical things: my back, my butt, my feet, but I don't know what you mean by 'dropping inside' or feeling something other than the physical?" Barry acknowledged.

"Okay, good. I love your openness," Taylor said. "Just follow my words and let's try, okay? So there is a big, loud, physical world out here; everything you can see and touch and smell. But if you get quiet, if you slow down, if you literally shrink your world down to a tiny, tiny size…there is an energetic world where all kinds of things are happening that most people are not aware of. It's the subtle world of energy and spirituality; it's a world behind the world, or a world within the world. Does that make any sense?"

"In theory it does," Barry commented. "I don't know if I've ever felt it myself."

"Would you like to try?" Taylor asked.

"If it'll help me heal and stay sober, then yes, of course," Barry answered. "I'll try anything."

"Good. You're going to be great at this," Taylor continued. "Feel the back of your arms resting on the couch, now imagine getting tinier and tinier and traveling inside your arms, so you can see and feel the blood moving through them."

"Like 'Honey, I Shrunk the Kids'," Barry said.

"Yeah, sort of like that," Taylor said. "Good. Keep letting yourself get smaller and smaller, keep slowing down more and more...now what do you feel inside your arms? Your chest? What is happening energetically inside you?"

"I feel some heat, and some cold," Barry replied, his voice soft and distant, "I feel a tightness, right over my chest. Is that normal to feel that?"

"That's perfect," Taylor responded. "That's exactly the kind of thing we're looking for."

"It's super tight, like a vice grip over my heart. Where did that come from?" Barry asked.

"I don't know." Taylor commented. "Why don't you ask it?"

"I thought you're supposed to be the healer," Barry quipped, half-awake as he was.

"I am, but that doesn't mean I have the answers. The best healers empower their clients to find their own truths, their own answers; otherwise, you become dependent on me."

"Fair enough," Barry said, his voice still soft and far away. "Where did you come from vice grip? What are you doing in my chest?"

Barry took a quick, sharp breath. He was back in his childhood home, it was a Friday afternoon, and his dad was chasing him around the dining room table. At first Barry thought it was a game, but one look at his father's murderous face and Barry knew it was no game. The carpeting was sky blue and Barry was maybe five. His dad, David Lemming, was cursing under his breath and darting this way and that, but little Barry was quick, scrambling between the chairs and then sprinting over to the living room behind one of the faded beige couches. His father's giant hand reached over the top and grabbed Barry by the neck, lifting him up over the couch and shaking him like a leaf. *Stop, Dad, stop*, little Barry said, the tears coming fresh now, Barry's small body shaking as his dad tightened his grip. *You little shit*, his dad was saying, *don't you ever fucking do that again, do you understand me? What did I do?* Barry cried. *What was it that I did wrong?* But then his dad was gone, dropping Barry onto one of the couches and marching upstairs to find Barry's mom and continue the interrogation. Little five year-old Barry slid off the couch and lay on the carpeting and sobbed, his snot and tears mixing in with the cloud blue.

"Fuck," was all adult Barry could say, opening his eyes and looking around Taylor's office.

"You okay?" Taylor asked, offering him a glass of water. "You were out for about fifteen minutes."

"It was my dad. He was chasing me and grabbing me and stuff. I thought it was play, but it definitely wasn't, at least not in this memory."

"What did it feel like?" Taylor asked.

"Like I was running for my life, and then when he caught me -- and he always caught me -- he grabbed me by the back of my neck and squeezed. Hard. Could that be why I get killer neck pains and headaches?" Barry asked.

"It sure could," Taylor said. "The body remembers."

"And why furniture freaks me out?" Barry asked.

"Furniture freaks you out?" Taylor asked.

"You have no idea. Patricia and I tried to go furniture shopping and I had a massive anxiety attack, right there in the store. I thought I was going to die; I couldn't catch my breath for anything. And then I got completely and utterly shit-faced about two hours later. That was one of the few times I actually drove drunk," Barry continued.

"So, Barry, I have a question: this memory that just surfaced, the one where your dad was chasing you: how did it end?"

"With me sobbing on the carpet and my dad going upstairs to go after my mom," Barry said.

"Are you happy with that ending?" Taylor asked.

"No, it sucks. But I think it's truthful. Things like that happened all the time. My dad was kind of a rager," Barry said, his voice lowering. "But I didn't remember it being that bad."

"And where did your dad grab you?" Taylor asked.

"All over the place: he'd grab me by the arm, yank me this way or that. In this memory, he was squeezing my neck," Barry explained.

"Lightly or like he meant it?" Taylor asked.

"Like if you were gripping something and trying to break it," Barry said.

"Barry, I know we're just starting to work together, but what you're describing is physical abuse. Have you ever thought of yourself as a victim of physical or emotional abuse?" Taylor was leaning forward, his face open and free of judgment.

"But my dad loved me, loved us," Barry countered.

"I'm not saying anything about love, whether he loved you or not. Abuse is often mixed with love, and that's why it can be so confusing."

"He loved me more than anyone," Barry said, nodding his head in a kind of rhythm.

Taylor bit his hip, waited.

"So the chasing and the grabbing and pulling and squeezing...that could really be considered physical abuse? That's not normal? I thought everybody had episodes like that," Barry continued, opening an eye and looking over at Taylor.

"No, Barry, not everybody lives through that. What you're describing can absolutely be considered abusive," Taylor explained. "Emotional and physical abuse, if you want to get right down to it."

"It's weird. I've never thought about myself as an abuse survivor. It was really important to my dad that we thought he was a good dad. I used to tell people all the time that he was the best dad in the world. I might have to re-think that one. Could all of this have something to do with my drinking?" Barry asked.

"What do you think?" Taylor asked back.

"Yeah, I guess it could," Barry said.

"Barry, I know you're still working out your issues with God or the concept of a Higher Power, but as you saw in our last session, healing can come from angels or light or a million different ways of lifting someone's heart and easing the pain of the past. This memory that we were just working on; are you okay leaving it where it is or would you like to do some healing with it?" Taylor asked.

"I guess I still don't understand," Barry admitted. "It already happened. How can we change it? Isn't that being manipulative?"

Taylor smiled. It took him years and years of meditating and studying to understand this concept. How can he transmit it to Barry in a few, short sentences?

"We can't change what happened in reality," Taylor began. "That will never change. On this one day when you were five, your dad did, in fact, chase you around the dining room table and grab you by the scruff of your neck and shake you. We can't change that. But the pain of it, the lingering negative emotional effects of what happened, that continues to live inside your head and your heart. It has a life of its own, and it – the pain – will continue to impact your present-life decisions and behaviors as long as it exists. It's almost as if the pain takes on a life of its own, gains its own consciousness. From an energy perspective, the energy of the pain knows no time or space, so it's still living inside you like it just happened. We can't change what happened in physical reality, but we can change your reaction to it, your inner experience of what happened. Does that make sense? By bringing healing to the pain, by asking God or allowing the "light" to literally lift the pain out of your heart, then you can truly be free from the past. And once the past is past, then you can actually be present with the present. Does that make sense? Washing what happened and allowing God to give you a clean slate, that is the true miracle. That is what we call healing."

"That sounds awesome," Barry said quietly. "How do we do it?"

"Remember that angel that showed up last healing? Let's see if that can happen again. Ready?" Taylor leaned forward again. He loved this transformation part more than anything else.

Barry nodded, closed his eyes, followed his breath down into his chest.

"Barry, go back to the memory, or what we call a picture, and in the picture, watch your dad chasing you, round and round, you getting more and more scared, but before he grabs you, I want you to picture a giant angel coming into the room, that's it, now just watch and tell me what happens..."

Little five year-old Barry was running for his life, he could smell and feel his dad's rage as he goes left, then goes right, running behind the dark brown table and then leaping over behind the couch, his dad's giant hand just about to grab him when a bright light appears...Little Barry getting up onto his knees and staring at a giant angel, all wings and beauty and light as the angel stretches seven feet out across the living room...the angel now lifting his father up by his neck and carrying him out the front door...his father yelling and cursing but then growing quiet as his shoulders sag and he slumps away down the street. The front door closes as a huge bubble of white light forms a protective barrier around the house. Barry runs up the stairs to get in bed beside his mom where they snuggle and are safe. Little Barry presses his face against her shoulder and she smiles down at him with warm, beaming eyes. Her skin is pink and soft, and after a few minutes, they both doze off peacefully. Barry hopes his dad never comes back.

"That's crazy," Barry said, opening his eyes. "Was that even real?"

"What happened?" Taylor asked.

"You couldn't see it?" Barry asked, raising up on one arm to turn towards Taylor.

"I can when I need to. I actually like to give people their privacy, so I help and support, but give you enough space to have your own experience," Taylor explained.

"The same angel came back, except this time he stopped my dad from grabbing me and threw my dad out of the house. Then he sent this amazing bubble of light all around the house so my dad couldn't get back in unless he was going to be nice to us," Barry said, filling him in.

"What did you do?" Taylor asked.

"My little five year-old self? I ran upstairs and snuggled in bed with my mom. She was safe and cuddly and we hardly ever snuggled like that. She was scared and usually too far-off for me to get close to her like that," Barry answered. "Could a memory like this make it hard for me to let Patricia get close to me? She complains all the time that I never hold her or let her touch me. And she's right. I'd rather be water-boarded by terrorists than snuggle in bed with her."

"That's exactly right," Taylor said. "These kinds of memories drive all kinds of defensive behavior. The cool thing is when the pictures change, behavior can change. How do you feel?"

"I feel amazing," Barry said. "Like a ton of tightness and worry is gone from my chest. I think some part of me was constantly being chased by my dad."

Barry grew quiet for a minute.

"Everything okay?" Taylor inquired.

"I just…I just worry or wonder about something: if we keep changing and healing all these painful memories from my past, will I still be me?" Barry asked.

"You'll be the best version of you!" Taylor exclaimed. "Yes, you'll definitely still be you. You'll still have the same memories, you just won't have the pain associated with them. In a way you get the best of both worlds because you retain the wisdom from different life events without all the limiting pain associated with them." Taylor paused, gave Barry a chance to digest what he was saying. "And as far as it being manipulative, it's something I've thought long and hard about over the years. I think as long as our intention is for healing and nothing else, and as long as someone is truly turning to God as the source of healing, then I think we're fine. If we're doing it from ourselves, or from our minds or our egos, then I would worry a little bit. That's why meditation is such an important part of healing; it brings you into a deeper part of yourself so you can know that you're more than just your mind or your ego."

"Meditation? We haven't talked about meditation at all," Barry commented.

"That's coming up in the next few weeks," Taylor said, smiling. "But that is all the time we have for today. You did great work today, Barry the car salesman. You are just rolling right along."

They shook hands, shared a deep smile, and Barry made his way down the stairs, leaving Taylor to look out at his boats and prepare for the next client. *How did he do this seven or eight times a day?*

Barry stepped outside onto Taylor's front porch. The sun was beaming. It was noon on a Thursday, and Barry had a good twenty-one hours until he needed to be at the dealership. Once again, he couldn't believe how good he felt: light, open, like he didn't have a care in the world. *Why didn't more people try this?*

He smiled, grabbed his car keys, and went to go find Patricia.

41

Barry took Patricia's hand as they walked. They were on the Santa Monica pier, just past the old merry-go-round, a slight breeze blowing into their faces. All around them, children shrieked, grandparents murmured back and forth.

"I love it down here," Patricia said.

"I know. Why don't we ever do this?" Barry asked.

"You're always too busy, Mr. Professional Sales Rep," she commented.

"Me?" Barry asked, genuinely surprised.

"Yes, you, Barry Lemming. Don't act all surprised. You only get a day or two off from the dealership, and whenever I suggest something like going for a walk, lying at the beach, anything non-productive, you give me a little speech about..."

"I know the speech," Barry interrupted. "That's just me being an ass. Feel free to throw a bucket of cold water on me the next time I pull that."

She gripped his hand a little tighter. "Sounds good. Seriously, though, I think it was hard for you to slow down, to actually not do anything."

"And why do you think that might be, oh Wise Doctor Meyer?" he asked.

Patricia smiled. "Do you really want to know what I think, or would you rather just tease me a little?"

"I really do want your opinion on this," Barry replied. They had made it half-way down the pier, people and fresh salt air all around them, when suddenly Barry's focus narrowed and it was just the two of them, talking. Barry loved it when it got like this.

"I think if you stopped rushing around all the time, being busy every single second, then you might actually feel something, and I'm not sure you'd like what you feel," Patricia offered.

"Or maybe I'd like it a lot," he said, smiling. "Slowing down has its benefits, or so I've heard."

"Are you flirting with me, Mr. Lemming?" she asked, lowering her voice and batting her eyes at him.

"Oh, definitely," he responded.

They started their stroll again, now passing the new add-ons to the pier: the roller coaster, the new games section. Barry and Patricia were content to just walk, let everyone around them hustle and bustle. Fifteen minutes turned into an hour. They stopped for bar-b-que brisket sandwiches at Crazy Larry's Downhome Southern BBQ, the sauce and grease literally running down their arms as they passed napkins and a large sweet tea back and forth. Barry hadn't had this much fun in years, and when Patricia suggested they head home, he was all in.

She lowered the blinds and lay down next to him. Barry was already shirtless on the bed, smiling and content.

"Don't you look like the bird who ate the canary," she said, slipping her shirt off and snuggling next to him.

"Can you blame me? Look where I was just three weeks ago, where we were, and where we are now."

"So, look, I want to take this slow, and I want you to let me be in charge," she said.

"In charge how? Like handcuff-me-to-the-headboard in charge?" he asked.

"Would you like that?" she responded, moistening a forefinger and circling it around one of his nipples.

He smiled for a bit, then took her hand and stopped her.

"What is it?" she asked.

"If you touch me like that, I'm going to cum fast," he said. All of the joking tone was gone from his voice.

"So then cum fast, Barry. I don't care. You can have your own rhythm. Just be present with me. Have four orgasms if you want…just stay with me."

She went back to circling his nipple, rubbing it between forefinger and thumb, then leaning over and placing his nipple in her mouth. Barry groaned. She ran a hand down into his pants, pressing on his thigh and inner groin, refusing to touch his penis, not yet. Barry bucked and twisted, willing himself towards her, but she slowed him down, pressing him flat back on the bed and returning back to his nipple.

"You're driving me crazy," he said.

"Good. I want you to practice containing it. Feel all of these good feelings, but don't take them somewhere, don't push it. You're afraid to feel, Barry. I think it's the root most of our problems, not to put it all on you because I certainly have my half of the equation. But I watch you numb out with alcohol and sports and sex, and then you wonder why I feel so alone." His face dropped. "I'm not trying to nail you. I'm trying to save you. The truth, remember? The truth will set us free. Now just breathe and relax and feel, don't try and take it anywhere."

Barry did as he was instructed. Patricia's fingers went back to his hips, his low belly, then eventually they found their way onto his penis, rubbing slowly up and down. Barry's breaths became shallow and stilted, he lost sight of the room and felt a weird spin begin to happen. She continued to suck and chew on his nipple and Barry felt like the top of his head was going to come off.

"Patricia, stop. Please. Stop."

"What if I don't want to?" she said in her most seductive voice, her hand and mouth working overtime.

"Stop goddammit!" Barry yelled, scrambling away from her into the corner of the bed. His breathing was ragged and his face was flushed; he felt like he was about to pass out.

"What the hell?!" she demanded.

"Jesus Christ, Patricia, I just tried to fucking kill myself! Do you have to push me like this?"

"Barry, Barry, will you look at me?" she asked, moving a bit closer to him on the bed.

"What? What is it?" he asked, sounding like a scared four year-old.

"I'm not trying to push you, except maybe I am. This is where we always stop, and we both get our feelings hurt and then go away for a week or two before we try again. What's so bad about trying it my way?"

He pressed his lips into a hard, straight line. "If I keep doing it your way, and you keep touching and stimulating me like that, I don't know what's going to happen."

"So?" she asked. "What's so bad about that?"

"I feel like the top of my head is going to come off," he admitted.

"Not really," she said.

"No, I guess not, but it feels like that," he continued.

"What do you think might really happen?" she asked.

"I might yell or scream or cry," he offered.

"Then yell or scream or cry," she said, taking his arm and pulling him back towards her. "Let me into your world, as awful as it might be. That's what true intimacy is about. I don't care if the neighbors hear, even though it's a Thursday afternoon and no one's home except old Mrs. Sousy across the street."

She laid him back on the bed and began again, first with her fingers on one of his nipples, then her mouth, then moving her hand lower and touching him, feeling him. Barry's breath became ragged and he resisted the urge to run. He felt himself stiffen and then it actually began to feel good.

"Just stay with me, Barry," she said through clenched teeth. "Don't push it or try to end it by going fast."

He stayed slow. He used the breathing technique that Taylor had taught him to breathe right through the feeling that the top of his head was going to come off. Instead, he thought of the beach, and the waves lapping on the sand, and of holding her hand while they walked in the warm sun.

It worked, for a minute. Barry felt peaceful and calm and was actually enjoying being in the room with Patricia. But then it changed. A darkness came over the room, the light beige paint turned to old wallpaper, and that was when Barry saw him. First it was in the corner of his vision, a far-off picture that had nothing to do with anything, but then it flipped and Barry was no longer an adult, no longer with Patricia, no longer in the safety of their Palisades home.

He was seven years old, wearing his favorite red-and-blue striped shirt, and his Uncle Paul was straddling him, all three-hundred-and-sixty pounds of him, with his eyes closed and a far-off look on his sweaty face while his hips gyrated away, little sixty-pound Barry pinned underneath him, being pressed down into the folds of the giant water bed, the blue sheet and the rolling water pressing up all around his neck and shoulders while his uncle continued to press down on him, Barry wanting to scream, wanting to stop it, wanting to call for his mom and dad who were out going for a walk after the large family dinner, and then little Barry was getting stiff and starting to enjoy it but it was his uncle and he was all sweaty and gross and huge and Barry couldn't catch his breath, couldn't make it stop, couldn't figure out exactly what was going on.

42

"You okay?" she asked.

He'd rolled away from her and was facing the wall, his thoughts quiet and dark.

"Did I hurt you?" she asked. "Push things too far?"

Barry turned back towards her. "Patricia, look, this is a super intense time for me. You don't have to go through this with me."

"Where am I going to go, Barry? You want me to put my life on hold, press the pause button for six months while you do your therapy? It doesn't work like that. I have a life, too, y'know."

"I know that," he said. "And if you want to move out on your own while I go through this, I understand. I really do."

She took his hand. "Look, Barry, being completely honest here, once I move out, I'm not coming back. So you might as well tell me what's going on."

A large lump formed in his throat, and he thought for a minute he wouldn't be able to speak. He swallowed, took a breath, tried to swallow again.

"It was my Uncle Paul," he began.

"The big one? What about him?" Patricia asked, her eyes big and round.

"I'm pretty sure he sexually molested me," Barry said without much feeling at all.

Barry knocked on the front door. It was late on a Friday afternoon. Wanda, Taylor's wife, answered.

"Hi, Barry. Come on in. Rasheed will be right with you," she said, turning back towards the kitchen.

Barry stepped inside, his eyes adjusting to the indoors. "Who's Rasheed?" he asked.

"Oh...Rasheed...Taylor. I get them mixed up sometimes. Rasheed is his spiritual name," she explained.

"He has a spiritual name?" Barry asked.

"Why don't I let Taylor explain it to you," she said as she lowered green beans into a colander and continued getting dinner ready.

Just then, Taylor's large frame appeared on the stairs. "I'm ready for you, Barry," he said.

"Right on time," Wanda exclaimed.

Upstairs, Barry shook Taylor's hand and sat on the edge of the couch. "Thanks for seeing me on such short notice."

"No problem," Taylor replied. "How's everything going?"

"I think my uncle molested me," Barry said.

"Whoa. Really? Did you have a memory? What makes you think that?" Taylor asked.

Barry recounted the events of the day before, starting with him and Patricia on the pier and leading all the way to Barry's flashback in bed.

Taylor didn't say much, just let Barry talk.

Barry talked and talked, and when he was done, he finished with, "If it's true, then I want to go kill that fucker. He's still alive; I know where he lives."

"Do you think it's true?" Taylor asked.

"I have no idea. Can you make stuff like this up? It would certainly explain a lot. I mean, for ten years now, Patricia has barely been able to touch me. I cringe whenever she comes near me, but then I get pissed when she keeps her distance and say she's ignoring me. It's been a total no-win situation for her. And if we are trying to be intimate, I have to be in total control. Otherwise, I freak out and hate it even more than I normally do. I'm fucked up, that's for sure."

"If this did happen," Taylor continued, "it sure would explain some of your drinking. Between your dad's rage, your mom's withdrawal and depression, and now your uncle...man, I feel for you."

"Yeah, me, too," Barry said, exasperated. He ran a hand through his hair and resisted the urge to run out of the room. He had no idea what to do next.

"This is part of the challenge of alcoholic or addictive behavior," Taylor said, "People think, 'Oh, just stop. Stop drinking, stop smoking, stop whatever.' But it's not quite that simple. There are reasons why people drink; people trying to numb out or ease the pain of certain things. As brutal as it is right now, Barry, it's a great sign that this stuff is starting to come up. It means you're ready to deal with it."

"Yeah, woo-hoo," Barry said, deadpan as usual. "Let's throw a parade. I'm even more messed up than I realized." He smiled in spite of himself.

"Tell me about your uncle," Taylor said.

"I really don't want to talk about him. Do I have to?" Barry protested.

"Do you want to get better?" Taylor asked.

Barry nodded.

"Then, yes, I think you do," Taylor explained. "Remember our analogy of letting light into dark, dusty rooms? Your uncle might be one of your big, dark rooms."

"Who's Rasheed?" Barry asked, trying to change the subject.

"Oh, you heard about my other name, huh? I'll make you a deal: tell me about your uncle and then I'll tell you all about Rasheed."

Barry took a deep breath. "Okay, here goes. My Uncle Paul is a big man; he weighs north of three-fifty, maybe three-seventy at his hay-day. And he had this teeny-tiny wife, Simone, who weighed maybe a hundred pounds dripping wet. They were the oddest couple. Anyway, he had this big, voluminous house down in Orange County and we were always going there on weekends. He was my dad's older brother. And a couple times he wrestled with me and ended up pinning me on his waterbed, literally all three hundred and fifty pounds sitting on top of me, squishing me into the watery folds of the bed, and I thought it was just horsing around. I liked him, I really did. I have fond memories of going there. But yesterday, when I freaked out as usual with Patricia touching me...I remembered something different with my uncle, this look in his eye, almost like he was gyrating on me – literally getting off on me – it was so creepy. Now I still don't know if it was real or energetic, to use one of your words, but there was definitely something going on. And then I remembered that my Uncle Paul was a psychiatrist and what was his specialty? Young boys.

He works with young boys of all ages, and that's when I started to put two and two together, and holy shit, maybe something did happen. It sure would explain a lot."

Taylor handed Barry a glass of water. Barry took a sip and tried to compose himself.

"How do I find out?" Barry asked.

"Find out what?" Taylor asked in response.

"What really happened? If he actually messed with me or if I'm just making all this up?"

"That's a hard one. You have your memories, your perceptions, but believe it or not, in the end, it doesn't actually matter," Taylor answered.

"Doesn't matter? Of course, it matters," Barry spit out.

"Okay, I didn't say that as delicately as I could have. Yes, of course, it matters," Taylor continued. "It matters a huge amount whether or not you were molested by your uncle or someone in your family. But it's not like you can drive down to his office and demand an explanation, although some people do confront their abusers, with varying results I might add. But what really matters as far as your healing is your memory, your perception of what happened. Because even if nothing happened physically, it sounds like something was definitely going on energetically and you just might have been sensitive enough to feel it. It could explain a lot, Barry: the alcohol, the binging, the addictive behaviors. Many "sensitive" people have a hard time dealing with the world and end up using substances just to get through the day. When they get sober, or start working on themselves like you are, they realize how sensitive they actually are, not only as adults but back when they were children. Learning how to cope with daily life without alcohol or drugs becomes an incredibly valuable life-skill and a huge hurdle to clear. You have to grow as a person in order to do it. But regarding your uncle and what may have happened…if you want, we can do healing work with these memories just like we have with everything else. A picture is still a picture, even if it's incredibly painful."

"It's not enough," Barry said, his mouth turning down in disgust. "I don't want to just feel better. I want him to suffer. If he really did these things, and God forbid did them with other boys, then someone has to stop him."

Taylor waited a minute, let Barry's words sink in.

"I understand how you feel, Barry," Taylor said.

"But what I really want, even more than figuring this stuff out with my uncle, is to be rid of that demon," Barry continued. "That's when I'm really going to feel free and my life is going to change. As long as that thing is hanging around, how free am I really going to be?"

"That demon is not a simple thing," Taylor explained. "In fact, it's possible that the demon and your uncle are related. Many sexual-abuse survivors end up getting plagued by demons or voices that come through during the abuse, especially if it happened more than one time. It's not just about the physical act of the abuse, it's having your spirit squashed by the experience, the taking away of choice and boundaries. Many abuse survivors feel like they have no voice or say in what happens to them. The pain of victimhood can lead to depression, addictions, irrational behavior, even suicide in some extreme cases."

Barry shifted his weight on the couch. "Tell me about the demon. What do I have to do to be rid of it?"

"It's not quite that simple," Taylor began. "Getting rid of something like a demon involves understanding a whole

paradigm, a way of looking at voices and non-physical beings. It would require some studying and learning some new
things."

"Can you help me?" Barry asked.

"Absolutely," Taylor replied.

"Okay, I'm game," Barry said. "Where do we start?"

"Remember 'The Matrix'? When Morpheus offered Neo
the red or the blue pill – told him he'd take him as far as he
was willing to go and the only thing he'd ever tell him was the
truth?"

"Yeah, I sure do," Barry said. "One of my favorite scenes
from any movie ever."

"Well, I'll make you the same offer," Taylor explained. "I'll
tell you everything I know about voices and demons and how
to get rid of them, but you're going to have to learn some stuff
that contradicts everything you've ever known or believed.
It's going to press up against some of your most deeply-held
beliefs, about the world, people, this physical reality…every-
thing. Do you feel ready to swallow the red pill?"

"That's the one Neo took, right?" Barry asked, laughing.

"Yes, that is most definitely the one Neo took," Taylor answered, laughing right with him.

"And what about the healing with my uncle?" Barry asked.

"We can do that whenever you're ready," Taylor replied.

∾

They were out on Taylor's back deck, overlooking the water
and the beautiful marina. Wanda had served them a delicious
dinner of wild salmon, rice pilaf, and green beans – Barry
couldn't tell but it seemed like food tasted so much better

after healing sessions – along with lemonade and corn muffins that she and the kids had made from scratch.

Barry was stuffed. "Thanks for having me," he said, starting to get up.

"It was wonderful to have you, Barry," Wanda said, smiling.

The men cleared the table while Wanda ran upstairs with the kids. Inside, Taylor washed and Barry dried. When they were finished, they went back out on the deck, each with a slice of warm cherry cobbler and fresh whipped cream.

"We're living it up tonight," Barry remarked.

"Yeah, I'm going to regret it in the morning," Taylor said, patting his stomach.

"Aw, you look like you do all right," Barry said. He took a bite of the dessert and moaned in delight. "Oh my God, this is good."

"It's Wanda's specialty. But she's also a professional speech therapist, specializing in kids with autism, just so you don't think she cooks and cleans and that's it," Taylor commented.

Barry raised his hands in self-defense. "I wasn't thinking any of that. I was just admiring a good dessert."

Taylor leaned forwards a bit. "Do you want to hear a bit about demons and voices and how to clear them?"

"That's why I'm here," Barry said, "along with the cobbler, of course."

"Back in the mid-nineties," Taylor began, "I'd hit a wall. I'd been working on myself since senior year in high school. Remember when I used to sit up in that crazy ivy?"

"How could I forget?" Barry replied.

"By 1996, 1997, I'd been meditating and using positive visualization for eight or nine years and I'd reached a plateau. It happens in personal and spiritual growth. I started looking around for a teacher, and I found a man named Robert Jaffe, MD. He's a spiritual healer and a medical intuitive and was giving lectures up and down the coast. He's based up in Napa Valley and was giving a talk down here in southern California. Well, I went. Wanda went with me; we were married by this point and I had just finished grad school at UCLA. His lecture was good. He was talking about personal growth and healing and how you can bring your heart back to the light. He talked about his own health challenges and some of the things he'd done to heal. And then, this is always a weird part, I must have had like angels or something covering my ears because he talked about a spiritual path known as Sufism, Shadhiliyya Sufism to be exact, and going over to Jerusalem to meet this spiritual guide known as Sidi, and I didn't hear a word of it. Like I literally don't remember him saying anything about that.

"Well, the lecture ended, and Wanda and I went up to meet him and introduce ourselves, and it was like he and I had this magnetic connection. I could feel him buzzing when I went and stood near him. It took all of about forty seconds for him to invite us to move up north and become his students and for us to say yes! We ended up wrapping up things down here in a matter of months and moved up to Dr. Jaffe's spiritual retreat center in a little place called Pope Valley, CA, which is about a half-hour north of Napa Valley."

"That's wild," Barry commented.

"I know. We didn't have any kids, didn't have a mortgage yet; it was the time to do something crazy like that. We lived there for five years. Looking back, it was one of the greatest times of our lives. Both Wanda and I grew an incredible amount. Her Sufi name is *Jamila*; it means the 'one with the beautiful heart.' Mine is *Rasheed*; it means 'one who is rightly guided.' A Sufi name is both your greatest gift and your greatest challenge; it's where you need to heal the most, but as you do, it'll be your best quality to give to others.

"I remember when we first got there; we drove up from LA, which is what, about a six-hour drive? It took us thirteen hours. I kept passing out and having to pull over and sleep, almost like I was leaving the material world and I knew it. It felt like I was going to the end of the earth, and when you visit Pope Valley, that's exactly what it feels like, except in a wonderful, familiar way.

"When we first pulled in – I knew I was going to Dr. Jaffe's "compound", that was all I knew, I didn't know anything about Sufism or any particular spiritual path – we drove up this long, winding driveway, mountains and desert all around, and pulled into the parking lot, and there's a man walking towards us with a large hat or head covering. It looks like a large *yarmulke*, y'know, what Jews wear to cover their heads. And I think to myself, 'Nice yarmulke.' We keep walking. Another ten feet, and there's a man in a jalaba, which is traditional Persian or Middle Eastern wear for men, but I think to myself, 'There's a man in a dress!' We walk another ten feet and someone comes over the loud speaker, singing the traditional Islamic call to prayer: "Allah Akbar! Allah Akbar!" It was beautiful but terrifying. And by the time he was done, Wanda and I were running for our car and speeding back down the mountainside, and that was our introduction to Shadhiliyya Sufism."

Barry was stunned. He didn't know what to say. He knew Taylor was different, but living at an Islamic Retreat Center? "So you're a Muslim?"

Taylor smiled, folded his hands. "Well, it's not quite that simple. We are Sufis, students of Sufism to be exact. We've both been studying it for eighteen, nineteen years now. We did convert to Islam about ten years back, but that was after tremendous study and understanding what Islam is and what Islam isn't. Most of the world has it wrong, especially here in the US. Islam is an incredibly peaceful religion; passionate, but peaceful. Much of the world is misusing it for their own agendas: to mistreat and subjugate women, misusing power and religious control, and don't even get me started on ISIS. That is not Islam, nor any religion, by the way. That is a bunch of cowards following the darkness and calling it something else."

"I, um, didn't expect all this. I've never actually met a Muslim person. You'll have to forgive me," Barry said, his world rocking just a little bit. "Is it important that I know any of this?"

"Well, if you want to defeat that demon, there are certain spiritual practices I'd like to teach you. You're going to have to find a way to change your mind, change your heart, learn to look beyond the physical world to see what voice or light is moving through you. It's not going to be easy, I promise you that, but you've shown terrific potential in our healing sessions," Taylor said. "The Islamic religion has a beauty to it that most of the world doesn't understand. What you see on the news, in the media – people blowing themselves up, women being mutilated – that is so far from the truth of Islam. Sufism is both a door into Islam and a vehicle to understand the unity of all religions. God is good, and God wants good things for His creation. That is the essence of any religion, and it is especially true in Sufism."

Barry looked out at the boats, at the ocean bobbing up and down ever-so-slightly. He rubbed his hands together and purposely took a moment before he spoke.

"Do I have to convert to Islam if I want to defeat this demon?" Barry asked.

Taylor laughed. "No, not at all, Barry! I'm sorry I gave you that impression. I don't really see you converting to Islam. You seem to be happy being Jewish and I would stick with that. Islam is not an easy religion; to really do it the way the Prophet was instructed requires incredible dedication and study. It is a completely different way of life, to tell you the truth.

"But, and this is a big but, there are certain Sufi practices that I would like to teach you. You're going to need them in order to change your heart to the point where you can defeat that demon. And that's exactly what it's going to take: you're going to have to defeat him. God will help you, and me and the angels, you'll have incredible support. But you've allowed something with pretty bad evil into your psyche; ultimately it's going to be you that's going to have to let it go."

Barry let these words sink in. He knew he was going to have to make a major change; he never dreamed it would be anything like this.

"We can't just do a healing session and picture the angels or the light getting rid of him?" Barry asked hopefully.

"The demon? No, it'll take more than that, unfortunately," Taylor responded.

"What kind of spiritual practices do I need to learn?" he asked.

"I'll teach them to you; they're easy to learn. Don't worry about that part. You'll do fine. The bigger part is expanding beyond the physical world. I'd like to teach you how to meditate if you're open to it; your heart is going to need that stability to go where we're about to go."

"It's just one little demon," Barry joked.

"I've seen your demon, Barry. There's nothing little about it," Taylor said, without a hint of humor whatsoever.

43

B arry straightened his back and tried again. It was six in the morning on a Saturday. Barry sat with four other students in Taylor's office, the sun barely creeping up over the horizon. They were sitting on hard circular cushions in a semi-circle; Barry could feel his sit bones pressing down into the cushion. He took a deep breath and tried to relax.

"Good morning, everybody," Taylor began. "Thanks for coming out early on a Saturday morning. I'm going to start this morning from the beginning. It's always good to go over your foundation, and we have a new student this morning. Welcome, Barry."

Barry nodded, smiled at everyone, felt like the biggest fraud ever.

"So, take a deep breath, let your spine elongate and take several deep breaths, allowing the air to pass all the way through your lungs down into your mid-section. Let's do that for several minutes." Barry watched his breath the way Taylor had taught him in their sessions; his mind continued to spin:

Patricia at home in bed, different transactions at the dealership, Chad still mucking things up. *And breathe, Barry,* he heard a voice inside himself say. *Who said that?* he wondered in a different voice, this one so loud he thought everybody else could hear it.

"Good," Taylor's voice was gentle and reassuring. "Now drop a level deeper, continuing to watch your breath. Don't try to control your mind, just drop below it. Allow your mind to do what minds do; minds are not good or bad, they just are. They churn out thoughts, they look at options, both positive and negative. They are wonderful for creating lists and crossing things off that list; they're not good for guiding and leading the heart...that's it. Dropping deeper, switching channels from the loud, chattering, world channel...getting softer...more subtle...gentler...good, that's better...what is going on inside you? What is wanting to open deep inside your heart?" Barry could feel himself starting to nod off. His head drooped, his chin dropped, and soon he was half-asleep.

"Closing your eyes to the outer world...so they can open to the inner one...and we're waking up now, Barry. This is time to relax, but not time to sleep."

And just like that, Barry was instantly awake. *How deep was Taylor inside his head? Who could wake people up like that?*

"This meditation is one of the foundational tools of Sufism. It is called Remembrance. As human beings, we tend to forget the Divine; this practice is a chance to remember. We are going to start in English this morning, as a review for everyone and as a way to ease Barry into the practice. The words I'd like you to use are: 'The One.' Just repeat that phrase: 'The One. The One. The One. The One.' You can inhale on 'The,' and exhale on 'One,' or you can take a larger breath and repeat the phrase all while holding your breath. Let's practice that now."

Barry did as instructed. He allowed his mind to ease, to literally switch to a channel where he was watching and following his breath and forgetting all about what other thoughts might be going on. The One, The One, The One, The One...

He found himself relaxing, and dropping to a deeper, quieter place, the words 'The One' echoing through his mind and heart, but somehow the words were *up there* and he was *down here*, where it was black, and peaceful, and quiet.

Taylor's next words came from far away. "Good, nice work everybody. Keep dropping in, keep hearing my words from far away. We are now going to switch to Arabic; this may be a stretch for a few of you, especially you, Barry, as a first-timer. The Arabic version of 'The One' is 'Allah.' *Allah* is the Arabic word for God, and it literally means 'The One': the one God, the one light behind and through all lights. *Allah-u* is the Aramaic word that Jesus used when he prayed and meditated. It then got shortened to *Allah* and actually pre-dates the Islamic religion. Allah has many heart-opening and healing qualities. It is one of the great mysteries of this world, the effect that chanting *Allah* has on the human heart. Let's begin that now."

Barry switched from 'The One' to 'Allah' and immediately felt his blood begin to boil. The calm, peaceful, black place was filled with red and he was suddenly incredibly angry. He continued the phrase, though, having learned from Taylor that whatever comes up during meditation is good. He tried to breathe, he tried to relax, nothing worked.

He raised a finger.

"Yes, Barry," Taylor asked.

"Um, everything was going fine until we switched to 'Allah.' Now I want to kill someone," Barry admitted.

"Believe it or not, that's good, Barry. Just keep saying the phrase and keep feeling your feelings."

"How could wanting to kill be good?" Barry pressed.

"It's not," Taylor answered. "But it was already in there. Using the Arabic phrase 'Allah' is not making you want to kill; it's pushing on something that was already there, some old anger or some old pain. Just repeat the phrase and see what comes up. You're doing great. Let's continue everybody."

Barry went back inside. He was literally seeing red. He could hear his parents, his grandparents, his great-grandparents who died in the *pogroms* in Russia…all of them screaming at Barry. *You're a traitor! Who says this word? This is the word of our enemies! Traitor! Traitor! Traitor!*

Barry decided to continue. *Allah. Allah. Allah.* He just said the word, watched his breath, and sank back down below. Some of the red had left the room, he was now standing on a giant wasteland, no buildings or landmarks in sight. There were mountains in the far-off distance, but nothing except dark barren earth extending in every direction all around him. He knew he was visualizing, or seeing a made-up scene, but it seemed so real. On the one hand, Barry knew he was still sitting in Taylor's office, meditating with a small group of students. But in this reality, red streaks shot through the sky and there wasn't the slightest hint of human habitation. How weird was this? *Allah. Allah. Allah.* Then someone was coming towards him, from far off. Barry continued to breathe, continued the phrase, continued to notice what was happening on the inside as opposed to up above. *Allah. Allah. Allah.* The din from his family and ancestors began to quiet down.

Barry took a deep breath, kept repeating the phrase, as the person or persons got closer and closer. *Allah. Allah. Allah.* Barry forgot all about Taylor's office and found himself one-hundred-percent present with the meditation. He stood and shifted his weight in the dark desert sand; he wanted to run, but he was also curious as to who it was. They continued to draw closer, now maybe five hundred or a thousand feet away. His deceased father? An angel? *Allah. Allah. Allah.* Barry even forgot what he was saying, that it was Arabic or spiritual or any thought or attachment to the Name at all. It was as if was something was now saying him instead of the other way around. The person got closer and closer, now maybe fifty feet away, but still hard to make out in the dark of the desert. *Allah. Allah. Allah.* Barry couldn't hear his Jewish ancestors at all; they had given up or left. Barry took a few steps forward; this was only a visualized meditation and he could feel that he had nothing to fear. Now twenty feet away. *Allah. Allah. Allah.* Barry looked up: it was a man on a horse. The horse was silky white with a beautiful, perfect mane. The man wore rich robes and carried a large sword at his side. Barry tried to look up, but could not see the man's face. He could only get as high as his chest. Barry was not afraid. The man had incredible power and grace; Barry watched himself kneel in the sand, even though he had no idea what he was doing. The man paused next to Barry, lifted out his giant sword, and touched the tip of his sword to both of Barry's shoulders. *Rise*, the man thought, putting the word directly into Barry's mind. Barry still could not see his face, but it wasn't unusual or weird. It just was. Barry rose out of the sand and felt stronger, more confident, like his spine had been strengthened. The man rode around him three times, then reared up on the horse and brandished his sword and yelled, taking off in a dead sprint towards the mountains in the distance.

Barry watched him go.

He had never had an experience like this, not in any way, shape or form. He didn't believe worlds like this existed, not until now, not until it happened to him.

"Good. Now gently begin to come back to the surface, allowing your breath to carry you back up," Taylor's words filled the room. "And when you are ready, begin to wiggle your fingers and toes, then stretch your legs and arms, and when it's right and you're ready, come all the way back."

Barry waited until class ended and everybody filed out. They had been in for over an hour, even though it only seemed like five or ten minutes to Barry. Taylor saw him waiting and came over to him.

"Hi, Barry. You did great! How was your first class?" Taylor asked.

"Well, good, I think. I liked it, that's for sure. But something funny happened, something that's never happened to me before," Barry said.

"What's that?" Taylor asked.

Barry related the whole event, from the dark landscape to his family's anger to the stranger appearing out of nowhere. He told Taylor every last detail; Taylor listened without saying a word.

When he was done, Taylor took a deep breath and smiled.

"Do you know who that was?" Barry asked.

"That, Barry, was the Prophet Muhammed coming to meet you, may the peace and blessings of Allah be upon him. He's here to help you kill your demon."

44

Patricia looked up at Lynn and smiled. They were out on her deck, enjoying the sun and the chips and guacamole that Lynn had set out.

"Tell me this again," Lynn said as she set down two mango mimosas on the glass table-top.

"Mango mimosas? My favorite!" Patricia yelped and raised her glass. "I'd like to propose a toast."

"What are we toasting to?" Lynn asked.

"Hmmm, to life, to Barry not having killed himself, to us possibly being happy together…and to him never hitting on you again," Patricia exclaimed with a wild look in her eye.

"That I will definitely toast to," Lynn said as they clinked glasses. They each took a sip of their drink. "How was it with Greg?"

"Are you kidding me? It was awesome! He's like a Greek God and he was all mine for a night," Patricia said, breaking off a chip and sticking it deep into the yummy guacamole.

"Just for a night?" Lynn asked.

"Remember a few years ago, when you and John were having problems and you came and talked to me? It's so hard when things are dark and it feels like years since you've seen or felt the goodness of a relationship...Greg was like seeing the sun again. He was warm and sunny and made me feel good all over. But then, when I got that phone call and Barry was down at St. John's in the ICU...I don't know. It's like the last ten years opened up and I realized it wasn't time for me to leave. I had...I have to see this through, one way or the other."

"Why was he in the ICU?" Lynn asked.

"Shock, trauma, loss of blood. He blew half his right ear off," Patricia said.

"Wait, what?" Lynn gasped.

"I didn't want to tell you over the phone. I haven't really been telling people," Patricia stammered.

"He tried to kill himself? Really?" Lynn exclaimed.

Patricia looked her best friend right in the eye. "Yep. He sure did. Doctors are still testing to see if he has any significant hearing loss." Patricia smirked. "He didn't use his ear that much anyway. But here's what's so amazing: he's changed, Lynn. They say having a near-death-experience can change a person. Barry Lemming is not the same man I've been living with for the past ten years. It's almost like he needed to get to such a low point that he was willing to do himself in. And it could have gone either way. But he survived, somehow, miraculously. And now he's on the other side of it. He's grateful. He actually prays before we eat!"

"Barry? Barry prays?" Lynn almost shouted.

"I know! I've never seen anything like it. He lowers his eyes and his voice gets all quiet and he says these words, I don't even know where they come from. Not out of a book, that's for sure. He had a true spiritual experience. That's the best way I can explain it."

They sat in silence for a sec. Both of them amazed at the recent turn of events.

"I'm really happy for you," Lynn said, finally breaking the silence. "I'm surprised. And happy. If you had told me a week or two ago that you were staying with Barry, I wouldn't have been totally stoked. But with what you're talking about…"

"I know. Me, too," Patricia said. "I've actually cleaned out the cardboard boxes in the hallway, put everything away. It only took me ten years to finally move into our house."

They sat for a moment in silence, both of them enjoying the sun, their friendship, and the possibility that Patricia and Barry could actually be happy.

"We're not out of the woods yet," Patricia continued. "He continues to get weekly healing sessions, and work on himself, and work on us. He's now all about personal growth. I can't believe it. It's almost like a part of him died that afternoon on the Bluffs, the part of him that drank and sabotaged and was afraid to be happy, but a new part of him was born. The real part."

"Unbelievable. I almost wouldn't believe it unless you were telling me yourself. What about Greg? Do you think you'll see him again?" Lynn asked, putting more chips on her plate.

"We're friends. That's it," Patricia answered. "I had to let him down easy."

"And what about you?" Lynn asked.

"What about me?" Patricia asked back.

"Well, what are you going to do now that your boyfriend has had this incredible breakthrough? Don't tell me working three afternoons a week at *Le Michele Boutique* is your real calling in life?" Lynn inquired. She was pushing a bit, and she knew it, but when you're best friends, you can get away with stuff like that.

"I don't know," Patricia responded. "Taking care of Barry's high's and low's and alcoholic adventures has been like a full-time job. I guess that makes me co-dependent, huh? Now that Barry is starting to take care of Barry, I actually have some room to think about other things. There's a writing program over at SMC Community College that I might be interested in. And you know I'd still love to have a baby. I wonder if that could happen now."

"I just can't believe it. Barry Lemming with a near-death spiritual experience. I guess anything is possible," Lynn remarked.

"I will drink to that," Patricia said as they clinked glasses and downed more of their mimosas. "You know what's amazing?" Patricia continued. "The whole time we were together, something felt off or weird, like it wasn't the real us. Back in college, when we first started dating, that felt like Barry. And I loved him. I truly fell in love with him. He's not perfect, God knows, but he has a realness, a genuine-ness that's hard to find. But when we got to LA, and he got into the whole 'I'm-going-work-for-Toyota-and-be-a-super-salesman' thing...it's just been off. I don't know what kept me hanging around, maybe the possibility of having kids, maybe because he's been generous and pays most if not all of the bills, but it had to come to a head and now it has. God, I hope this sticks. If he backslides and starts drinking again, I swear to God, I'll kill him myself."

They finished their drinks and moseyed out onto Lynn's semi-private tennis court, the one she and John shared with a neighbor up the street. Patricia felt a little tipsy as they rallied, but she didn't care. It was a Monday afternoon, she was at her best friend's house, the sun was sparkling down on the ocean and Barry was now sober and working on himself full-time.

What could possibly go wrong?

45

Mja-bukeppe-wae-Balthusra.
My name is Balthusra.
Ittz-vcch-me-nene-pa-pu.
It makes me sick to make your acquaintance.
Hae-la-uuh-tuk-tuk-ma-nae-uh-sma-na-pu-pu.
Your kind is weak and we show our dominance over you.
La-lu-pa-pa-utz-be-keppin-mi-na-ha-ho-grr-slo-na-bada.
I have chosen this one for my own; I am his master.
Kee-mo-sala-mai-mau-be-pa-pa-tow-be-ma.
Do not be foolish and try to rescue him.
Keeh-la-man.
He is mine.

46

Barry drove slowly away from Taylor's house, the dust rising in small billows behind his Mustang.

Did all that really just happen? Did I just meet a man on a horse wearing silk robes and touching me with his sword? Was that really Prophet Muhammed?

Barry's mind was spinning. He felt giddy and nervous, like he was standing on the edge of a cliff and driving at the same time. *Alcohol, fighting with Patricia, arguing with that demon out on the Bluffs...*it all seemed a million miles away. There were so many better things to think about! Worlds to explore, new meditations and phrases to learn. Taylor had opened up brand new worlds for him.

Then why aren't I feeling better? Barry wondered.

Because I'm not out of the woods yet, he realized. *That demon is still alive, still around or near me. Patricia and I haven't worked all of our stuff out yet; I mean, jeez, she still can't touch me in bed without having me go ape-shit. Did my uncle really molest me? Did I make that up? And if I did, then why am I so messed up when it comes to intimacy and sexuality?*

Barry continued to drive. He slipped in an old cd, one of his favorites, *Talking Heads*, and just let himself drive. It was early on a Saturday and he still had an hour or two before he needed to be at work. He hopped on the 405 and drove north towards Westwood, got off on at Sunset Blvd, turned left over the overpass, and then got right back on the 405 heading south. *Who did stuff like that?* Barry Lemming, that's who, remembering his love for driving and why he got into car sales in the first place. He loved to go fast, he loved to get places, he loved to make money, and he loved to help people get what they want.

All qualities of a great car salesman.

He pulled into the dealership, smiled at April at the front desk, and made it back to his cubicle. Chad was waiting for him.

"What's up, Chad?" Barry asked.

"Can I talk to you for a sec?" Chad looked nervous: his eyebrows were pinched together and there were dark circles under his eyes.

"Yeah, sure," Barry said.

"Stan just pulled me aside and said if I didn't have a killer week this week, he was going to let me go," Chad said.

Barry sighed. How quickly the world comes rushing back in. "How many sales do you have this month?"

"Two," Chad answered.

"Two? For the whole month? My grandmother could have five and she's dead!" Barry felt bad for saying what he said, but he could no longer hold his tongue. Around anyone.

Chad looked down and toed the carpet. "Yeah, I only have two, unless you want to give me some of yours."

Barry looked up over the walls of his cubicle. It was a few minutes before nine and the place was just starting to fill up.

Paulino came dragging in, looking hung over or like he'd been up all night have sex with a co-ed. Orzo was already at his desk, firing away in Arabic over the phone and probably securing his first sale for the day. "Chad, look, I'm going to level with you. Life is short, and precious. You can do anything you want in life: you could open your own restaurant, you could go back to school, you could be a tour guide at Disneyland. But the one thing you cannot do is sell cars. And I don't mean that as a character flaw; not everyone is cut out for this business. It's a mean, vicious business and I wouldn't wish it on my best friend or my worst enemy. You're too nice a guy; you don't have that killer instinct. Do you know what I mean?"

Barry looked up. Chad was crying, small sniffles that he was trying to keep in.

"Jeez, man, I didn't mean to make you cry," Barry said, handing him a Kleenex box.

"It's not you," Chad blathered. "I told you my girlfriend is pregnant. She really wants me to be good at this, but I hate it. I hate being here. I hate the dealership and all the pressure and that big dick-head Stan! This job sucks!"

"I know," Barry said, patting Chad on the shoulder and standing up with him. "It's just better that you found out now. Shoot, you could be here five years and then realize how much you hate it. Look at how much time you just saved yourself."

"Right. That's a good way of looking at it," Chad admitted, still sniffling a bit and thumping a wadded-up Kleenex into the trash.

"Any idea what you're going to do?" Barry asked.

"My uncle's offered me a waiting job back at his place. They do ribs and stuff. That'll hold me over til I figure something else out. Thanks, Barry, for everything. I really appreciate it. You were always good to me."

They shook hands. Chad looked him square in the eye and smiled before walking away to gather his things.

Just then, Stan came rolling down the aisle-way, heading straight for Barry.

"Stan, what's up?" Barry asked, shifting weight and trying to gauge Stan's mental frame of mind.

"Barry Lemming, that's what's up! #2 on the board, still a few days left to gun for Orzo and the #1 slot. How many cars you going to sell today?" Stan hollered.

"Twenty-five!" Barry responded.

"That's my guy," Stan said without slowing down for a second.

𑀫

It had been a good day. Barry closed one deal, had two others that were just about to go. He'd probably wrap them up Monday night, often known as the best night in the car business when people have a night or two to sleep on it, realize their neighbors and family members aren't going to be ooh-ing and aah-ing over their ten year-old station wagon, and come in sheepishly after work to ask if the new Camry or Rav4 can be detailed before they take it home.

He looked at his watch. It was just past five. The sun was out, the birds were singing, Patricia wouldn't be home until seven, and he had a couple hours to kill. He hopped in his Mustang, fired her up, and took off down Lincoln Blvd.

Should it be the Talking Heads? General Public? Eric Clapton? To have a great drive, you have to have great music.

Barry smiled. *May these kinds of decisions be the biggest things I have to face for a while.* He slipped in a Joe Cocker CD, leaned his seat back a bit, and just drove, heading down Lincoln, cutting up a small connector street to avoid the afternoon traffic, then turning left onto little Santa Monica.

He must've spaced out, or been listening to the music, or been thinking about something far-off, because somehow, he looked up and was parked with the engine off in the Gaslight parking lot.

Jesus Christ, Barry thought. *What am I doing here?*

Other than the Tiki Hut down in Playa, the Gaslight was his regular drinking hole. He'd probably driven here five hundred times on automatic pilot after finishing work, and somehow, he'd just done it again.

He reached for the keys to fire the ignition back up, almost smiling to himself at his mistake, when a little thought came into his head: *I could go inside, see if anyone's around. Doesn't mean I have to drink, just because I set foot on the property...*

He gripped the steering wheel a bit tighter. He knew what he should do. He knew what he ought to do. He knew what Taylor and Patricia and probably everybody else out there wanted him to do.

For addicts, true addicts, life comes down to a series of choices. Some are big, some are small, some are life-saving, and some are heart-breaking.

Barry thought about Patricia, about how good things had been, about the love they'd been sharing and how tender she'd become recently. He knew he was the cause for the change, knew that she was softening because he was growing, and knew for damn sure that if he went inside and had just one drink, she would leave him and never come back.

Start the car, Barry, a voice said behind his right ear. The voice was warm and reassuring and gave him a strength to do what was right.

Fuck you, Barry thought from a dark place inside his heart. *No one controls me.*

He went back onto automatic pilot then. He watched himself take his keys out of the ignition and climb out of the car. He watched himself close the door, lock it, and stride inside the Gaslight, the whole time a part of him screaming: *No! You idiot! You're throwing everything away!*

Shut up, Barry thought. He felt mean, vicious, untouchable. It was a good and familiar feeling.

He opened the wood-paneled door and stepped inside. It was darker than he remembered. The floor was dirty and dusty, a few stragglers sat at the bar, a few more of the tables were filled with customers. Barry almost threw up at the smell and feeling inside the bar, but he took a step forward anyways. It had been more than a month and he was glad to be back.

"Barry! Long time no see! Where you been hiding?" It was the same regular bartender, the long-haired blonde hippie with a giant chest who missed his calling as a WWE wrestler.

"Oh, y'know, I've been around," Barry said. *Rum? Tequila? Vodka? Which should it be today?* And then suddenly he swooned and leaned to the side, catching the bar-top to stop himself from falling. He was standing outside himself, watching himself go through the ordeal again: the arguing on the Bluffs, the giant demon looming over him, the flash of light not coming to save him this time, and Barry's pale, deceased body inside a coffin at his funeral. He could see it clear as day. And Patricia, crying on Lynn's shoulder as they lowered him down into the earth.

Barry shook his head. "What was the question?"

"What'll it be?" the bartender asked. "This one's on the house, good to have you back."

Barry looked up at the bar. He couldn't believe he was still standing here. He was about to answer when out of his side view, to the right in a silhouette form, he could see the demon standing beside him: he was huge, and fiery red, and grinning from ear-to-ear.

Good, Barry. Welcome back, the demon said, with awful gross flesh dripping out of the sides of his mouth as he spoke.

That was enough.

Barry turned and sprinted out of the bar, banging into the door and letting it slam on his way out.

Outside, he turned and puked into one of the bushes, the wretch and bile coming too fast for him to control. He vomited several times, emptying his stomach's contents from earlier in the day, until he was dry heaving and crying but also laughing at the same time.

Almost, Barry thought. *You almost got me, you bastard. But your time is coming, just you wait.*

47

"Okay, demon-killing time," Barry said, sitting on the edge of the couch and looking right at Taylor. "You're serious today," Taylor replied.

"Serious as a heart attack. It almost got me, the demon. I drove back to the Gaslight, one of my favorite haunts, and before I knew it, I was standing at the bar about to order a drink. And the demon, the fucking ugly, blood-sucking demon, was standing right beside me, smiling. And all this gross flesh was dripping out of his mouth and I want him gone now." Barry was talking a mile a minute, rubbing his hands together and anxious to get started.

"Have you been doing the Remembrance?" Taylor asked.

"Every morning," Barry said. "Not quite as long as you suggested, but a good 15-20 minutes every day before I go to work. I'm almost reconciled with the fact that I'm a Jew, living in west LA, using the Arabic word for God."

Taylor smiled. There was only one Barry. "Any alcohol of any kind?" Taylor asked.

"Not a drop," Barry said.

"How long has it been?" Taylor inquired.

"Coming up on sixty days," Barry responded.

"Congratulations. That is a huge accomplishment. You should be really happy with yourself," Taylor said.

"I am. Why are we not killing the demon? Why the small talk?" Barry pressed. He had come to know Taylor's nuances during their weekly sessions.

"Look, Barry, this is hard to say, but you're not quite ready. You're doing great, don't get me wrong, but you try and kill that demon right now, I don't know, I just know it's not time yet."

"Really? What else do I have to do? What if that demon gets me before I get him?" Barry blurted out.

"Okay, look. I'm going to level with you. What you've done in two months takes most people a year. You've stopped drinking, you're doing weekly sessions, you're meditating daily, you've even cleaned up your relationship and getting everything back on track. But killing a demon, even seeing a demon, is pretty advanced work. I would feel better if I teach you a few more foundational things before we go there."

"Jesus Christ," Barry muttered.

"Yes, that's one of the things we need to talk about," Taylor responded.

"Seriously?" Barry asked. "Taylor, I don't mean to be impolite, and I am incredibly grateful for everything you've taught me, but my life is at stake here. I know it. That demon is going to get me if we don't do something, and do it quick. So teach me whatever I need to learn. Shit, I'll move in with you and Wanda if I need to. We just need to hurry up the process a bit, if we can." Barry was leaning forward as he spoke, his eyes open and large.

Taylor took a deep breath. The truth is he had never helped someone defeat a demon before. He had tried, several years ago, and it had ended with the patient taking his own life before he and Taylor could emerge victorious. Taylor had become distraught over the ordeal, even moving back up north to re-study with his teacher, Dr. Jaffe, for a month.

Taylor took a deep breath. "Barry, I had a patient a few years ago, similar to you in many ways. He, too, heard voices and thought he was being followed or bullied by a demon. We started facing it too soon, even earlier than you," Taylor explained.

"What happened to him?" Barry asked, afraid but also needing to know the answer.

"He took his own life," Taylor said quietly, crossing and uncrossing his legs as he spoke.

"How?"

"Um, in the bath. He drowned himself in the bath. He was here one day, working with me and facing this stuff, and then the next day his mom was calling, and me and Wanda were going to the funeral. I know how real this is, Barry. Trust me. I want you to defeat this thing as soon as humanly possible. I just need you to be a little stronger first."

"Okay," Barry relented. "I understand, and I appreciate the caution. What's next?"

"What's next," Taylor began, "is to understand voices, where they come from, and how to navigate the world of thoughts and choices. I won't charge you for today because this is part of my introductory class as opposed to a healing session."

"Taylor, charge me for whatever time we spend together," Barry interrupted. "You're worth your weight in gold."

"Why do you say that?" Taylor asked.

"Because you're still spending time with me, it's still time away from your family or boating or whatever it is you do to relax, and trust me, you are still helping me save my own life," Barry answered. "Look how much I've grown in two months! Patricia thinks I'm like a different person. And a lot of that is due to you and the wisdom and patience you've shown me. Don't ever undersell yourself, please."

"Okay, Barry, thanks," Taylor responded. "I appreciate that and I appreciate your trust in me. My patient's name was Jim, the one who took his own life. I just wanted you to know that for some reason. You ready to start?"

"Ready," Barry replied, pulling out a notebook and jotting down notes as Taylor spoke.

Taylor stood up and pulled out a rolling whiteboard, using a black dry erase marker as he talked.

"Voices. The whole world thinks you're nuts if you listen to voices. But everyone listens to voices, they're just usually the voice of the self, the ego. People hear a voice inside their head that sounds like they're own, and they usually follow that when making decisions. No one thinks that's crazy, right?"

"Right," Barry confirmed.

"One voice that most people know is the voice of the self. The Arabic word for that is *nafs*. Everything that makes you you – your thoughts, your feelings, your perceptions – those are *nafs*. Your dreams and desires, passions, good and bad feelings; all of that comprises the *nafs*. *Nafs* are not necessarily bad; it is the part of you that makes you you. But until you tame your *nafs*, until you learn that there are deeper places to make your decisions from, then the *nafs* can run the show, and that is where people get into trouble. There is a Sufi saying that anyone who claims an easy victory over their *nafs* is a liar or a fool, or both."

Barry chuckled. He was starting to appreciate Taylor's sense of humor. He also knew he was nowhere close to claiming victory over his own *nafs*.

"In the beginning of someone's spiritual awakening, they know this world, this physical, material world. We call that *mulk* – what you can see and smell and touch. Most of the world lives in the physical world, the world of *mulk*. That is the first level of reality in the Sufi paradigm."

"The matrix," Barry interjected. "What looks real, but is actually illusion."

"Exactly. Very good. As you start to open up and meditate, or do healing sessions or somehow begin to travel beyond this physical world, now other realities can begin to open up to you. You got a taste of this when Prophet Muhammed, may Allah's peace and blessings be upon him, came to visit you. The next world, the world of light and color and beauty, is called *malakut* – it means the world of the angels. And it is so much more incredible than the physical world that most people think they've arrived: heaven, peace, even enlightenment. But they really haven't; they've just traveled to the next world beyond this one. That's not meant to diminish their accomplishment because leaving *mulk* and reaching *malakut* is still a major movement in one's spiritual development. But to get wrapped up in *malakut* and fall in love with the beauty and the angels to the point where you stop progressing…this can blind a student and prevent them from continuing on the journey. They can literally become enamored with the beauty and stop walking. *Malakut* is amazing and much more refined than *mulk*, but it is still only the second world."

"Can I ask a question?" Barry asked.

"Of course," Taylor replied.

"What does it mean to 'walk'? You've used it before and I didn't know what it meant then, either," he said.

"Walking is a spiritual term; it means to develop or transform. The Sufi paradigm, at least the Shadhiliyya branch of Sufism, is based on stations. Spiritual stations. Very much like stations on a route for a train, you progress from one to the other. You go from one station to the next, although it's more holographic than linear. Each station requires you to come into a deeper level of truth and understanding; by letting go of falsehood, by shedding false beliefs about yourself and the nature of reality, your being will progress from one station to the next. It's an awesome, incredible experience and one that I highly recommend," Taylor explained.

"How do you do it?" Barry asked.

"There are books. Our Sufi guide, Sidi al-Jamal, who sadly just passed away two years ago, has left behind more than 35 books for his American students. Two of them, <u>Music of the Soul</u> and <u>He Who Knows Himself Knows His Lord</u>, have actual stations in them. <u>Music of the Soul</u> uses a 28-station model, while <u>He Who Knows Himself</u> employs a 7-station model. Both are effective for moving a student closer towards God."

"Okay," Barry stammered. "Can I get one of these books?"

"Sure, I have a copy downstairs," Taylor answered. "I'll be happy to give you a copy. Want a drink?"

Barry looked up. Taylor was holding a bottle of Ginger Brew Natural Soda.

Barry chuckled.

"What's funny?" Taylor asked.

"I thought you meant a different kind of drink," Barry said.

"No, fortunately or unfortunately, Ginger Brew is about as wild and crazy as we get around here," Taylor said, handing Barry a soda. "Want to take a break? Stretch your legs for a minute?"

Barry got off the couch and joined Taylor over by the large bay window. Several sailing boats pushed off from the dock and skittered out towards the open sea.

"It's quite a view," Barry acknowledged, taking a sip. "Oh, that's good. Spicy. Do you ever look out there, Taylor, at everyone going on about their life not worrying about all this personal crap, and envy them? I do."

"Y'know, I used to. When I was sitting up in that wet, damp, stinky ivy day after day, trying to figure everything out, I'd look down at our high school class, everyone romping around, having a great time, partying, getting laid. I knew I was missing something, but I was also gaining something," Taylor said.

"I'd say," Barry quipped. "I'd say you gained quite a lot."

"Remember Christopher Reeves?" Taylor asked.

"The actor who played Superman?" Barry said.

"He helped me figure something out. We were living up at Dr. Jaffe's retreat center, Wanda and I, and I was just having a helluva time. The spiritual wringer, as it were. It seemed like I couldn't do anything right. No matter where I turned, what I thought or felt, Dr. Jaffe kept telling me I was following my *nafs*. *Nafs* is not high praise in Sufi parlance. I'd try this, try that, and Dr. Jaffe would just shake his head and say, 'Still *nafs*.' After a few months, I was totally ready to give up. It was pretty rough. And I remember reading about Christopher Reeves in the news: he was rich, he was famous, he seemed to love what he was doing, and he was marrying some beautiful actress. And there I was: broke, no sign of a real career, in love with my wife but stuck at a Sufi spiritual retreat center in the hills of northern California without any sense of where my life was heading. And I remember thinking, "'Why God? Why does someone like Christopher Reeves get whatever he wants and I'm here struggling on what seems like every single level?' The next week, he got in that bad horse riding accident and was paralyzed. His life was never the same."

"I remember that. It was awful," Barry admitted.

"And I realized that all of us get humbled in one way or another. It seems that every single human being ends up on their knees begging some Higher Power for help. Some do it early, some do it late, some willingly and some kicking and screaming. But either through illness, divorce, bankruptcy, depression, every one of us has to face rough circumstances and realize our life is changing. In some cases, it needs to change. But whether we like it or not, we need to accept that it's never going to be the same. It is a humbling and often humiliating experience. Some people just give up, throw in their cards, get cancer or some major illness and check out without a fight. Others, like you, like me, push through and keep pushing until we come face to face with God. And I mean the One Big God. It doesn't matter what you call It/Him/Her; doesn't matter what name you use, what language you pray in. What matters is that you admit and acknowledge that there is something bigger than yourself guiding the Universe. That admission is required to make this type of change. To move from the *nafs* to the heart, and then the heart to the soul. In acknowledging that, in bowing your head and your heart and admitting that you need help from something bigger than yourself, that returns you to the right relationship with the

Divine. In Sufism, we call that *'sajda,'* or literally putting your head on the floor and bowing to God. That's the right relationship between us and God, the one position where our head is below our heart.

"When that happened with Christopher Reeves, I realized that everyone goes through their own trial. Everyone. I realized that God wasn't punishing me, or denying me, while I was seemingly broke and lost at the retreat center. He was giving me a chance to walk willingly, to plow through my *nafs* and learn about these different levels before I had to, which was a huge blessing, actually. I didn't have a divorce, a bankruptcy, a major illness. What I had was sadness and a longing in my heart to know the truth. That was it. After that, I put my head down, did what Dr. Jaffe taught me, and went through the stations pretty quickly as far as most people go.

"But that moment when each of us needs to get on our knees and face God, that is a crucial moment in a person's life. I had mine up at the retreat center in Pope Valley. Christopher Reeves had his toppling off a horse. You're having yours now, after battling with a demon and almost blowing your head off."

Barry was quiet for a moment. "I'm lucky to have found you, Taylor. Truly. Thank you for sharing all this with me. It's a great help to know I'm not alone in all this."

48

Taylor cleared his throat and took another sip of his drink.

"When it comes to voices, Sufis divide everything up into three major voices: the voice of the self, or *nafs*, that is Voice #1. It's the easiest to identify because it's the one that most people know. It's what you hear inside yourself, what you think or feel when you make decisions or have observations: *I have to go to the bathroom. I like the Chicago Cubs. I am tired.* This is all *nafs*. It is the lens of your *self* that you see the world through. It's not good or bad; it just is, a certain level of perceiving or witnessing that most people have no idea is just their *self.* Another word for *nafs* is ego, which in Sufi terms stands for Edging God Out." Taylor and Barry both chuckled. "We take our humor where we can find it. And don't worry, I'm not quitting my day job anytime soon.

"Voice #2 is the voice of God. As you go deeper in the Remembrance, as you spend time repeating the Name and begin to truly turn your heart to God in prayer and worship, it is possible to begin to hear a subtle, beautiful, guiding voice.

Now this is a bit tricky, especially from a semantics standpoint. As students of Sufism, we never want to claim to hear God's voice. That would be arrogant and the exact opposite of what Sufism stands for. Remember, the hallmark of a student of Sufism is humility, true realization of who we are in comparison to who or what God is. Our Sufi guide, Sidi, used to talk about being sober on the outside, but ecstatic on the inside. Cultivating a true, intimate, personal relationship with the Divine is the highest achievement that we can reach as human beings. It is literally beginning to experience Heaven here on Earth. Not easily attainable, and also not easy to maintain once you've reached it. It takes constant work, cleaning the weeds of your *nafs* out of your garden, so to speak.

Taylor cleared his throat, got a far-off look for a second, then continued.

"Instead of claiming to hear God's voice and risking arrogance, we use words like guidance. *When I pray about it, the guidance I get is...As I sat in Remembrance, the guidance that came to my heart is...*Does that make sense? Plus, not everybody hears a voice. Some people get pictures or images, some people get a feeling, some people just know what they're supposed to do and don't know exactly how they know. God speaks to everyone in different ways. How the information is received is totally between that person and God."

"You truly believe that God speaks to everyone?" Barry asked.

"All the time. There are different channels in the Universe, just like on a giant television. The physical world, the noisy world of the material, what we call the world of *mulk*, has about 97% of the channels. They are so loud and seductive and alluring that it takes real dedication to begin to listen to the other channels. The *nafs* grab a few of the channels, Voice #3 takes a few of the channels, and that leaves just one channel left open for God, or what we Sufis call Allah. It is the least-chosen channel because:

a) It is hard to find.
b) It takes true dedication.
c) It doesn't promise immediate gratification.

Taylor looked at Barry, watched him take the information in. he was looking for signs of stress or recognition, much like when Morpheus was explaining the Matrix to Neo.

"Do you understand?" Taylor finally asked.

"I think so. It sure explains a lot," Barry responded.

"Like what?" Taylor inquired.

"Like why so many people are having a hard time. So many divorces, illness, almost half the population on some kind of anti-depressant," Barry explained. "People are having a hard time because they're listening to the wrong channel, going after the wrong things. It's not even like they're making a wrong choice; they don't know there is a choice."

"Exactly!" Taylor exclaimed. "I knew you were the right student, Barry Lemming! Once you have a true brush with death, once you realize how instantaneously this could all be over, your priorities can re-align very quickly. This whole material world drives you for immediate satisfaction, getting what you want, becoming the Co-Creator of your life." Taylor had a very serious look on his face, his eyes narrowing. "That is the first level of spirituality, a New Age approach that is very immature from our perspective. Sufism is different; we don't believe in *'Co-Creation.'* What we believe in is surrender;

turning your *nafs* and yourself and your will back to the Divine and surrendering to God's Will for you. By truly putting your head at God's feet, everything can begin to change for you.

"God's voice is different. God opens the possibility of certain things, but they are for your soul, for the development of your spirit, not necessarily what's best for your bank account. Although, if you believe in an after-life, then what God offers is absolutely good for your long-term bank account."

Barry looked up and Taylor had a twinkle in his eye.

"How do I begin to hear God's voice?" Barry asked, rubbing his hands together in anticipation.

"Keep doing what you're doing. Keep doing the Remembrance every single day, and then if you want, begin asking God questions. It doesn't mean you have to like the answers. You might not even believe the answers at first. Just gather information. Turn your heart to God and have a conversation, just the way you and I are speaking now," Taylor instructed.

"You make it sound simple," Barry said.

"It actually can be," Taylor replied. "One of the Sufi sayings is, *'God is a hidden treasure wanting to be found.'* The simplest way, Barry, is to turn your attention away from the material world and find the depth of what God is offering. It's a treasure worth finding. I promise you that."

"What if I just don't believe?" Barry asked.

"Tell that to God," Taylor offered. "It's time for you two to work this out."

Taylor put down his dry erase marker, signaling the end of the lesson. Barry stood up, stretched his legs.

"Hey, you never went over Voice #3," Barry commented.

"I know," Taylor replied. "Voice #3 will be next lesson."

49

Barry leaned back against the living room couch and straightened his spine. He took a deep breath. It was early, barely five-thirty in the morning and Patricia was still asleep in bed. *The nice warm bed.* Barry looked out at the dark outside his windows, shook his head, took another breath, and tried to concentrate.

It had been four months since his last drink. He was proud of himself, happy in a way that he hadn't been in a long time. He was actually getting sober and getting his life back on track.

"Allah," he said, barely above a whisper.

He took another breath.

"Allah," he said again, still feeling like a phony, visions of Isis and suicide- bombers dancing around in his brain.

Have I joined a cult? he wondered.

Is Taylor secretly part of a rebel cell for Isis?

Then why does he seem so peaceful?

Are suicide-bombers peaceful?

Am I losing my mind?

He still hadn't told anyone what he was doing, not even Patricia. It was something between him, Taylor, and God at this point.

Okay, talk to God just like we are having a conversation, Barry thought.

Okay, God, since you know everything and can hear and see everything, you know I'm struggling to believe in you.

I know, a voice said inside of him.

Who said that? Barry wondered quickly, the whole exchange taking place in less than five seconds.

"Allah," Barry said again, this time a little softer.

Is that you talking to me? Barry asked inside his head.

Yes, the voice answered. It was warm and gentle and Barry wondered how anyone could be afraid of it.

Jesus, Barry thought out loud, but still inside his head.

Close, the voice said.

Oh, great, Barry thought, *my God does stand-up.*

Barry heard a laugh. *Just who was he talking to?*

"Allah," Barry said again, this time dropping deeper into his heart. He could feel the drop down, something he'd been practicing the past few weeks. Everything began to drop away then: Patricia, work, even his sessions with Taylor.

A world opened up inside him: he was standing on a mountaintop, a literal mountaintop, and a black-blue-green sky swirled all around him.

"Allah," Barry heard himself say from his physical mouth.

Why did you put me here? Barry-on-the-mountain-top asked.

It's your time, the voice said. *Your time to learn, time to walk, time to live.*

Are you real? Barry asked.

Are we having this conversation? the voice responded.

I guess so, Barry said.

I guess we are, the voice said.

And you really are God? Barry asked.

The answer came in the form of images: Barry could see himself as a newborn, see his parents with their 70's haircuts driving home from the hospital with their little bundle of joy; Barry as a four-year-old riding his new bike up and down the cul-de-sac in front of their house; Barry at his bar mitzvah, hugging and greeting everyone; Barry meeting Patricia in the Quad at Riverside, spilling the sloppy joe down the back of his jeans; Barry at his father's side moments before he passed away.

Tears formed in Barry's eyes. This was truly God. He knew absolutely everything there was to know about Barry, he had never left him for one second, and for the first time in adult Barry's life, he knew was not alone.

He also could feel that this voice he was speaking to wasn't actually God, but a representative for God. That if the real God came down in all His glory, the light would be so bright it would burn Barry to a crisp, right there on the couch in the living room of their Palisades alphabet street home.

God can send representatives, ambassadors, if you will.

Barry felt this whole concept come into his brain as a single thought, and he immediately understood.

God was real.

More real than Barry could even imagine.

He'd been such an idiot, waging this war against an unseen God all of his life. He'd wasted time, wasted opportunities, been living completely on his own when it didn't have to be that way.

All of this he understood in a flash, and with that he started to weep.

And he wept, and he wept, and he wept.

I'm so sorry, Barry said. *I've made such an incredible mess of things.*

It's okay, the voice said. *You are human. I made you to make messes.*

Can I ask you something? Barry asked.

Of course, the voice said. *Isn't that why we're talking?*

Why did my parents divorce? Was it my fault? Barry asked, the words flowing out of him without any thought at all.

The voice paused a sec. It wasn't as if the answer wasn't there; it was more like the voice was waiting until Barry was ready.

Are you ready to hear this? the voice asked.

I think so, Barry said.

Your parents divorced because they could not hold the Love. It had nothing to do with you. Both you and your sister tried to make it about the two of you, tried to insert yourselves into the equation, so you could help work things out. But it was always between your parents, Barry. I did what I could. I opened doors and softened fights, but in the end, both of your parents made their choices, and those choices resulted in divorce. It was actually as simple as that.

When people fight, and block the Love, and close their hearts, and choose other people even for a brief time, the Love can literally shrivel up and die between two people, and then that's it. It's over. And if it doesn't come back, then after a time I give permission for separation. It does not make me happy when two people choose this, especially when children are involved, but I have given you humans free will, and I keep my word, no matter what the cost.

Barry took this in. *It wasn't my fault? You're not mad at me for what happened?*

Not one bit, the voice said. *But your relationship with Patricia, that is a different matter.*

What do you mean? Barry asked.

That is your responsibility. It's of your making. But you're on a good track now: you've apologized, you've stopped drinking, you're getting to know Me. And that's good. Keep caring for her and giving to her and soon you'll have a family, God willing. The voice laughed.

You laughed! Barry said.

Why can't God have a sense of humor? the voice said. *You do. Who do you think gave you that sense of humor?*

I love you, Barry said, tears forming in his eyes.

I love you, too, Barry Lemming, the voice said. *Very much.*

Barry opened his eyes then. Over an hour had passed, even though it had only seemed like five minutes.

His meditation over, Barry stretched and smiled. Three weeks of Sufi Remembrance and he just had his first authentic conversation with God. Incredible.

His life would never be the same.

50

Two days later, Barry was back in Taylor's office, telling him piece by piece about his meditation and conversation with God.

"That's unbelievable," Taylor said.

"I know! What an idiot I was!" Barry yelped. "But it's getting better now. Thank God."

"You're starting to sound like a believer," Taylor commented.

"Bit by bit. Are you ready to tell me about Voice #3?" Barry asked, leaning forwards a bit on the couch.

"Ah, yes, good old Voice #3. Voice #3 is the voice of the *shaytan*, Arabic for the devil or the evil whisperer. The *shaytan* has many minions or foot soldiers; the demon you are battling is one of his loyal followers."

"You believe in the devil?" Barry asked, surprised.

"You don't?" Taylor replied.

"I don't know what I believe anymore. I can't believe we're even having these conversations," Barry said, smiling in spite of himself.

"I never did believe in the devil, or evil. I wanted everything to be good," Taylor continued. "But then I had the hardest time explaining why certain things happened. Things like murder, rape, child abuse, people hungry and starving while others dumped their leftover caviar into the trash. It didn't make any sense, especially once I found my belief in God, then it really didn't make sense."

"What is the *shaytan*?" Barry asked. "Did I say that right?"

"Yep, you sure did. The *shaytan*, or whisperer, is a tempter. He will try and lead you towards temptation, the wrong path, the one that turns you against yourself. His goal is to come in between you and God, to try to make you lose faith in yourself. That's how I'd describe him. Whereas God is constantly calling us to our highest version of ourselves, our most loving, most kind, most creative; the *shaytan* is doing the exact opposite, pulling us to our most basic, most animalistic, most self-centered, lowest version of ourselves. In the beginning, it's a big deal when you realize how much the *shaytan* is talking to you, and how much we listen! It's embarrassing really. Sidi talks all about it in <u>Music of the Soul</u>. There's a great chapter on Adam where Sidi accurately describes what the *shaytan* is, where he came from, and how to defeat him."

"There's a way to defeat the *shaytan*?" Barry asked.

"Absolutely. Over and over and over again. He's nothing if not persistent," Taylor explained. "Most people believe the devil or *shaytan* is a fallen angel, one who let arrogance get the better of him. But according to Sufi lore, the *shaytan* is actually a hidden servant of Allah, forcing the human being to choose between the light and the dark. That's what this whole world is about: learning to choose. If there was no *shaytan*, no darkness, how would we see the light? How would we develop as spiritual creatures? And that's why you see people struggle so deeply, because they are still learning the lessons of choosing goodness over everything else. That is why God has to be first, because the *nafs* and the desires of the self actually open the door for the *shaytan,* and once *shaytan* gets a foot-hold in your being, well, you're seeing it right now in this battle you're in. Not easy to win, is it?"

Barry shook his head. "No, it's not, even though I'm doing well right now. So how do you defeat *shaytan?*"

"There are different methods. The best one, and the one I'm going to teach you this morning, is called *tawba.* It literally means 'to return.' To return back to the truth, back to the light, back to the safety of God's love."

"How did you learn all this?" Barry asked.

"It's a lot, isn't it? While everyone else was out partying and getting high and shopping and saving for their retirement accounts and watching football on the tube, I was stuck up in the mountains getting my butt kicked by an awesome pair of spiritual teachers. I read, I studied, and I walked, just like you're doing now."

"Okay, just so I understand," Barry cleared his throat and stood up, walking around as he talked, "What you're telling me is that the devil is real, he talks to all of us just like God does, and I'm not crazy for hearing these different voices."

"Right," Taylor said.

"You are definitely the strangest therapist I've ever heard of," Barry admitted.

"It's part of why I dropped my license. My views are outside the norm, to say the least. But as a spiritual healer, I'm supposed to talk about this stuff! The battle between the light and the dark, the human heart caught in between trying to choose, getting seduced by the devil who offers you the bright, shiny lights of the material world. Great stuff, isn't it?"

"I can't talk to too many people about this, can I?" Barry asked quietly.

"No, not too many. Too bad it's not in a book. Wait, it is, Music of the Soul by Sufi Master Sidi al-Jamal!" Taylor exclaimed.

"When's your book coming out?" Barry asked.

"I'm working on it," Taylor admitted. "It's not quite finished yet, but it will be soon. Can we get back to you and your healing session? Gotta watch you like a hawk."

Both Taylor and Barry smiled. They were truly enjoying each other's company and their newfound partnership.

"So, defeating the *shaytan*…" Taylor began.

"Right. Thanks," Barry acknowledged, sitting back down.

"Are you ready for this?" Taylor asked.

"What do you mean?" Barry replied.

"I mean, are you ready to be happy? Free from the negativity and gunk you've been living with?"

"You mean it can actually get better than some of the breakthroughs I've been having?" Barry asked.

"It can," Taylor answered. "A lot better."

Barry turned towards Patricia and smiled. He slid his hand onto her arm and they sat that way on their living room couch, not speaking, for a good minute or two. Patricia turned the page in her book and leaned back against him, enjoying their company together.

"How are your sessions with Taylor going?" she asked.

"Incredible," Barry answered. "I can't believe it, actually. I never thought I would learn some of the things I'm learning."

"Like what?" she asked.

"You really want to know?" he replied.

"Of course! I'm always interested in what you're interested in," Patricia said. "Unless it has to do with a piece of dead leather being chased after by ten hulking, steroid-ridden guys and then thrown through a hoop or dragged across a chalk line."

Barry smiled. "Taylor is teaching me how to be truly happy."

"Well, that sounds like a very worthwhile pursuit," Patricia acknowledged, putting down her book and smiling. "Are you going to share these pearls of wisdom?"

"I'll tell you as much as you want to hear," Barry replied.

"Voice #3, the voice of the *shaytan*," Taylor began, standing back at the dry erase board, marker in hand, "is a liar. The devil or the tempter lies to the human being to get him or her to give up on themselves, to literally turn away from the goodness of God and begin to lose hope in their situation. That is the hallmark of the *shaytan:* loss of hope. Anytime me or one of my clients gets really discouraged and down in the dumps, I know the *shaytan* is involved. And it's tricky because the *shaytan* often comes through people or situations, so you actually have to look behind people or circumstances to find where the *shaytan* is wreaking his havoc."

"What do you mean? Can you give me an example?" Barry asked.

"Sure, let's make it practical for you and your life. Think of a situation where you were caused some pain. Let's not start with the biggest or hardest one, like whether or not your uncle sexually molested you. Pick another one," Taylor explained.

"How about when my dad used to chase me around the living and dining room and then squeeze my neck when he caught me?" Barry asked.

"Perfect," Taylor answered. "Now even though we've done a healing or two on this, there still might be a *shaytan* that came through during that experience that is still making trouble for you. Some of those times when you wanted to be more present in your intimacy with Patricia, or maybe when you had that anxiety attack at the furniture store."

"Oh, I hate furniture stores," Barry admitted. "That's my version of hell: being trapped in a furniture store for the rest of eternity."

"Can I ask a side question?" Taylor inquired.

"Sure, anything," Barry responded.

"Why is furniture so upsetting? Because your dad used to chase you around the furniture? Because furniture was in the room?" Taylor asked.

"I don't know. It doesn't make sense, even to me. Maybe because I had to blame the furniture instead of my dad? Because my dad needed to be perfect, so instead of putting the blame where it belongs – on him – he insisted that it wasn't his fault. He used to tell me, and have me tell other people, that he was the best dad around. Crazy, huh? A total mind-fuck is what it was. And I loved my dad, loved him fiercely. But I'm starting to wonder if he was a narcissist, and like any true narcissist, it can never be about them; it's always everyone else's fault. So in this case, since there was no one else there, just me and him, my five-year-old mind had to make it about the furniture so my dad could remain perfect in my eyes and I could reflect that "perfection" back to him. Does that make any sense? Am I actually blaming furniture for my dad's behavior?"

"I think it's a wonderful, deep insight," Taylor responded. "You ever think about getting into therapy?"

"As a career?! No, I'll stick with sales for now," Barry continued, laughing a bit. "But whether my theory is right or not, regarding furniture, all I know is that if I picture myself standing in a row at a furniture store, I get anxious and weepy and have to run out of there," Barry said. "It's happened like three times. Patricia and I are completely unable to go furniture shopping. As a result, we still have cardboard boxes everywhere and our house always feels half-finished. I should tell her to go pick out stuff without me."

"Okay, let's start there," Taylor said. "And remember, this exercise is for healing, but also to learn how to defeat the *shaytan*."

"This is so cool," Barry acknowledged. "How many are there of you Sufi guys?"

"Worldwide, about six million, at least in our Shadhiliyya group. But here in America, people like me who are doing Sufi healings and teaching people this stuff? About twenty. We all trained under the same teacher, Dr. Jaffe. Okay, you ready? Take a deep breath, drop inside, and picture yourself in a giant furniture store," Taylor instructed.

"Nooooooo!" Barry feigned a scream.

"Can you see the furniture?" Taylor asked.

"Unfortunately," Barry replied, his voice dropping lower.

"Okay, good. Now keep dropping in. Remember, it's never really about the present, it's about what the present triggers from the past. So, standing in this furniture store, surrounded by all these tables and couches and chairs, what does it bring up in your heart? What is the picture or memory that is getting activated?" Taylor asked.

Barry closed his eyes, allowed his breathing to slow, and then all of a sudden he was five years old again, his dad was breathing down his neck and chasing him top-speed around the dining room table. Barry squirted underneath one of the chairs and made it over to the blue-carpeted living room, ducking behind the arm of the flowery couch when his dad's giant hand reached down and picked him up, literally lifting him off the floor, squeezing the back of his neck. Hard. Young Barry whimpered. His dad stared down at him, red filling the pupils of his eyes. Barry felt his blood go cold.

"Okay, I have the scene," Barry mumbled.

"Is it about your dad?" Taylor asked.

"Yeah, his eyes are blood red and he's squeezing me. Right here," Barry explained, putting a hand on the back of his neck.

"Okay, good," Taylor continued. "Now look behind your dad. Sometimes it's behind, sometimes to the side. What do you see?"

Barry went back inside and looked past his dad. A few feet away, to the left, this thin fiery creature was waving his arms and reaching through his dad's body to grip young Barry by the neck. Barry couldn't believe what he was seeing. He literally shook his head and looked again.

"I see this fiery looking dude. Different than the demon I faced before. This one's thinner, and he's talking to my dad. And I don't know if I'm making this up, but it's almost like the fiery-guy is reaching through my dad to get to me. Could that be? Does that make any sense?" Barry asked.

"It makes perfect sense. Now trust what you're getting. Just watch for a minute as your dad continues to simmer or yell, and the *shaytan* reaches through him to get to you. Feel how it feels," Taylor said.

"Well, it's awful. Do you I really have to watch this?" Barry asked.

"Just for another minute. Then we'll start the healing, I promise. But this feeling you're getting, how would you describe it?"

"Like my blood has gone cold. Like my dad could murder me and not even be upset about it. He is not himself, that's for sure. And here I've been blaming the furniture for what he did. It's not the furniture's fault; this is all my dad," Barry acknowledged. "Except it's not really even my dad, it's this thing reaching through him. It's almost like my dad starts it, or opens the door for it, and then this fiery-thing takes over and makes it a hundred times worse."

"Good, Barry. That's really good. That is what the *shaytan* does. Okay, ten more seconds of witnessing the scene and then we'll start the healing," Taylor offered.

Barry kept watching. Curse words and yelling continued to fly from his dad's mouth. He was so mad that actual spittle started coming out of his lips. His eyes were blood red and distant, almost like something else had taken him over completely.

"Okay," Taylor said, "Excellent, Barry. You are really getting the hang of this. Now the official way to defeat shaytan is an ancient Arabic phrase: *'Audhu bi'laahi min ash-shaytani ar-rajim.'* Translation is: I take refuge from the devil who should be stoned. But I'm going to save that one for a bit and teach you a simpler phrase; we call it *tawba* and it's only three words. *Tawba* is the master cleaner. You can use it to clean emotions or pain, wash things from your heart and mind, and also to defeat *shaytan* and clean up things from the past. *Tawba* literally means 'to return,' to return from the pain of the created world and all the people in it back to the goodness of God. The three words are again in Arabic: *'Astaghfir allah alazim.'* I'll say it a few times, then we can do it together. The first word is the hardest; once you get that, it's all downhill from there. *Astaghfir* is pronounced: uh-staag-fear. Uh-staag-fear. Some people leave the 'g' out, but then it's not grounded enough for me. Want to try and say it with me?" Taylor asked.

"Uh-staag-fear," Barry said.

"Good. Say it again," Taylor continued.

Barry said it three or four times, getting it right or close enough each time.

"Good. The second word you already know: allah. Allah means 'the one,' or 'the one God,'" Taylor explained.

"Allah," Barry said.

"Right. And the last word has a couple different pronunciations: ala-zeem or ala-theem, depending on where you're from. I say 'ala-theem.' I like the way the 'th' feels on my tongue," Taylor said.

"Ala-thim," Barry tried.

"Make it a double ee on the end," Taylor instructed. "Ala-theem."

"Ala-theem," Barry said.

"Perfect!" Taylor exclaimed. "Good. Fast learner. Now put all three words together, and there's even a little tune or rhythm you can use. Uh-staag-fear allah ala-theem. Uh-staag-fear allah ala-theem. Uh-staag-fear allah ala-theem."

Barry joined in, saying it three or four times until he got the hang of it.

"Sounds good, Barry. You're doing great," Taylor said.

"Okay, what do we do?" Barry asked.

"Now we're going to say it a hundred times into your dad and that fiery dude behind him. Don't worry about whether anything happens or not, leave that up to God. You just show up, be present, be in neutral as much as you can, and let the prayers do their work," Taylor instructed.

"Will this really do anything?" Barry asked.

"Watch and see," Taylor said, a hint of a smile on his lips.

They started singing or repeating the phrase together, Barry getting the words mostly right as he dropped back inside and went back to the scene:

His dad was still grabbing him, the fiery shaytan thing was still gesticulating wildly and reaching for him, small bursts of fire escaping his body in all directions. Yuck! But as Barry and Taylor repeated the words, tiny piercings of white light started to fly into both his father and the fire being. They both looked like they were being pelted with light, the fire being getting the worst of it as his body started to collapse and disappear.

Uh-staag-fear allah ala-theem.

Uh-staag-fear allah ala-theem.

Uh-staag-fear allah ala-theem.

Both Barry and Taylor continued to chant, this time the fire being backing up from his dad and trying to stagger away. But the bolts of light got stronger, knocking the shaytan to the ground and ultimately causing his death right there, less than five feet away from his father. Barry couldn't believe it. It was like magic! They continued the chant, this time the words and bolts of light entering his father, the redness leaving his eyes and causing his dad to shake his head. He immediately put young Barry back on the ground and let go of his neck.

Uh-staag-fear allah ala-theem.

Uh-staag-fear allah ala-theem.

Still shaking his head, Barry's father knelt down and hugged him instead, apologizing and getting Barry a glass of water. Young five-year-old Barry cried for a minute, eventually putting his arms around his dad and hugging him. Adult Barry, sitting there in Taylor's office, felt a huge weight leave his chest as real tears began to flow.

They continued with the chant, as Barry could see with his inner-eye his now-deceased father and the five-year-old version of himself walk outside the house and start to play catch with a football. In real life, when his father had finished smashing him with his verbal and physical assault, he had gone upstairs and given the same treatment to his mom before leaving the house for the last time. But in this version, with the shaytan gone and his dad coming back to his real, rational self, the outcome was very different: young Barry was smiling and feeling better as they tossed the ball in the yard.

Barry shook his head and came back to the room.

"How did it go?" Taylor asked.

"Unbelievable, actually. Is this stuff real?" Barry asked.

"What happened?" Taylor asked.

Barry told him in detail exactly what occurred. Taylor nodded and smiled and folded his arms across his chest.

"That's about how it goes," Taylor said when Barry had finished. "That's the power of healing."

"But how? I don't understand," Barry exclaimed.

"God works in amazing ways. These three words – *astaghfir allah alazim* – are three of the most powerful words in the world, in any language, from any tongue. They literally mean, 'Dear God, please forgive me,' and they can wash very deep pain from the heart and the past," Taylor explained. "This kind of scene, it doesn't know time or space, so when we do these healing chants here today, the light and energy literally travels back to your five-year-old self and takes the pain out of your heart. It not only re-writes your memories, it washes them completely."

"It's unbelievable. I wouldn't believe it except that it's happening to me. But why are we asking for forgiveness? I certainly wasn't to blame in this scenario," Barry said.

"I know. The forgiveness part can be difficult for people. We are literally asking for forgiveness for letting things or people come in between us and God. It's a way of removing the creation from between us and our Creator," Taylor tried to explain. "It's a pretty advanced concept, usually for people who are on the path for a year or two. But there's another translation that works better for most people: 'Dear God, please take this from me.' And you can use that with anything, any blemish, any pain, anything that we've done or witnessed or experienced that is still causing us pain," Taylor again explained.

"That's better for me," Barry agreed. "Dear God, please take this from me. Dear God, please take this from me. How often can I say it?"

"As often as you like," Taylor answered. "Wow, look at the clock. Our hour is up, Barry. Same time next week?"

"Thank you, Taylor, from the bottom of my heart," Barry said.

"You're welcome, Barry. Truly," Taylor replied, shaking Barry's hand and locking eyes for a moment.

Barry walked outside and stood on Taylor's front porch. The sun was out and the birds were chirping and once again, the healing had worked its magic. There seemed to be no end to the amount of relief he could feel.

God, if you're there, thank you, Barry said, somewhere inside himself.

You're welcome, Barry. There's much more where that came from, Barry heard a warm voice say.

Barry smiled, grabbed his car keys, and wondered just who exactly he was becoming.

EPILOGUE

Patricia ran her hand over the dining room table and looked over at Barry.

He was standing a few tables away, admiring an extended oak table that had pretty brown spots in the wood.

Patricia smiled. They were in a furniture store. Barry wasn't hyperventilating, freaking out, or running out of the store.

He has truly changed, she thought. *Or is changing.*

"Are you sure?" she asked.

"If that's the one you want," Barry responded.

"But do you like it?" Patricia asked.

"I like them both. What I care about is if you like it," he said.

"That's not fair. What if in a year from now you decide you don't like it?" she pleaded.

Barry turned and faced her. They were standing outside the store. Traffic whizzed by on Wilshire, the breeze from the cars moving both their hair.

"Honey, I love you. I love that we are living together and I love that you want a dining room table. Beyond that, I could truly care less which table we get. It doesn't make any difference in the world to me. Pick the one you want. And if, a year from now, I begin giving you grief for which one you picked, I swear, you can tie me up and do anything you want to me."

"You would like that anyway," she exclaimed, biting her lip and smiling. "You really don't care which one I pick?"

"I really don't," he answered.

"You've changed," Patricia commented.

"Changed good?" Barry asked.

"You really have to ask?" she said, kissing him on the cheek and heading back inside the store.

Barry sipped his tea as he leaned against the kitchen counter. Patricia flitted about this way and that, directing the huge, beefy guys as they carried the table in. They were buying a dining room table! Barry smiled deep inside himself; another hurdle crossed. He had so much to make up for, so many things he wanted to give her.

They were lying in bed. It was a Sunday morning and Barry opened his eyes to find Patricia's head on his shoulder, tucked there just like a small bird. Barry tried not to move. They hadn't slept this close in years. He wiggled his toes and tried to scoot a bit to the left; a small line of drool dribbled from the left side of his mouth and he wiped it with the back of his hand.

"Morning," Patricia murmured, keeping her eyes closed.

"Morning," Barry said. "Nice to have you close."

"Nice to be close," she returned, stretching and letting him get up to go to the bathroom.

He stood over the toilet and peed, staring at the Kobe Bryant poster on the wall above the toilet. *What wife let her husband have a Kobe poster in the bathroom? Wait a minute, did I just call her my wife? It's a Sunday, nothing to do today, I wonder if we can get lucky in a few minutes...*

Men are such dogs, he thought as he snuggled back into bed.

She had rolled over, was now facing away from him and towards the windows. Their bedroom looked out on the backyard, their giant wooden fence, and then the Palisades and the ocean beyond that.

"It's too early," she said.

"Too early for what?" he asked, running a hand under the back of her shirt and feeling the warmth of her gorgeous skin.

"You know what," she replied, pushing his hand away. "Let me sleep."

"I have a question for you; it's a serious one," he said.

"Too early for serious questions. Go get on the Stairmaster for a half hour and let me sleep. Then maybe you can get lucky when you come back." With that, she turned over and went back to bed.

Barry jumped out of bed, threw on his pale blue UC Riverside sweats, and hoofed out to the corner of the living room and his single favorite piece of exercise equipment: the

Max Trainer by Bowflex. A thousand-dollar piece of machinery that he was paying off a month at a time. He filled a water bottle, stepped up onto the machine, hit User #1, plugged in the earbuds from his iPhone, then hit Play on the phone and Enter on the Max. Off he went for the greatest 14-minute workout known to man.

Afterwards, in the shower, he thought about how much had changed:

- He'd been sober six months. Not even a hint of a drink.
- He was still doing weekly sessions with Taylor.
- He was meditating every morning.
- He and Patricia were actually getting along. Better than that, in fact. They were falling in love all over again.

He realized, kind of slowly, but a dawning realization as he toweled off, that he had wanted their relationship to change, but the truth is he needed to change. He had wanted to make it about her, and she had her small part – say 5%? – but he was the main reason for their discontent, meaning that it was within his power to make things right.

"Can I ask you my question now?" he asked, getting down on his knees so they were on eye level. Her eyes were closed as she was still ninety percent asleep.

"What?" she barked. "Sleeping woman here."

"Patricia Meyer, I have thought about this a lot, and I don't know why it took me so long..."

"Wait, what are you doing?" she opened both eyes and stared at him. "What are you doing, Barry?"

"Will you make me the happiest man in the world and be my wife?"

She blinked, now more than fully awake, and stared at the gorgeous ring he was holding in his hand.

"Are you sure about this?" she asked. "Do you know what you're doing?"

"I know exactly what I'm doing. These past six months have been out of a dream, and you have been the most loyal, most patient partner ever. I love you, Patricia. You make me a better person, and in my case, I have certainly needed it. I should have done this a long time ago; will you make an honest man out of me and be my bride and give me lots of babies?"

She shrieked and threw her arms around him and cried, first a few gentle tears, and then the floodgates opened and they cried together, sobbing and hugging and realizing they had finally made it. They were finally going to be a family.

An hour later, after they had cuddled and cried some more and held each other for a while, Patricia rolled onto her side and faced him.

"Took you long enough," she quipped, kissing him on the lips and then on the cheek, tenderly. "But yes, I will be your bride and I will be your partner for life, til death or alcohol do us part."

"I love you," he said.

"I know," she said, grinning widely from ear to ear. "Now get back in bed and let's start working on those babies."

He stripped down in two seconds flat and jumped back into bed.

"Hold on, Mr. Eager Beaver," she said, tousling his hair and then lifting her pajama top over her head. "There's something we need to talk about first."

"What's that?" he asked, squirming in the bed and anxious to get to it.

"If we are going to do this, get married, make babies, be a family, then our love- making has got to change."

"What's wrong with our love-making?" he asked.

"You're kidding, right?" she said, looking right at him.

"Oh, the whole you're-not-having-any-orgasms thing?" he said, lowering his eyes.

"Yeah, kinda sorta that thing," she said, smiling in spite of herself.

"I thought we were over that because you hadn't brought it up in a while," he said.

"I haven't brought it up because we had bigger fish to fry, like keeping you alive. Look, Barry, I know you and every other man on the planet loves sex. It's the way God made it to ensure our species' survival. But if this is going to work, if I'm going to actually spend the rest of my life on Earth with you, then you have to make one big dramatic change."

"And that change is?" he said, totally afraid of the answer.

"Our having sex can no longer be about you getting off. Your perpetual need for an orgasm is going to have to take a back seat," she said, folding her arms across her naked chest.

"How can you sit there, topless and incredibly gorgeous, and tell me my orgasm has to take a back seat?" he said.

"Forget it, just forget it," she said, lifting up the covers and jumping out of the bed. "Why did I even try?"

"Please, Patricia, wait a sec. Hold on. I was kidding. I joke when I'm uncomfortable. I need help. I need your help. I know I need to change; Lord knows I've had to change in every other area of my life. I am willing to change around this. I just literally have no idea what to change to." She stopped in her tracks. "Will you help me?"

She stared at him, thinking. "That's not my department."

"Then whose is it? Taylor's? I'll do healing sessions with him around this, I promise. But we need to work this out together. We are partners, in every way. Help me. Show me what you need, what you want. I promise I'll do the best I can," Barry said.

"You promise?" she asked.

"I swear on my father's grave," he said, making the sign of a cross, which is a funny thing for a Jew from West LA to do. *But no funnier than using the Arabic name for God when he meditated*, he realized.

She hesitated. "You're not saying this just to get laid, right?"

"I just gave you a ring, didn't I? You want to set the date for the wedding right now?" he bartered.

"No. Men. Can't live with you, can't kill you," she lamented, kissing him on the cheek and snuggling in next to him.

"Now do we get freaky?" he asked, raising his eyebrows and smiling.

"No, now you chill out and let me be in charge. If this is going to work, we're going to have to do things my way for a while," she said, putting a hand on his shoulder and beginning to rub.

"If I do this, if I let you be the leader in the bedroom, how do I know what's going to happen? And how often?" he asked.

"You don't. That's part of the healing here, you not always needing to be in control. If you love me, if you trust me, then you actually have to let me give to you, and then you're going to have to give to me. Slowly. Slow enough for things to build inside my heart. Women are different from men, Barry. For you, it's almost all physical. It's really different for women," she explained.

"Okay, what's first?" he asked, squirming again, glad that she'd gotten back in the bed and not stormed off.

"Why do we make love?" she asked him, lifting the covers and dropping her pajama bottoms off to the side.

"So we can be together, give to each other," he said, trying to keep a straight face.

"Okay, Mr. Jack Ass, what's the real reason? Why do you watch all those pornos and whack off whenever I'm not around?"

"So I can feel good," he said.

"Yes. Exactly. Thank you for saying that. So you can feel good, get some relief, take the edge off things. Our love-making can't be for that anymore." She looked straight at him. "I mean it. If you try it my way, if you give instead of take, I think you're going to feel better. But it's got to be about merging. You have to give to me and care for me and help fill my heart with all the love you say you have for me. I need to feel it. When we make love, I feel you wanting to get off. That's about it. That doesn't do it for me anymore and if it's going to stay that way, then I'm finding myself another man."

Barry thought about it a minute. "They don't say this in any of the books," he said.

"I wouldn't know," she said. "Do you think you can try this?"

"I'll try. What if it's over kind of quick?"

"Then we'll practice. I'm not asking you to be perfect. I just need to see some positive movement."

Barry smiled. "Where do we start?"

They lay together in the bed. Patricia guided him gently into his heart, and then as she moved on top of him, she kept talking him out of his head and down into his body, then from his body back to his heart, away from the fantasies and back to the reality, until he held her and was with her and they switched positions and he got on top and then he was inside her, moving her, carrying her, until she began to feel the floodgates open inside of her and he still had not orgasmed but was moving with her, in synch with her, her heart and her spirit remembering this was her man, this was her partner and together they were working on making something beautiful.